A

Paul the Puppeteer

with

The Village on the Moor and *Renate*

THEODOR STORM (1817–88) was born in Husum, a small coastal town in the duchy of Schleswig, then under Danish rule, where he established himself as a lawyer. Exiled after the unsuccessful rising of 1848, he entered the Prussian judiciary. During the rising of 1863/4 he was elected *in absentia* to the esteemed post of *Landvogt* (combining judicial and police powers) and returned to Husum. After Prussia's annexation of Schleswig-Holstein in 1867, to which he remained bitterly opposed, he settled for the modest post of *Amtsrichter* (District Court Judge).

In 1846 he married his cousin, Constanze Esmarch, whose unexpected death after childbirth in 1865 affected not only his life but also the character of his later works. His second marriage to Dorothea Jensen, however, the daughter of a Husum senator, helped to overcome her tragic loss. He left Husum in 1880 to retire to Hademarschen, south of Husum, where he died in 1888.

A major exponent of the German literary movement known as Poetic Realism, Storm wrote over fifty Novellen, most of them strongly rooted in the North Sea coastal region in which he lived. He has long been accorded a leading place, with Theodor Fontane and Gottfried Keller, among German-language writers of the second half of the nineteenth century; in recent decades his international stature, comparable with that of far better known writers of other nations, has been increasingly recognised.

DENIS JACKSON is a freelance translator specialising in the work of Theodor Storm. Among his previous translations are *The Dykemaster* (*Der Schimmelreiter*, 1996) and *Hans and Heinz Kirch: with 'Immensee' and 'Journey to a Hallig'* (1999), both published by Angel Books. He is a member of the Bundesverband der Dolmetscher und Übersetzer, Berlin-Brandenburg.

ANTONY WOOD is the publisher of Angel Books and a translator from German and Russian.

THEODOR STORM

Paul the Puppeteer

with

The Village on the Moor

and

Renate

Translated with notes by
DENIS JACKSON

Introduction by Denis Jackson and Antony Wood

ANGEL BOOKS
London

For Janet
and in memory of my sister Moya

First published in 2004 by
Angel Books, 3 Kelross Road, London N5 2QS
1 3 5 7 9 10 8 6 4 2

Translations and notes copyright © Denis Jackson 2004
Introduction copyright © Denis Jackson and Antony Wood 2004
Maps drawn by Ruth Knight copyright © Denis Jackson and Angel Books 2004

The moral right of the translator has been asserted

British Library Cataloguing in Publication Data:
A catalogue record for this book is available from the British Library

ISBN 0-946162-70-0

This book is printed on acid free paper conforming to the British Library
recommendations and to the full American standard

Grateful acknowledgement is made to Inter Nationes, Bonn for a grant towards the cost
of translation

Typeset in 10½ on 12½ pt Monotype Ehrhardt by Ray Perry, Woodstock, Oxon.
Printed and bound in Great Britan by Biddles Ltd, King's Lynn, Norfolk

Contents

Acknowledgements

I AM most indebted to Professor David Artiss, Memorial
University of Newfoundland, for his generous assistance and
loan of numerous books, theses and articles on the stories
included in this volume; to Frau Dr Anja Nauck for her hospitality in Berlin and continuing valuable assistance in the
resolution of a number of translation difficulties; to Herr Fiete
Pingel, Nordfriisk Instituut, Bredstedt, for information on
witchcraft in Schwabstedt, on the artisans and journeymen of
nineteenth-century Schleswig-Holstein and on the construction
of the farmsteads in the region; to Ruth Knight for her
painstaking work in the preparation of the maps; to Herr Holger
Borzikowsky, Stadtarchivar, Husum, for historical information
on the St. Marienkirche, Husum, which greatly assisted in the
provision of notes to the translation of *Renate*, and for his
permission for the use of an historical map of Husum from:
Holger Borzikowsky, *Husum in alten Bildern*, Verlag Boyens
& Co., Heide, 1993, p. 44 as a base for the map that appears
on pages 36–37; to Herr Fritz Fey of the Museum für
Puppentheater, Lübeck, for his generous hospitality during my
visit and for greatly increasing my insight into the marionette
theatre in nineteenth-century Schleswig-Holstein; to Herr
Nikolaus Hein and staff of the Puppentheater-Museum, Berlin,
not only for their information on the marionette theatre, but also
for their assistance in finding the cover picture for this volume;
to Juliet Rogers and Gren Middleton of the Puppet Theatre
Barge, London, not only for inviting me to a performance on
their delightful barge on the Thames, but also for providing me
with details of their lives and work as puppeteers, and whose

most generous personal gift of the memoirs of the nineteenth-century puppeteer Richard Barnard greatly assisted my understanding and appreciation of the extremely difficult life of such an artist at that time; to Janet my wife without whose untiring support, tolerance and encouragement such a project would never have been possible; and to Antony Wood, the publisher, for his professional guidance and support throughout the project for which I am sincerely grateful.

Denis Jackson
October 2003

Introduction

WHILE OTHER European literatures were exploring the novel, German-language writers were concentrating on a briefer, more economical form of prose narrative, the Novelle, focusing on a single event or chain of events, with a turning point which brings surprise. In the nineteenth century it was the major fictional genre in German, and to list its practitioners is practically to take a roll-call of the best-known prose-writers and poets of that century: Goethe, Tieck, Kleist, Hoffmann, Eichendorff, Droste-Hülshoff, Stifter, Grillparzer, Mörike, Storm, Keller, Meyer, and Hauptmann. And twentieth-century writers who have written Novellen include Schnitzler, Hofmannsthal, Kafka, Thomas and Heinrich Mann, and Günter Grass.

Theodor Storm (1817–88) was a great master of the Novelle, and ambitious in his claims for the genre. 'The Novelle,' he wrote to his friend Gottfried Keller in 1881, 'is the strictest and most unified form of prose fiction, the sister of drama. And like drama, it deals with the most profound problems of human life. It accepts and makes the highest demands of art.' Storm's finest Novellen substantiate that claim.

Storm was a leading exponent of the German literary movement known as Poetic Realism (1840s–80s), which concerned itself with what was seen as significant or valuable in life, as distinct from the international movement Naturalism, exemplified by the novels of Zola and Gissing and the plays of Strindberg and Hauptmann, which set out to depict 'life as it is'. The fiction of Poetic Realism typically focused on the microcosmic community, the village or small town, an orientation usually termed 'regionalism' rather than 'provincialism', as

German lands were not dominated by a single capital city until unification in 1871. It also contained a strong element of symbolism, going with the belief that true meaning lies below the surface of things.[1]

Theodor Storm, a lawyer by profession, began his literary career as a lyric poet, and both his verse and his *Novellen* are strongly rooted in the North Sea coastal region of the primarily Danish duchy of Schleswig where he spent most of his life,[2] through political vicissitudes which saw military conflict and eventual annexation by Prussia in 1867. Storm stood at the heart of a society in flux, under the pressures of far-reaching political, economic and social change, and in many of his *Novellen* he carefully recorded a rural and small-town life and values that were still lived but fast being swept away. 'Always at the heart of the Realists is the awareness of *time*,' it has been said, 'for essentially they were concerned not to record reality as they saw it, but to preserve the ideal image of the old world before it disappeared forever.'[3] In the three *Novellen* in this volume, topography, as so often in Storm, is close to actuality, which goes with this 'recording' aspect of his writing. The immediate land- or town-scape is always given full weight in Storm's fiction, setting the essential backcloth of tone and colour against which his stories unfold. Both *The Village on the Moor* and *Renate* are set in his home town of Husum and in a village a few miles away, and in the vast wild moorland that lies in-between. *Paul the Puppeteer*, too, is set in Husum and also further south in the small town of Heiligenstadt in north-central Germany. The

[1] For a more detailed account of Storm's life and of the German Novelle and Poetic Realism, see the introduction to *Hans and Heinz Kirch: with 'Immensee' and 'Journey to a Hallig'*, translated by Denis Jackson and Anja Nauck (Angel Books, London, 1999). See also Clifford Albrecht Bernd, *German Poetic Realism* (Boston, 1981), pp. 29–36.

[2] According to population statistics for 1831, some 65 per cent of the inhabitants of the duchy were ethnically Danes. Clifford A. Bernd, *Theodor Storm. The Dano-German Poet and Writer* (Oxford and New York, 2003) explores the extent of Danish influence on Storm's life and later works.

[3] J. M. Ritchie (ed.), *Periods in German Literature* (London, 1966), p. 193.

essential features of each surrounding landscape – the moor, rivers, forests and hills – and of specific streets, churches and other buildings in the towns and villages are precisely described in each narrative, just as many of them are still to be seen today. As in Thomas Hardy's novels, this topographical solidity contributes to the strong sense of the life of communities that Storm gives.

Storm's first important Novelle, *Immensee* (1850), set the pattern for the first phase of his fiction, the idyllic Novellen of *Stimmung* (mood or atmosphere), and has remained a favourite with both German and foreign readers ever since; indeed, for many decades it was a foreigners' gateway to German literature. His second phase was characterised by his friend the writer Paul Heyse as 'painting in oils' as distinct from the idealised, one-dimensional plane of the first, 'watercolour' phase. The works of Storm's 'oil' period, that of his full maturity, engage objectively with 'the real world', and show an acute awareness of socio-political forces. The central characters possess a far greater strength of will than those of the first phase, and pit themselves against fate and a hostile world; here Storm finds true scope for tragedy. The first story in the present selection, *The Village on the Moor* (1872), is the first fully-fledged Novelle of Storm's 'oil' phase.

Storm's relationship with his reading public from this time onwards, involving the nature of the work he submitted and what was eventually published, was complex. He had not only to satisfy the needs of his publishers and public, but also to meet the increasingly restrictive demands of the authorities. During his lifetime, Germany rapidly progressed from an illiterate to a literate nation. It has been said that while France had its political revolution and England its industrial, Germany's revolution was one of reading, primarily among the educated wives and daughters of a rising middle class with an insatiable appetite for poetry, tales of country life (*Dorfgeschichten*) and Novellen of middle-class life.[4] Fearing, however, that the rapid growth of the reading public might lead to civil unrest, state authorities were quick to adopt numerous forms of censorship. And among a predominantly female readership there arose an equally strong demand for 'respectable' and 'morally good' literature, in particular that which stressed the moral value of the family and its social importance. The resulting tone of the family journals upon which authors like Storm depended was therefore highly moral, orthodox in religious matters, and often extremely politically conservative.

The effects of such combined constraints cannot be overlooked. Writers and publishers ignoring them could suffer imprisonment, bankruptcy or dismissal. Conflicts arose between writers and editors over 'improper' material, and editors, including Storm's, would on occasion alter texts without the author's permission or insist that passages be withdrawn before publication. In *Paul the Puppeteer* some passages concerning Lisei's preference for confessing her sins to her husband rather than to a priest in a nearby town, and the effects of Catholicism in Heiligenstadt, were removed on first publication but later restored.[5] Storm not only considered the nobility and the established church as 'poison in the nation's veins'[6] but also held Materialist and Darwinist views. He therefore had to toe the line or rely on narrative devices, such as the time-frame, to distance himself from actions or opinions expressed by his characters.

The device of the time-frame (where a second narrator tells the main story), exemplified in this volume in *Paul the Puppeteer* and *Renate*, and in over half of Storm's Novellen, besides its literary purpose, allowed him to mask his direct authorial involvement. The distance created by the time-frame

[4] David Blackbourn and Richard Evans (eds), *The German Bourgeoisie* (London, 1991), p. 3. The ratio of non-readers to potential readers is estimated to have reversed from 3:1 around 1800 to 1:3 by 1870.
[5] Gerd Eversberg, '"Pole Poppenspäler" – zensiert', in *Schriften der Theodor-Storm-Gesellschaft*, vol.38/1989 (Heide, 1989), pp. 55–62.
[6] Storm to Hartmuth Brinkmann, 18 January 1864.

creates the impression that the narrator is simply an intimate *observer* of actions or events in the past and not expressing his personal views about them. The reader is thereby left free to interpret them as he/she wishes. The device was adapted to times of strong censorship, to mask an author's true political or religious views expressed through the characters and the story.

Nearly all Storm's Novellen from the mid-1860s onwards were first published in monthlies and quarterlies before appearing in book form. Most notable of these were *Westermanns Illustrierte Deutsche Monatshefte* and the exclusive *Deutsche Rundschau*, in which *Renate* appeared. These two journals alone published over half of Storm's works for a readership that contained an increasing proportion of women, at a time when the periodical constituted the real focus of reading culture in Germany.[7] Female response to Storm's work was critical, and central to it was the portrayal of women.[8] Failure to recognise and present the expected or traditional role of women in contemporary society would lead to rejection, and if a writer's personal opinions on the subject were at variance with such a view, they were best not publicised.

The ideal woman projected throughout late Romantic German literature had the qualities of mother, sister and willing servant.[9] Example in high places, notably at the Prussian court,

---

[7] The number of periodicals published in Germany increased from 800 to 1800 between 1833 and 1846. The best-known German illustrated family weekly, *Die Gartenlaube* ('The Summerhouse'), founded in 1853 and to which Storm contributed, lasted until 1918; its circulation in 1861 stood at 100,000; by 1873 it had risen to 282,000.

[8] 'Storm paid careful attention to women's reaction to new works when he read them out in the home or at a social gathering. Even if the verdict was only that a work was charming or delightful, such a reaction was reassuring' (David A. Jackson, *Theodor Storm. The Life and Works of a Democratic Humanitarian*, Oxford, 1992, p. 217).

[9] On this subject as on much else, see Eda Sagarra, *A Social History of Germany 1648–1914* (London, 1977). The *Conversations-Lexikon oder Handwörterbuch für die gebildeten Stände* ('Concise Brockhaus Encyclopedia for the Educated Classes', Leipzig, 1815) offered a neat division of the roles of the sexes: 'Man

had helped to inspire this ideal. Men were held to be rational creatures, women the repositories of feeling and moral strength. The idea of the woman as mistress and lover is generally absent from nineteenth-century German literature.

The church authorities in particular were never in doubt as to where a woman's duty lay: to her lord and master, her husband; a view fully shared by Storm, who was nevertheless sharply critical of the church's involvement in the regulation of marriage and its interference with the relationship within it. The idea of a wife confessing marital secrets to a priest, as in the Catholic church, was to him a form of adultery, an issue he confronted in *Veronika* (1861). At the same time he saw no impediment to a union between a Roman Catholic and a Protestant, as occurs in one of the stories in this volume. In line with the times Storm's early work displays mainly compliant, unworldly young women whose stories end in resignation or death, whereas the female characters in particular in his later Novellen are generally more self-confident and strong-willed,[10] as in the narratives in the present selection. They are presented, however, indirectly, through surrounding circumstances and *Stimmung*, and dialogue is kept brief and economical.

For Storm the highest value in life is love. Through love, both death and transitoriness, themes common in his later works after the death of his first wife Constanze in 1865, are overcome. In both his life and his writings, he saw love as the key to true human happiness, a 'true religion' as he defined it in a letter he wrote as a young man to Constanze,[11] a belief given clear expression in both *Renate* and *Paul the Puppeteer*. That Storm could also portray love's destructive qualities, as in *The Village on the*

---

obtains, woman sustains. [. . .] man resists fate itself and defies force, even in defeat. Woman, however, submits willingly and finds comfort and succour, even in her tears.'

[10] For a detailed treatment of female character in Storm's Novellen, see Grace Joubert, *Mädchen und Frauen in Storms Novellen* (thesis, University of Pretoria, 1978).

[11] Storm to Constanze, 24–28 April 1844.

Moor, underlines his artistic powers, and the capacity of the genre to 'deal with the most profound problems of human life'.[12]

After more than a decade of political exile (for acts of local patriotism rather than nationalist activities) in Prussia and central Germany following the unrest of 1848 and its aftermath, Storm returned to his home town of Husum in 1864 to take up the post of *Landvogt*, which comprised the duties of criminal and civil court judge, chief constable and guardian of wards in chancery. A year later the death of Constanze left him a shattered man. To add to his difficulties, following Prussian annexation of the duchies of Holstein and Schleswig in 1867 his new post was abolished, and he was faced with a choice between the administrative or legal side of the civil service. He settled for the modest post of *Amtsrichter* (District Court Judge), which produced a typical day in court in which he would deal with cases of arson by a thirteen-year-old girl, fraud, attempted poisoning and thefts of firewood as well as taking action on a report that a farmer had been half beaten to death. Storm's court work was a rich source of contact with persons and events that provided subjects for his writing, and there is little doubt that the resulting insights into the best and worst of human behaviour were a stimulus to his new realism and conception of tragedy. There is no better example of this than the Novelle *Draussen im Heidedorf* (*The Village on the Moor*).[13]

By 1871, when Storm began to write this story, the tale of village life, the *Dorfgeschichte*, had become a favourite genre in German literature. In place of the imaginative world of the late Romantics, such as Eichendorff and E. T. A. Hoffmann, it

---

[12] Storm to Gottfried Keller, 14 August 1881.
[13] Written between the end of 1871 and March 1872, the Novelle first appeared in the *Salon für Literatur, Kunst und Gesellschaft*, X/2, May 1872, and in book form, together with a series of 'cultural-historical sketches', in a volume entitled *Zerstreute Kapitel* ('Loose Chapters', Berlin, 1873).

opened up a whole new dimension of actuality – the self-contained world of the *Bauerntum* (peasant community), with its own laws, customs and traditions reaching back to the Middle Ages, a world of which there was no equivalent in nineteenth-century England. It was a natural genre for many German-language writers in the second half of the nineteenth century who were rooted in a specific locale – among others, Storm in Schleswig, Auerbach in the Black Forest and Keller in a Swiss canton.

The material for *The Village on the Moor* derived from a judicial enquiry of five years earlier while Storm still held the post of *Landvogt* in Husum. He related the details of the case, and of the enquiry that he pursued, in a letter written at the time to his future second wife Doris Jensen.[14] His account gives the bare bones of the storyline of *The Village on the Moor*, concerning the disappearance of a young farmer from a village near Husum after his marriage to a wealthy girl for financial reasons, and his relationship with a 'bewitching' but penniless as well as in other ways unsuitable girl he has long loved. In the events of this case Storm found 'a drama of passion in the country'. It marked the beginning of a new phase in his writing. Of this work he wrote to friends: 'It has a completely new tone',[15] and 'I believe I have proved I can write a Novelle without a pre-imposed *Stimmung*.'[16] Storm does away with overall *Stimmung* – the elegiac mood of resignation and loss, for example, that pervades *Immensee* (1850) – to achieve a more objective narrative, related through the eyes of the investigating lawyer, the district judge that he himself had been some five years earlier.

Storm's technique in this Novelle has been called 'the broken line style of narration', in which 'there is no continuity in the course of the external plot, but the inner continuity is fully

---

[14] Dated 2 April 1866.
[15] Storm to Ludwig Pietsch, 15 October 1874.
[16] Storm to Emil Kuh, 24 February 1873.

maintained [. . .]'.[17] The opening cameo scene, its details observed one night by the lawyer-narrator in swaying lamplight outside a coaching inn, not only introduces the general ominous tone of the work (now arising firmly from the story itself and not imposed from outside) but also sets out the whole situation, like a compressed first act of a tragedy, with the young farmer Hinrich Feyse in the company of Margret, the 'bewitching' Slovak girl he has long been passionately in love with, and whose effect on him makes him behave at this moment with petulant violence. The glimpse we have of him on the first page of the story, with his 'brooding look' and broad brow 'that protruded so far that it almost obscured his eyes', graphically portends his future. The lawyer-narrator is involved in the next event to be related, the settlement of Hinrich's inheritance on his father's death and sanction of his marriage arranged by the village sexton. At the narrator's third sighting of the young farmer a year later, buying a pair of jades in the horse market, it is clear that all is not well with him and we learn that the Slovak girl's hold over him is as powerful as ever. The next event is Hinrich's disappearance, and the beginning of the narrator's professional investigation. The rest of the story is a masterful exercise in multiple narration, the witnesses, including Margret herself, building up a vivid picture of Hinrich's life and his relationship with the Slovak girl. The reader is pitched into the heart of events, the tragic denouement actually occurring as the last witness is still being interviewed, in an atmosphere of mounting tension. Such is the detail that has swiftly emerged that by this time, as one critic has observed, 'Storm has told us just as much as the writer of a long novel.'[18]

Two key factors contribute to the impact made by this story. The first is a daemonic leitmotif. The Slovak girl's sharp white teeth are repeatedly mentioned, even taking on, towards the end,

---

[17] Franz Stuckert, *Theodor Storm, Sein Leben und seine Welt* (Bremen, 1955), p. 271.
[18] Margaret Mare, *Theodor Storm and his World* (Cambridge, 1974), p. 161.

bestial aspect; and the narrator associates her with a legendary 'white demon' which rises from the moor at night and sucks its sleeping victims' souls out of their open mouths. The second factor is symbolic nature description. Though this tale is shorn of the extended lyrical descriptions of nature found in Storm's earlier *Novellen*, the bare glimpses of the stark landscape play a significant part in the whole. A passage describing the moor, past which the district judge drives on his way to the village where the Fehse family lives, powerfully images the lone vastness of Hinrich's passion.

> [. . .] we were driving along by the edge of the so-called 'Wild Moor', which at that time stretched to the north as far as the eye could see. It seemed as though the last rays of the sun remaining on earth had suddenly been swallowed up by this gloomy steppe. Amongst the dark-brown heather, often beside large or small pools, single stacks of peat loomed out of the barren expanse over which the occasional melancholy call of a solitary plover would sound out of the sky. That was all that could be seen or heard.

There is a further dimension to this extraordinarily pregnant story. It was written at an historic moment in German history – unification under Bismarck and the birth of the new German Empire. The two legal characters, the village sexton and the narrating district court judge, represent the old and the new Germany. The former acts in the interests of the village community, aiming to ensure the smooth continuity of the local economy by an arranged marriage; the judge brings Prussian centralised uniformity to the whole region and seeks to understand things in a wider context. These two have subtly different takes on the situation they are dealing with, and the overtones of their, at times, slightly prickly collaboration gently anchor the story in historical time and place.

Storm spent some seven years of his exile in the small, staunchly Catholic town of Heiligenstadt, in the wooded Thuringian hills in central Germany, in the post of *Kreisrichter* (district judge). Although the town's population was only four and a half thousand, it boasted three churches, two Catholic and one Evangelical, and a grim stone prison. It was not on the rail network at that time and had to be reached by coach from Göttingen. The three gates in the town walls were closed each night, and a watchman blew the hours from a church tower. Street lighting was non-existent; in the main street water was drawn from the gully flowing past the houses. The area was economically backward, poverty rife and on a scale Storm had never dreamt of, much of which he put down to the role of the Catholic church and the townspeople's strict piety. Storm's residence was situated opposite the prison, where he and Constanze were frequent visitors, he on judicial business, she in connection with washing and other matters.

Winters in Heiligenstadt were often many degrees below zero, and on one such day during Storm's last year in the town there occurred an episode that remained in his memory for many years. He described it in a letter to his parents:

> One afternoon about four weeks ago, when we had the coldest weather here, we heard the loud crying of a child in the street; and looking out of the window, we saw across the road a young gypsy woman with two children outside the prison being driven away on to the street with a dog whip. Her husband was in the prison accused of theft (he was freed a few days later) and she had been trying to force her way into prison with him. Now she wandered about the street chilled and weeping, and the elder boy cried loudly for his father; night was beginning to fall, outside it was 17 degrees below zero. The poor people were without a roof; not a soul took pity on these vagabonds. Then we, as was proper for a writer's family, brought the wandering gypsy girl with her two children to our table and revived them with hot coffee and rolls. But the black-haired young woman wouldn't take anything; all she could think of was how 'him over there' would be worrying about them. [. . .] But when at last these people were fed and warmed, we still hadn't achieved much. Then Hans [Storm's eldest son] stepped in. He went with them around the

small hostels and argued with the landlords; but since no one would take them in, he went to the town hall and spoke to the mayor, and in the end, on the mayor's personal instructions, had them taken into the local poorhouse. By this time the woman was in such despair that she was ready to lie down in the cold with her children in front of the town gate.[19]

Besides showing Storm as a 'true Christian', however radical his views on the established church of the day may have been, the incident described in this letter prompted the key scene with which the second part of *Pole Poppenspäler* (*Paul the Puppeteer*) begins.

This Novelle, Storm's best known after *Der Schimmelreiter*, is another 'realistic' narrative. The impulse for its composition was unusual. In autumn 1873 Storm was commissioned, along with other well-known writers, to contribute to the new Leipzig monthly journal *Deutsche Jugend* (German Youth). He completed the Novelle in January 1874 and it appeared with illustrations by Carl Offterdinger in the journal later that year. Tales of adventure and patriotism accounted for most German literature for the young written at that time. Storm addressed his new story to both a young and an adult audience. He explained his approach in an afterword to the story on its first publication in book form in 1875:

The whole problem of 'writing for young people' confronted me. If you are going to write for the young, the paradox occurred to me, then you should *not* write for the young! For it is inartistic to change the treatment of your subject-matter according to whether you think grown-up Peter or little Hans is going to be your reader.

With this in mind, the field of possible subject-matter was considerably narrowed down. What was needed, without worrying about the readership and handling it strictly according to intrinsic requirements, was subject-matter that was equally suitable for adults and for the understanding and involvement of the young.

The above tale was written at last. Whether it bears out my theory, or, even if it does so overall, whether my imagination might not have

_____

[19] Storm to Johann Kasimir and Lucie Storm, 8 February 1864.

played tricks on me in certain details in telling the story, making me
unwittingly place myself closer to the younger readership originally
intended – in either case the gentle reader will be better able to judge
than the author himself.[20]

Storm's intention of reaching *both* an adult and a young readership has long been ignored in discussion of this Novelle, which
used to be regarded simply as a charming children's story, and
presented as such by publishers and illustrators alike. Not until
1955 did it begin to be seen by its author's compatriots as something more like 'the story of an artist, with the conflict between
artistic genius [*Künstlertum*] and bourgeoisie [*Bürgertum*] as its
focus.'[21]

Storm set the story in Husum and in Heiligenstadt in the first
decades of the nineteenth century, during and after the
Napoleonic Wars when first French and then Russian troops
occupied Schleswig-Holstein, when there was high regional
unemployment and food was scarce. He modelled his travelling
puppeteer, Tendler, on one of the most celebrated marionette
proprietors of the time, Georg Geisselbrecht (1762–?1826), who
performed puppet plays across Europe, including Husum in
1817, the year of Storm's birth.[22] Tendler's wife is presented as
Geisselbrecht's daughter. An announcement of Geisselbrecht's
forthcoming performance of the popular play *Doctor Faust* in the
Husum weekly paper, of which Storm was a keen collector of
back-numbers, may have led to the idea for his story. The name
'Paul Paulsen', given to the story's narrator-figure, a master
craftsman, appeared in a notice adjacent to Geisselbrecht's.

The life of the travelling puppeteer and his family was a
bitterly hard one in those times. Apart from the dangers of open
travel on the roads, nomadic show people had always been

---

[20] *Waldwinkel, Pole Poppenspäler, Novellen* (Braunschweig, 1875), pp. 107ff.
[21] See Stuckert, pp. 317ff.
[22] Details of Geisselbrecht's career and of the life of travelling puppeteers given
here and in the end notes are taken principally from John McCormick and
Bennie Pratasik, *Popular Puppet Theatre in Europe, 1800–1914* (Cambridge,
1998).

regarded with mistrust. State authorities stigmatised puppeteers, grouping them together with gypsies, thieves and vagabonds. In 1810 Friedrich Wilhelm II of Prussia even issued a cabinet order that puppeteers found without a permit to perform were to be arrested and thrown into prison. The low social status of the puppeteer was further reduced by social misfits and discharged soldiers taking up the occupation from sheer hunger and need in the great depressions during and following the Napoleonic Wars. Given such adverse social attitudes, every attempt was made by puppeteers and their families to prove their respectability. As many references as possible were collected from respected citizens who had seen their shows, to be presented to the authorities in the next town visited in order to obtain the necessary permit to perform. To avoid the stigma associated with puppetry, many puppeteers registered themselves under another trade if they possibly could, some, like Tendler, choosing to call themselves 'mechanicuses', or operators of a 'mechanical theatre'. It is not by chance that the respectability of the Tendler family is repeatedly emphasised in Storm's Novelle.

The family was a complete production unit. The cash-desk at the front of the often make-shift booth or community hall was usually occupied by one of the womenfolk, who also made the costumes. The menfolk made and carved the puppets. The women usually dressed and prepared the female marionettes, the men the male ones. Each puppet would be painstakingly researched, created and carved for a particular part, as much time and effort being devoted to the task as to any part in a full-scale theatre play; puppet plays could take up to five years to prepare and stage. Many puppeteers claimed not to have scripts, texts being seen as part of their capital and associated with the secrets of their profession. Most knew their repertoire extremely well and had memorised an incredible number of plays; those who forgot their lines would simply improvise. Parts would often be passed down orally from one generation to the next, and seldom written down. Many such historical details are turned into art in the fabric of Storm's Novelle.

An equally vivid historical aspect of the story is the sense
given of the power of the guild system prevailing in pre-industrial northern Germany at the time, a system whose significance
amounted to more than simply that of a collection of organised
crafts. The craftsmen's guilds were an integral part of society,
governing many aspects of daily life, from the smallest villages to
the largest towns, in intimate detail. They determined a man's
ability to work, his training, his income and the status and
ranking of his entire family within his community. A guild
formed a fellowship for its members that went well beyond
representing their particular craft; it often performed the role of
a friendly society, assisting members falling on hard times. In
1834 there were eleven craft guilds in Storm's home town of
Husum, some with their own hostel for the temporary accommodation of members and journeymen.

The guild system was a finely graded hierarchy in which men
and women were acutely aware of their precise relation to those
immediately above and below them. Master craftsman, journeyman, apprentice, widow or wage-worker – each of these
distinctions, besides their relation to securing a living, also
conferred a social identity. After 1848 it became fashionable in
German lands to address the craftsman class as *Bürger;*
Bismarck even described such people as the backbone of the
middle classes.[23] A guild imposed strict rules on its members in
return for its protection. To be recognised as a master and take
his place in the community, a craftsman first had to have a wife,
yet he should not marry before he was qualified. His wife had to
come from his own social class: to marry the 'wrong' wife could
lead to expulsion from the guild, with severe consequences for
future employment. Guild ordinances even demanded of every
master that he be 'conceived of legitimate parents in a proper
marriage bed'.[24]

Against such a background, Lisei's position as a daughter of

---

[23] See Ritchie, p. 181.
[24] See Sagarra, pp. 71–2.

'travelling folk' takes on a much sharper significance in relation
to Paul the master craftsman. That he is pejoratively nicknamed
'Paul the Puppeteer' by some of his fellow townsmen for his
association with such 'travelling folk' is a telling pointer to the
strong social context of Storm's tale. Storm was acutely alive to
the issues of the day, and the story of Paul, Lisei and the travelling puppeteer, besides being a literary masterpiece, also
operates as a powerful social-historical 'documentary'.

Storm's tale gives a thoroughly convincing picture of the life
of a puppeteer family at the historical moment that sees the
beginning of the travelling marionette show's decline. The
strongly drawn characters are not idealised. Frau Tendler's
manner towards her daughter is distinctly harsh, and she pres-
ents 'stern expressionless features' towards the outside world,
though later softening a little. Storm's life-long association with
the world of puppetry clearly lies behind his success in creating
a milieu arrestingly alive in every detail: a puppeteer's constant
appetite for scraps of material for the puppets' dress, deep devotion to the puppets, resourcefulness in coping with an on-stage
emergency, and knowledge of a wide repertoire of plays.

The story is straightforwardly structured: in more or less
continuous reminiscence, the main narrator, Paulsen, tells a
young boy the story of his association with the puppeteers in
boyhood and in a later period in his life. Although a story for the
enjoyment of the young, it also belongs fully to the adult world,
taking the conflict between artists and townsfolk, *Künstlertum*
and *Bürgertum*, as a central theme. In a number of subtle ways
throughout the story, the puppeteer's family is set apart from the
townsfolk. The Tendlers speak a South German dialect, their
daughter Lisei particularly strongly, making them stand apart
from the inhabitants of the northern town; on first appearance,
Tendler's family is immediately classified among those 'not entitled to stay at the tailors' hostel as guests of the guild'; in the
more sombre second half of the story, old Tendler, when
arrested, is greatly humiliated by being made to 'trot beside the
policeman's horse' all the way back to the town, and his impris-

onment, although he is innocent, tellingly associates him with those outside the law in the eyes of the townsfolk. Such repeated emphasis on the separation of the puppeteers from 'respectable' society heightens the social distinction between Paul the master craftsman and Lisei the puppeteer's daughter, a relationship at the very heart of the Novelle.

Some two years later, in 1876, Storm began to write historical Novellen (*Chroniknovellen*). *Aquis submersus*, a story of tragic passion, is the first of a series of narratives in which he vividly recreated the past, often with skilful simulation of the language and style of discovered 'documents'. He immersed himself in chronicles and local histories of Husum and its surrounding region, some of which eventually found expression in *Renate*, a dramatic and powerful frame-tale set at the beginning of the eighteenth century. An item Storm discovered in a chapbook relating to this period[25] provided him with the main structure of the Novelle: an orthodox pastor's son's love for the daughter of a neighbouring farmer suspected of the black art; the witch craze of the period; the son's promise, when he too became a pastor, to the dying father never to marry his beloved; and his later departure from the village to live with his brother. Storm worked in details derived from many other sources and set the story in the beautiful village of Schwabstedt, which he often visited from Husum. It first appeared in the *Deutsche Rundschau* in 1878.

It has often been asked whether Storm was religious. Taking the term at its widest, including high ideals and the desire to live morally and helpfully to others, the answer has always been in the affirmative. But from the standpoint of orthodox religion, it has been decidedly in the negative. Storm was nevertheless extremely tolerant of others' beliefs, had numerous friends amongst the clergy, and never denied any of his children a

---

[25] H. N. A. Jensen, ['Scenes from the Life of a Pastor'], in *Volksbuch für die Herzogtümer Schleswig, Holstein und Lauenburg, 1850*.

Christian upbringing. This general tolerance, together with his deeply-held humanitarian rationalism,[26] may be reckoned a good starting-point, combining the ability to empathise and a critical attitude, for the writing of a tale of superstition and bigotry in the early-eighteenth-century Lutheran church.

The witch craze lasted some five hundred years across Europe, from the first attacks by the church against witches and wizards in the thirteenth century to its cessation in the eighteenth. It reached its zenith in Europe between 1560 and 1660. Wars – such as the Thirty Years War (1618–48) – bad harvests, famines and plagues provided the breeding grounds on which the witch craze could thrive. Belief in witchcraft served as a means of accounting for the otherwise inexplicable misfortunes of everyday life: lacking natural explanations, men turned to supernatural ones, and a whole variety of deaths, diseases and disasters were attributed to witchcraft, with the assistance of the church which ascribed such events to the work of the Devil.

It has been argued that the church freely used witch-hunts as a means of social control and retention of its power over the faithful;[27] and the point is powerfully demonstrated in *Renate*. The wording of interrogations and required responses and methods of torture and execution was laid down in minute detail in the *Malleus maleficarum* (*The Hammer against Witches*, c. 1486), issued under the authority of Pope Innocent VIII, which was followed to the letter by most European churches well into the eighteenth century. The last execution in Germany occurred in 1775. The slow rise of scepticism and rationalism eventually put a stop to witchcraft persecutions; this is the period in which Storm sets *Renate*.

The overwhelming majority of accusations of witchcraft were against women, particularly the old and alone, midwives, and females set or living apart from the community, and many tens of

---

[26] See Jackson, op. cit.; and the same author's afterword to Theodor Storm, *The Dykemaster (Der Schimmelreiter)*, translated by Denis Jackson (London, 1996).
[27] Geoffrey Scarre, *Witchcraft and Magic in 16th and 17th Century Europe* (London, 1987), p. 49.

thousands were accused, horrifically tortured and brutally killed during the craze. Women were considered to be far weaker than men, both spiritually, physically, and in sexual restraint. They were therefore thought to be easy prey for the Devil, by whom they were believed to be easily tempted into sexual relations and demonic pacts. Today, writings such as the *Malleus maleficarum* are deemed the ravings of sexually frustrated monks; in their time they led to the deaths of numerous unfortunate women.

Renate takes the form of a memoir – discovered years later by a descendant – written in old age by a retired Lutheran pastor, Josias, who looks back on his days as a theological student and his affection for the daughter of an enlightened farmer-landowner (*Hofbauer*) whose household is held by the local community to be in league with the Devil. Storm creates, both in the village community and in the minds of Josias and his father, the mindset of belief in witchcraft and in the Devil as a living entity typical of this period, strongly reinforcing its impact by the introduction of an historical character as a friend of Josias's father – the fanatical pastor Petrus Goldschmidt, devout enemy of the Devil and all his works. Josias writes in the baroque style of his time, which Storm modernised slightly after first journal publication.

The conflict that takes place in this rural orthodox Lutheran pastor is all the more powerfully convincing because it is presented from the inside, in his mind and in his heart. His upbringing and the influence of his father are challenged by the enlightened Hofbauer's household, his daughter Renate being a free spirit like her father. And at the recently founded Halle University, Josias is exposed to the new Protestant rationalism. From Josias's memoir the reader has the full emotional pressure of this conflict and the impossibility of its resolution, and here Storm's narrative strategy is brilliantly apt. The memoir breaks off with the impasse unresolved; Josias leaves the area to take up a living elsewhere. His story is completed in another discovered document – a letter written by a nephew of Josias who used to see him in old age.

To the general outline of events Storm found in the chapbook he added a further incident from another source which he fashioned into the opening scene related in Josias's memoir, in which he first meets Renate. Resting one evening, after a hard day's exercise, in the old town church in Husum, the fourteen-year-old Josias is attacked by an enormous black guard dog, and takes refuge by mounting a statue of St George and the dragon. About to succumb, finally, to exhaustion, he is rescued by the dog's owner, the young Renate, whom in his swooning state he imagines as an angel flown down to him from the top of the church's celebrated altarpiece crucifix. This scene has a key place in the structure of the Novelle, being balanced by the return of the 'angel' at the close of the story in one of the most moving moments in German literature.

Fellow writers placed *Renate* extremely highly; Theodor Fontane found it the most successful of all the Novellen that Storm had written to date.[28] Its success lies first in its powerful and completely convincing portrayal of the mindset of superstition, and secondly, in the supremely elegant and human manner in which the narrative brings transcendence of this mindset. All three narratives in this book, in fact, stand at the highest level of Storm's achievement. Together with other recently published translations of selected Novellen by Storm,[29] the majority of them appearing in English for the first time, they will give the English-speaking reader opportunity to judge whether Storm is a writer to be placed among the greatest classic European authors.

Denis Jackson and Antony Wood

---

[28] '. . . excellent, without qualification,' Fontane wrote to Storm on 2 November 1878, 'This is how to write.' Gottfried Keller and Paul Heyse also communicated early enthusiastic reactions to Storm.

[29] Translated by Denis Jackson and published by Angel Books: *The Dykemaster* (*Der Schimmelreiter*, 1996) and *Hans and Heinz Kirch: with 'Immensee' and 'Journey to a Hallig'* (1999).

Translator's Note

THEODOR STORM is a writer as deeply rooted in time and place as Thomas Hardy. To read and translate his narratives is to take many a journey into a past that is vividly alive, into a North Friesland, on the west coast of Schleswig-Holstein, that is a tight-knit community cherishing its own history. Besides their value as literature, his Novellen are vast tapestries of the life and times of his region, and no contemporary economic, social or political factor that could affect his characters is overlooked.

In order to translate his stories adequately, it is necessary to have 'been there', in Storm's country, to have a thorough understanding of historical events and associations – often lying behind rather than in his text – and to have visited and studied the history of his native coastal region and of the usually specific locations of the Novellen, so that localities can be 'seen' as the characters might have seen and experienced them. A journey across the wild lonely moor to Schwabstedt, the picturesque village to the south of Husum by the river Treene, settings for *Renate* and *The Village on the Moor*, to visit the fine twelfth-century church with its high belfry nearby and the still visible remains of the thirteenth-century bishop's residence there, takes the translator into the heart and soul of Storm's fiction. It is not difficult to imagine the presence of will-o'-the-wisps and the 'white demon' out on the moor or the fanatical devil-hunting priest striding through the streets of the small village. And the building that once housed the Riflemen's Guild in the narrow Süderstraße in Husum, in which Herr Tendler performs in *Paul the Puppeteer*, is still to be seen.

Storm is a writer of immense descriptive and poetic powers

('My craft of fiction grew out of my lyric verse,' he once wrote, and he remains one of the most popular lyric poets in the language). His vocabulary extends to half as many words again as Shakespeare's.* He uses different narrative styles to match the periods, subjects and settings of his works, each significantly different from the other. Leitmotifs reinforce his characters' distinguishing qualities; symbolism or folklore gives depth and dimension to a scene or event; and words are frequently chosen for their sounds as well as their meanings.

To translate the contrasted forms and styles of the narratives in this book – the judicial style of the investigating magistrate in *The Village on the Moor*, the narrative level pitched to both a younger and an older reader in *Paul the Puppeteer*, and the early eighteenth-century style of *Renate* – demands the use of every aspect of historical and local information available. It demands precisely seeing the images in the text, walking in the steps of the characters, transporting oneself into the period, and feeling the atmosphere of the setting. It requires, too, a knowledge of how the author uses particular words and phrases and in what contexts. Computer technology now makes such information readily available to the translator; an author's entire works can be scanned in seconds to study how specific words or phrases are used. This technology too has enabled the creation of my own lexicon of Storm's vocabulary for ready access in translating.

With *Renate*, besides the research needed to assimilate the details of belief in witchcraft in Germany at a particular historical moment, and the attitudes of church and community towards it, there was a basic stylistic challenge. I have endeavoured both to reflect Storm's simulation of early eighteenth-century language and at the same time not to depart from the colloquial, everyday idiom in which the pastor-narrator writes, especially evident in the dialogue.

With *Paul the Puppeteer*, a major translation issue arose in

---

*A. Procksch, 'Der Wortschatz Theodor Storms', *Germanisch-Romanische Monatsschrift*, VI, 10/11, pp. 532–62. Shakespeare's vocabulary extends to some 15,000 words, Storm's to 22,500.

regard to Storm's use of dialect. Lisei in particular, a child for most of the narrative, speaks in strong dialect throughout. Storm himself clearly recognised the difficulties of choosing and writing an appropriate and understandable dialect, especially in the mouths of characters who would have acquired a mixture of dialects during travels around Europe. After he had written a draft of the story, he wrote to the Stuttgart literary historian Georg Scherer:

> I would simply say this: I have imagined the dialect to be from the region between Berchtesgaden and Munich; Bavarian and Austrian can often be confused. Also, the characters should on no account speak pure dialect, though the child might do so, for they are moving from one place to another across Germany . . . A word of dialect should never be used that cannot be understood by someone who simply knows written German. That I have used dialect is an indescribable impertinence by me, as it is not my own.

Dialect not only immediately identifies a person's geographical region or social class but generally exists only in speech, seldom in writing. The difficulty of writing in dialect is that no standardised spelling exists, and use frequently has to be made of a makeshift orthography. This in turn leaves the non-dialect-speaker confused over exact pronunciation, leading to serious distraction from the flow of the narrative. It is also impossible for the translator to find in his own culture any 'equivalent' to the dialect that Storm intended to be 'from the region between Berchtesgaden and Munich'; for whatever dialect is selected, the characters adopting it, here the girl Lisei and her parents, are immediately associated with a specific geographical region or social class within the reader's present-day culture, and *not* with the one intended by the author. The reader is therefore transported to the wrong setting, away from the one originally intended, to the serious detriment of the whole impact of the work.

For these reasons I have not attempted to render either Lisei's or her parent's dialect, which so characterises them in the

German, into an English regional or rural dialect. I have rendered Lisei's speech throughout in the simple and direct language and vocabulary of a child. There is therefore an unavoidable loss in translation here, but no loss, I hope, in Storm's moving story and masterly characterisation of Lisei and her parents, a tale of the enchanting world of the puppeteer and his marionettes that has been read and enjoyed in the German-speaking world by both young and old in over a hundred editions.

Storm's fiction is still comparatively little known to the English-speaking world. Few English translations have appeared since the early 1960s. The only previous translation of *Renate* was published in 1909. The other two stories in the present selection appear for the first time in English.

As in my two previous volumes of Storm's fiction in translation, it seemed essential for a fuller understanding of Storm's world to provide the reader with some background information on historical, topographical and folkloric references, and this is given in the end-notes. In addition, locations of many of the places that feature in the stories will be found in the three maps on pages 34–39.

The texts I have used, by kind permission of the publisher, are from the four-volume critical edition *Theodor Storm: Sämtliche Werke*, edited by Karl Ernst Laage and Dieter Lohmeier (Deutscher Klassiker Verlag, Frankfurt am Main, 1987–88), special edition, 1998, volume 2, edited by K. E. Laage, *Novellen. 1867–1880*: *Draussen im Heidedorf*, pp. 69–101; *Pole Poppenspäler*, pp. 164–220; and *Renate*, pp. 523–87.

Denis Jackson
Cowes, Isle of Wight
June 2003

Maps

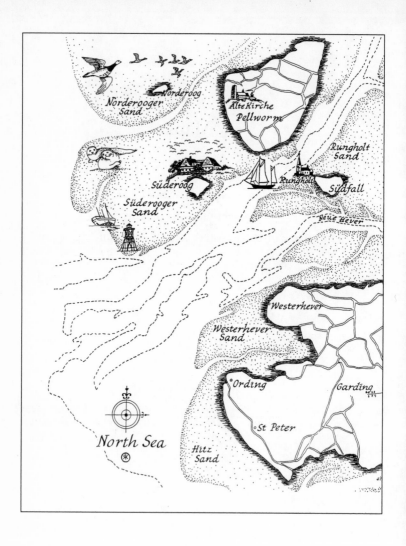

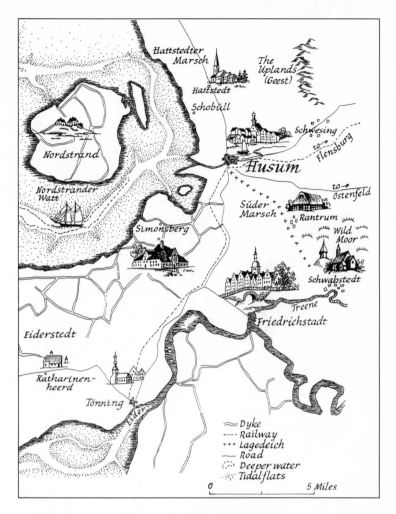

The west coast of Schleswig. The eighteenth- and
nineteenth-century settings for *The Village on the Moor*,
Paul the Puppeteer and *Renate* are all in this region

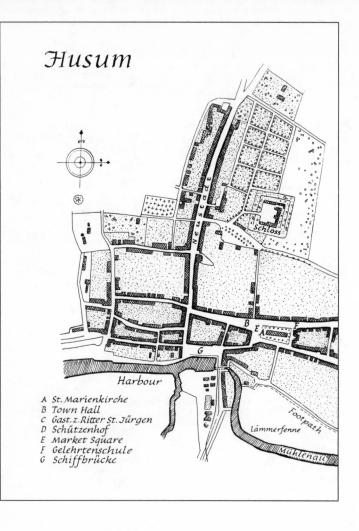

Husum

Schloss

Neustadt

Harbour

Footpath

Lämmerfenne

Mühlenau

A St. Marienkirche
B Town Hall
C Gast. z. Ritter St. Jürgen
D Schützenhof
E Market Square
F Gelehrtenschule
G Schiffbrücke

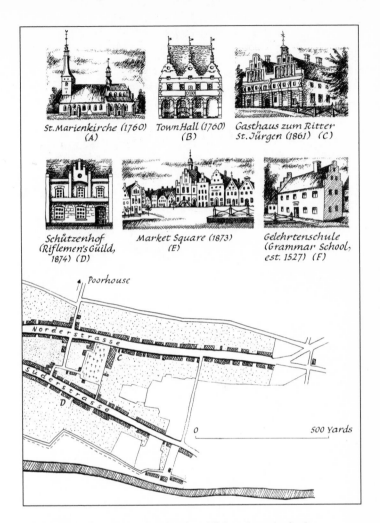

St.Marienkirche (1760) (A)

Town Hall (1760) (B)

Gasthaus zum Ritter St. Jürgen (1861) (C)

Schützenhof (Riflemen's Guild, 1874) (D)

Market Square (1873) (E)

Gelehrtenschule (Grammar School, est. 1527) (F)

Poorhouse

Norderstrasse

Süderstrasse

C

D

0   500 Yards

Street map of Husum, showing in addition the principal buildings and locations that feature in stories contained in this book. (Based on a street map of 1862)

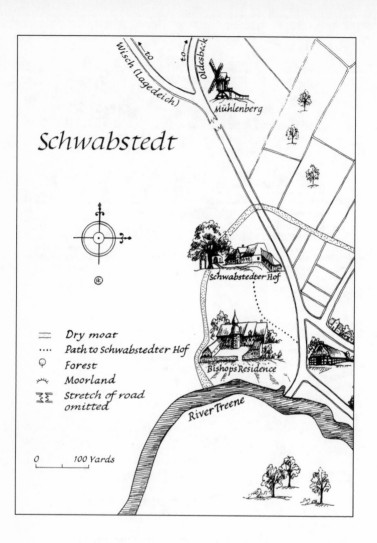

Wisch (Lagedeich)

to

to Oldesbeek

Mühlenberg

Schwabstedt

Schwabstedter Hof

Bishops Residence

River Treene

=== Dry moat
.... Path to Schwabstedter Hof
♀ Forest
⋏⋏ Moorland
ꙅꙅ Stretch of road omitted

0   100 Yards

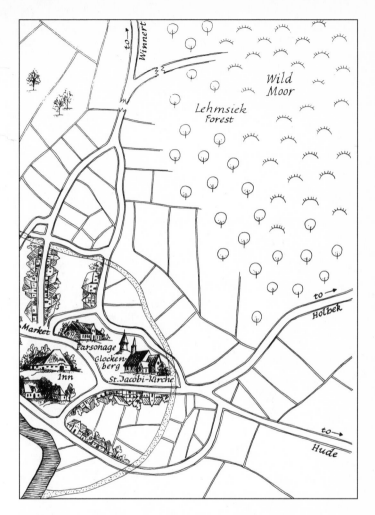

The village of Schwabstedt and the surrounding region (ca 1700), containing the settings for *Renate* and *The Village on the Moor*

The Village on the Moor

IT WAS an autumn evening. I had been at the district judge's office questioning a couple of wood thieves who had been brought in at midday, and was now walking slowly home. Gas lighting was not established in our town then; only small hand lanterns swayed about in the dark lanes like will-o'-the-wisps. But one of these lights remained firmly fixed in the same spot, drawing my idle eyes towards it.

As I drew closer I saw a harnessed farm wagon drawn up outside the inn then used by farmers arriving from villages east of the town; the old ostler stood next to it holding the stable lantern while the people prepared to leave.

'Hurry yourself up, Hinrich!' a voice called down from the wagon. 'You've spent time enough shilly-shallying! Carsten Krüger's and Carsten Decker's wife are both nearing their time; I can't stop worrying about them.' The rather elderly voice came from a stout, apparently female figure wrapped in scarves and coats and sitting motionless on the rear seat of the wagon.

Instinctively I had stopped at the turn-off in the road. After hours at work, it is always interesting to watch others acting out a scene like this, and the ostler held the lantern high enough for me to observe everything.

Next to a youthful female figure, whose appearance was in striking contrast to the stocky build of our usual country girl, stood a young farmer with tightly curled blond hair springing from beneath his cloth cap; in one hand he held the reins and whip, with the other he gripped the backrest of a wooden chair placed close to the wagon as a step. There was a brooding look in the face of the young man; the broad brow protruded so far that it almost obscured his eyes. 'Come on, Margret, get on up!' he said, as he reached for the girl's hand.

But she pushed him away. 'I don't need your help!' she cried. 'Just look after your horses!'

'Now stop fooling about, Margret!'

At these hardly concealed words of impatience, she turned her head. By the light of the lantern I saw only the lower part of her face; but those soft pale cheeks had hardly ever been left to the mercy of the weather during the sowing and reaping seasons; what particularly struck me were the pointed white teeth now exposed by the smiling lips.

She had not responded to the young man's last words; but by the attitude of her head I could guess that her eyes now gave him the answer. At the same time she set her foot lightly on the wooden chair, and when he now put his arm round her she let herself gently fall against his shoulder, and I noticed how their cheeks rested against each other for a while. I also saw how he tried to urge her towards the front seat of the wagon; but she slipped away from him, and in an instant had settled herself on the seat at the rear of the wagon next to the portly woman, who again called out from beneath her scarves: 'Hurry yourself up, Hinrich, hurry yourself up, lad!'

The young farmer, as though undecided, remained standing by the wagon. Then he pulled at the girl's clothes: 'Margret!' he exclaimed in a dull voice. 'Come and sit at the front, Margret.'

'Thanks, Hinrich!' she replied loudly, 'but I'm quite comfortable where I am.'

The young man pulled harder at her clothes. 'I'm not leaving, Margret, if you won't sit beside me!'

She now leaned down towards him over the edge of the seat; I saw a pair of dark eyes flashing in the pale face and the white teeth were again visible between the full lips. 'Won't you hurry up, Hinrich!' she said softly, with almost amorous promise, 'or must we go to town with Hans Ottsen next time? He's pestered me often enough.'

The young man murmured something I did not understand,

then sprang up wildly between the horses on to the front seat of the wagon, cracking his whip angrily and snatching at the reins so that the bays reared high in the air. And immediately, to the accompaniment of cries from the women, the vehicle rattled away into the night, hitting the chair with a wheel so that it shattered into pieces on the cobbles. The old ostler stumbled backwards with a 'God in heaven preserve us!', then disappeared grumbling with his lantern through the door of the inn.

Like a shadow play everything came to an end, and lost in thought, I continued on my way home.

* *

About six months later the district judge's office was informed of the death of Hinrich Fehse, resident of the community and proprietor of a large holding in one of the villages to the east of the town which I knew to be heavily encumbered. Since he left behind him, besides his widow and a grown-up son of the same name, two under-age children, the entire estate had to come under judicial process. In the absence of close relatives and in accordance with the wishes of the widow, the former sexton of the village was appointed guardian to the children; a man who during the discharge of his previous duties had concerned himself less with the young entrusted to his pedagogic care than with his already not insignificant agricultural ventures, but who since relinquishing his post had been all the more helpful to his former pupils in life's affairs with his often all too worldly-wise advice.

When I entered the court on the day of the settlement of the inheritance, I found this influential figure sitting by the parish representative's desk already busily scrutinising the documents. After he had recognised me through the round lenses of his spectacles, he carefully brushed the side hairs over his bald head and stood up to greet me in his characteristically dignified manner. At the same time he pointed to a young man who had also risen from his seat at my entry, and said: 'This is Hinrich

Fehse, Herr Amtsvogt,* the eldest son of the deceased.'

At that moment I felt as if I had already seen this angular head before somewhere, only when and where I could not remember. But never before had I seen such a sullen look of indifference on a youthful face; the grey deep-set eyes appeared hardly able to make the effort to raise their eyelids towards me.

Against the wall sat an elderly farmer's wife with hard features and dark eyebrows, her grey hair tied back beneath a small black cap; she sat motionless, her hands holding a pocket handkerchief and resting on a blue-printed linen apron. This was the widow of the deceased farmer Hinrich Fehse.

I had good reason to discuss the somewhat complicated affair first alone with the sexton, and so accompanied him to my adjacent office.

'The family will scarcely be able to keep the farm,' I said, opening out the inventory of the estate before him. 'We shall be forced to sell it, I fear.'

The sexton fixed his round bespectacled eyes upon me. 'I'm not of that opinion!' he said in his weighty, schoolmasterly tone.

I pointed out the long list of debts recorded in the inventory. 'When the widow's rightful portion is included, there won't be sufficient remaining to cover the siblings' shares of the inheritance.'

'Indeed not!' And the dignified man pressed his thick lips together and looked confidently at me as though he already had the complete solution in his pocket.

'And in spite of this,' I continued, 'you want him to take over that large farm?'

'That would be my view!'

'And the money, where would you get that from?'

'That should already be quite taken care of!' And he named the daughter of a wealthy farmer from the same village. 'Yesterday,' he went on, 'we celebrated the engagement, and the

---

*District judge – an old Schleswig-Holstein post incorporating legal and administrative responsibilities.

Fehses' farm can now be taken over jointly by the young couple.'

The sexton folded his hands behind his back and, with head raised, awaited my expression of amazement. But at this disclosure it suddenly became clear to me where I had previously encountered the young Hinrich Fehse. I saw him standing again by that dangerous-looking girl next to the wagon and heard him gloomily exclaiming: 'Margret, Margret!'

'I have the feeling,' I said at last, 'that I've already met your bridegroom somewhere! Has the midwife in your village an especially attractive daughter by any chance?'

'Herr Amtsvogt knows about that too!' replied the sexton, somewhat surprised. 'Well, we've engaged the girl as a sewing maid twenty-four miles away in the town, and she leaves for there tomorrow. The young lady's never wished to involve herself with heavy farm work in her life.'

I had to laugh. 'And how have you managed to arrange all this?'

The self-satisfied smile on the face of the sexton was as broad as his round cheeks would permit. 'If I may say so, Herr Amtsvogt, even the Devil can be got to dance for money, so why not an old woman!'

'Indeed, you are right; and the midwife's daughter is presumably without means?'

'That smooth skin of hers, Herr Amtsvogt, was no use to us, and anyway, she has nothing to put into the farm. Besides,' and he lowered his voice to a confidential whisper, 'her grandfather was a Slovak from the Danube, and God knows how he ended up here with us; and what's more, the old midwife with her card-reading and spells for swellings she relieves fools of their money with – that wouldn't have suited an old farming family, I can tell you!'

'Did Hinrich let himself be so easily separated from that girl, then?' I asked.

The sexton's worldly-wise head struck a pose. 'If I may speak frankly,' he replied, avoiding the issue, 'it was doubtful whether the girl would have accepted him; there are others she strings along who count for much more. But the young woman won't be badly served with him, for you've got to grant it to him, he's a farmer through and through!'

Our discussion came to an end. From the legal point of view there was no possible objection to the proposal put forward; on the contrary, every difficulty was immediately overcome by it.

By the time we returned to the court, the bride-to-be had presented herself with her father. She must have been almost ten years older than the bridegroom arranged for her; her face was finely formed, but unappealing, as is usual among those who have worked in childhood; it was evident that the ash blonde hair had been exposed to the sun and all weathers. The bridegroom was now sitting opposite her against the other wall; head lowered, hands folded in front of him between splayed legs. During the proceedings that now followed he indicated his full agreement with everything; a mere 'Yes' or 'No' or 'That must be so then' was all he could find to express this agreement with, however, while wiping his brow from time to time with the back of his hand as though there were something there to wipe away. Finally, when everything had been discussed with all the parties assembled and the agreement set down on paper, there followed, according to law, the signing of the protocol.

Hinrich Fehse too stepped up to the parish representative's desk when his turn came and carefully wrote his Christian name in steep, irregular letters beneath the protocol; but then, with a deep sigh, he put down the quill and stared motionless in front of him. A girl's beautiful head may now have entered his thoughts; perhaps the disruptive idea of breaking with the bonds of the old farming tradition crossed his mind. But the sexton, who had not let him out of his sight during the entire proceedings, now went up to him, hands in pockets, and said quietly: 'Just your surname, Hinrich; just your surname!'

And Hinrich, as though dragged by the iron cable of necessity, now also wrote in 'Fehse' in his elongated hand after his Christian name.

Actum ut supra, Transacted as above, and a sprinkling of sand on it; the matter was settled. Hinrich Fehse left the court a made man; together with his wife-to-be he had the working capital for the farmstead in his hands; if he did his duty as a farmer, he would lack for nothing. And soon afterwards I heard that the wedding had been celebrated with all due pomp of rural tradition.

* *

The impression these events made on me gradually faded. At first I particularly noticed that when the young farmer drove past me with his wife on market days I would receive a nod of the head from the latter, while he himself, without looking round, simply whipped on his horses. A good while afterwards, late one evening, I saw him again in the lit entrance hall of that inn on the corner, and the thought struck me: 'What is he doing in the town at this hour!' But I gave no further thought to it. Then it was autumn again, November was approaching, and I was returning from my morning walk along the Neustadt where the horse market was being held. The handsome animals were standing tethered as usual in front of the inns on both sides of the street, and I was just forcing my way through a crowd of sellers and buyers and excited town youths when loud sounds of shouting and hand-slapping came towards me from one of the inns. When I approached I recognised Hinrich Fehse, engaged in keen business with a Jutland farmer. The matter in hand, it soon became clear to me, was a pair of most wretched-looking horses standing nearby, their heads lowered, while the Jutlander, in high praise, pulled the tail of one of the animals to one side.

'Well, all right,' said the other, without even looking at them, 'the old nags will just about do.'

'Hundred 'n' thirty for them both?' the Jutlander shouted back.

But Hinrich withdrew his hand. 'Hundred 'n' twenty,' he said gloomily, 'not a schilling more.'

And with a slap the hands came together. Hinrich Fehse untied his large leather money-bag, put the ready thaler coins into the other's hand, then prepared to unbind the purchased animals from the hitching post.

When I had moved on and the outline of the scene had become clearer in my mind, it appeared to me as though since our last meeting the young farmer, as they say here, had lost the game. His face was severe and drawn, the already small eyes had almost disappeared beneath the protruding brow. All in all, I now found something very striking in the commonplace event I had just witnessed, so that when I later entered the court I could not help raising the matter with my well-informed parish representative.

From his high desk stool the elderly official's hand motioned his extreme concern.

'So,' I said, 'things are looking bad?'

'Not just looking!' he replied. 'For the last six months Margret's been back in the village, and almost every evening Fehse's been found at the midwife's place; he chased after her even in the town at Whitsuntide, when she was working at her sewing in the harbour square. And in the meantime he's sold what he has of value, animal feed and rye seed, so that come winter his empty barns will stay empty; even the fine brown geldings have gone the same way today – that were valued, you know, Herr Amtsvogt, at five hundred thaler in the inventory – and he's replaced them with a pair of old Jutland jades. And now here's the midwife's girl parading herself around the village out there in silk jackets and gold brooches; she's carrying all Fehse's oats around on her!' And the old man took a large pinch of snuff.

'And that pair of geldings too, Brüttner!'

The short grey-haired man stuck the quill behind his ear and sailed round on his revolving stool to face me fully. 'Well,' he said, smiling to himself, 'and who gains from it in the end won't be too difficult to guess!'

'How is it you know so much about it?'

Brüttner was about to answer when the court messenger

entered the room. 'The sexton sends his regards, he's not able to come again today, but next Thursday; and then he's going to bring Fehse's wife and mother along with him.'

'The sexton's been here then?' I asked.

'Hm, yes, he has,' retorted Brüttner, 'and I thought, after recent events it would be best if the two women placed Herr Fehse under close guardianship; he'll explain it all, Herr Amtsvogt.'

* *

However, before the sexton could implement this bold plan, I received a written report from the Bauernvogt* – it was on a Wednesday – that Hinrich Fehse, resident of the community, had been missing since the previous Sunday evening. In the opinion of some he had left Hamburg on an emigration vessel with the money recently received from selling horses; others feared that he might have taken his own life. Apart from the known relationship with the midwife's daughter, no particular event had been heard of that could explain his disappearance. Inquiries made so far had yielded no results.

I decided to inquire into the matter that very afternoon. In order to be less restricted I did without a clerk of the court and simply took the court messenger for company. We drove in an open carriage; for it was a mild autumn day, the kind that our region is always granted before the final onset of winter. The sturdy hedgerows, which we had on both sides of the road during the first hour, still bore some of their foliage; here and there between hazel and oak bushes a spindle-tree pushed itself forward, the graceful red priest's-hood seedcases still hanging on its slender branches. As we drove on, my eyes took in a scene that was both peaceful and sad; yellow leaves, beneath the still warm

---

*Leading member of a village community whose duties combined public administration with representation of the interests of the peasantry.

rays of the sun, continually broke loose and sank to the ground, and from time to time a late thrush, shrieking in alarm, would flutter through the bushes away from the snorting of our horses.

But the landscape changed; the low hedgerows with cultivated fields behind them ceased. Instead we were driving along by the edge of the so-called 'Wild Moor', which at that time stretched to the north as far as the eye could see. It seemed as though the last rays of the sun remaining on earth had suddenly been swallowed up by this gloomy steppe. Amongst the dark-brown heather, often beside large or small pools, single stacks of peat loomed out of the barren expanse over which the occasional melancholy call of a solitary plover would sound out of the sky. That was all that could be seen or heard.

I was reminded of something I had once read – I think about the original Slav settler tribes that still populated the steppe of the lower Danube. At dusk a thing would rise up out of the moor there resembling a white thread, which they called the 'white demon'. It would move towards the villages, steal into the houses, and when night came, rest on the open mouths of sleeping persons; then the thin thread would swell and grow to a monstrous shape. There would be no sign of it the next morning; but when a sleeper opened his eyes, he had become an imbecile in the night; the white demon had drunk the soul from his body. It would never return to him; the dreadful thing had carried it far off into the moor, into the dank deep ditches between the heathland and the peat bog.

Not that the white demon was found in these parts; but the mists of these moors would thicken into no less eerie things that sought to confront many a villager, especially the older ones, at night and at twilight.

At the southern edge of the Moor lay our destination, the village, the church spire and dark straw-thatched roofs of which had long been visible to us. When we arrived at last, I stopped the carriage outside the old sexton's house in order to learn something more from him about present circumstances in the Fehse household. I met him with his farmhand busy loading a pile of dung on to a cart, in his buttonless blue woollen work jacket, fork in hand, but he was no less dignified for that, once he had exchanged his 'pile of gold' for level ground. 'I'll tell you something, Herr Amtsvogt', he began, after he had first prepared his vocal chords with a few attempts at a firm cough: 'He who can't be advised can't be helped! This Hinrich fellow quite clearly didn't know his luck; God only knows if the situation can still be saved by a guardianship!'

Meanwhile, we had entered the house and gone into the living room. Beside the stove, where a fire was burning despite the mild weather, sat a frail-looking little old woman almost wholly concealed by a large piece of knitting which she held with her bony fingers. She apologised for being unable to get up from her armchair to greet me, complaining that it was because of her back-ache; then from her chair she opened the nearby kitchen door and called out in a sharp voice: 'Kathrin! Put the kettle on, Kathrin!' And immediately I heard the trivet being dropped on to the range in the room next door and the fireplace raked.

The sexton's wife pulled the door to and continued with her knitting; but her small dull eyes constantly followed our movements as her husband and I walked up and down in conversation.

'If you will allow me, Herr Amtsvogt,' she said at last, pushing her knitting to one side: 'there was an omen in the days when my husband was still in office . . . I'm very fond of roses,' she continued, coughing slightly; 'it must have been the day before the ring-lancing at the school, when, with special permission, there'd be dancing and merrymaking at the inn in the evening – I suddenly found all my roses had been plucked. I knew perfectly well where the thieving rascal was to be found; but at school Hinrich was so good at twisting and turning with my husband, he was the schoolmaster then, that the cane was deflected on to his back. And that girl was sitting as quiet as a mouse reading her hymnbook.'

'But mother,' interrupted the sexton, 'you shouldn't be telling Herr Amtsvogt old children's tales!'

'You think so, father?' she retorted. 'It was shortly before their confirmation; there's only *one* trail, and it still leads there to this day.'

I politely asked her to continue her story.

The little old woman nodded. 'I still had my health in those days, Herr Amtsvogt,' she began again, 'but on that following evening, as soon as I had set foot in the inn with the pastor's wife, I could see that Hinrich had had his way; for in the garland that the Slovak girl wore on her black hair, there were my red roses; and she'd been twirling about with him so, sweat was running from the clumsy fellow's cheeks.

'Now, now, father!' – she interrupted herself as the sexton made a new comment. 'I know very well the fun didn't last long; but I'll tell the Amtsvogt everything. There was actually one of the older lads who was not infatuated with the midwife's girl like the others, although she had done her best to make herself noticed by him – this was the son of that wealthy Klaus Ottsen here! – Just as the musicians began a new waltz he comes swaggering up in his blue jacket with pearl buttons, with a silver watch-chain over his waistcoat, and looking round among the girls as though they were all standing there just for him. But he made a neat figure with his brown hair, and even today he still thinks a lot of himself. He stopped in front of Hinrich and Margret, who were about to rejoin the dancing, and looked down at them scornfully. "Stealer and receiver?" he said laughing. "Rosy Hinrich and Slovak Margret? You make a fine pair together!" The girl glared at him with her dark eyes. "Are you going to let him insult me, Hinrich?" she cried. And in a flash Ottsen received two punches in the neck from him. "That's for Slovak Margret! And that's for Rosy Hinrich!" And the musicians played on and the children danced and stumbled over Hans as he picked himself up from the floor; and amongst all the noise I heard our pastor's voice and saw him grasping Hinrich by the collar and holding him against the doorpost. "I want you to know, Fehse!" I heard him say, "the dancing's over for you this evening!"

'He stood there and bit his lip till it bled, and Margret lifted her head of black hair and searched the hall for another dancer. It's a strange thing, the human heart, Herr Amtsvogt! For some time I'd observed Hans Ottsen standing there as though he wanted to devour the girl with his eyes; and it didn't help at all that the stolen roses went so confoundedly well with her fine impudent stubby little nose. And that's how it was! Now she had him on a string too. "What d'you say, Margret?" says this show-off in a low voice. "Do you want to spend the evening with *me* now?" At first, when he had snatched at her hand, she had pushed him away and behaved like a wild cat; but when she noticed how serious he was, she was all affectionate, laughing and showing her white teeth, and she danced with her fancy Hans straight past the poor fellow as though there had never been a Hinrich Fehse for her in the whole world. He just stood there as though he was nailed to the doorpost; only his small eyes followed the couple; it was lucky they weren't loaded with shotgun pellets!

'What happened in the hall after that,' she continued, after spending a while regaining her breath, 'I didn't see; the pastor's wife called me into the room at the back where our menfolk were playing cards. Time passed; the evening had just been called to a close, I was standing by the window and listening to the wild geese in the sky above, for it was a mild night and the birds were flying over the Moor towards the sea on the tidal flats – then someone suddenly said: "Where's Hinrich Fehse?" Hinrich Fehse wasn't there. "I saw him outside in the road," someone else said; "he'll have gone home." But his mother came in all distressed; he wasn't at home either. Old Hinrich Fehse, standing up for his son in spite of all, was at the front of the dense crowd in the taproom. He banged his glass down on the table, only the stem was left in his hand, and raged at the pastor; he was not having his son picked on, even if he couldn't cover him with watch-chains and pearl buttons like the rich farmers; no by God, that he was not going to tolerate!

'I'd gone back to the dance hall where the musicians were just putting their fiddles away into their leather bags. The midwife's girl was still standing there on the empty floor with Hans Ottsen; she seemed to be the only one completely unconcerned. "Margret," I said to her, "don't you know where Hinrich's got to?" – "Me? – No!" she said abruptly, taking off one of her small shoes and adjusting the red bow on it; then she flashed her dark eyes at Hans again and playfully slapped his hands: "You've covered me in dust, you have! You're so wild; just wait, I'm not dancing with such a hothead any more!"

'And that was Margret for you, Herr Amtsvogt. But Hinrich still didn't come home the next morning either. They said the midday meal would bring him home; but that was wishful thinking; the whole village took to their feet, they searched for him with ladders and poles. And in the end! Where do you think he'd been, Herr Amtsvogt? – He'd been sitting with the toads all night, out there on the Moor by the Dark Pool. Finkeljochim, he cuts his brooms there, came running into the village and told us. Then they fetched him home, with rheumatic pains in his arms and legs from the damp of the Moor. He was confined to his bed for a few weeks, and when the doctor could do nothing, they used all kinds of local remedies; and then as they say, three cups of camomile tea and a few handfuls of churchyard earth soon put everything to rights again.'

The coffee had meanwhile been brought in, and the sexton reminded his wife, not without apparent concern, that the Amtsvogt still had to speak to him.

'I don't want to be in the way, father,' she retorted, filling the cups from her armchair. 'I'm just saying, and I've already told the pastor: once the girl was home again from the town, Hinrich immediately ran round to the midwife's house, and the girl was delighted to have someone in tow again, even if only to annoy his young wife; and since old Klaus Ottsen's been on his deathbed and can no longer keep a firm hold on things, his Hans too can find his way there at nightfall. I'm not at all surprised that Fehse's run off again this time; for he's never been able to learn to live with himself, which is the greatest gift in life by far. I can't fathom why there's so much fuss about it in the village; he'll come back, when he's had enough!'

The frail little woman, whose pale cheeks had recovered their colour during her lively narrative, fell silent and attempted to liven up the coals in her stove with the tongs. I put certain questions to her and then let the sexton, his dignity visibly restored once we were outside, accompany me to my carriage.

'Of course, Your Honour,' he said, as though coming to the conclusion of a lengthy thought process, 'I've had a lot to do with this marriage, but a person shouldn't count on the world for thanks! Just look to that girl Margret; she'll be able to tell you everything.'

In the meanwhile he had buttoned up the leather guard in front of my seat, and I gave a dignified departing wave of the hand as my carriage rumbled off along the poorly cobbled village street.

Beyond the church lying to the right, on the granite wall of which, in passing, I read the year 1470, a cottage with green shutters looked out from now almost bare elder hedges.

'That's the midwife's,' said the court messenger in answer to my question, turning towards me from the coachbox. 'They keep it spotless; I've been there a few times on business.'

The cottages on the left of the road came to an end after a while. The farmsteads, which continued to stretch a good way to the church side of the road, faced west and were separated from the Moor by only the road and some bounded fields and meadows; the last of them, in an isolated spot some distance away, had already been pointed out to me as Hinrich Fehse's.

I noticed groups of people in front of many of these houses, who seemed to be in lively conversation, occasionally pointing towards the Moor with outstretched arms. It was evidently a disturbing time for the villagers.

At last we drove on to the Fehses' farm. The house, standing some hundred paces back from the road, bore visible fruits of the prosperous marriage: the northern half with its great barn door and semi-circular stall windows had evidently been built hardly a year before; the other half, by contrast, containing the living quarters, might well have passed down in its present form from father to son since time immemorial. In front of the low windows, upon which a heavy dark-brown straw-thatched roof bore down, an almost bare patch of garden stretched down to the road.

Since no member of the household appeared when we drew up at the barn door, I sent the court messenger into the house, and he presently returned to the carriage in the company of an old woman. I began to greet her as the widow Frau Fehse, but she replied that she was only a neighbour looking after the house; the elder and the younger Frau Fehse had gone to see the Bauernvogt; for Finkeljochim's daughter had said that she had seen Hinrich the night before, just as the moon had risen, out on the Moor. At this news people had been sent out in search of him again.

I enquired more closely.

'There won't be anything in it, Herr Amtsvogt,' said the old woman. 'The girl's a bit simple; and ever since Hans Ottsen put ideas into her head last winter, she's become a complete scatter-brain.'

'But where is this girl to be found now?'

'You can't see her now, Herr Amtsvogt. She's out on the heath with the others showing them where it was.'

For the present, shown into the living room by the old woman, I had a table set up in the middle of it, on which I laid out the writing materials I had brought with me for making the necessary notes.

It was a low-ceilinged but spacious room; the white sand in the hallway, the shiny brass knobs on the stove, everything displayed cleanliness and order. Opposite the windows were two curtained wall-beds; in front of one of them, upon which the words: "East or West, home is best" were painted between forget-me-nots, stood a now empty wooden cradle.

So as not to lose any time, I told the court messenger to find the midwife's daughter, who lived nearby, while the old woman undertook to fetch the Fehse women from the Bauernvogt's house some distance away. I now found myself alone in the house; from the wall came the harsh tick of a Black Forest clock; awaiting what was to come, I had walked over to the window and was looking into the yellow autumn sun which was already low on the Moor.

The rustle of women's clothes roused me from the thoughts in which I had begun to wrap myself. When I turned round I saw the slim shapely figure of a girl in town clothes, whose small and, so it seemed to me, shaking hand was just slipping a black head-scarf from her neck.

I was in no doubt who it was I had before me; for the first time I saw that girl's bewitching head uncovered.

'You are Margarete Glansky?' I said.

A hardly audible 'Yes'.

I sat down opposite her at the table and took the pen in my hand.

'You know young Hinrich Fehse?' I continued.

'Yes', just as quietly.

'I mean, have you known him well?'

She did not answer. When I looked up I saw she was deathly white; I could hear her small white teeth chattering. Fear of external responsibility springing from perhaps inner feelings of guilt might have been gripping her.

'What are you afraid of?' I asked.

'I'm not afraid – but the farmers' wives, they all hate me.'

'This is not about you, Margarete Glansky, but about the young man who has been missing for some days.'

'I don't know anything about it; it's not my fault!' she burst out, still wrestling for breath.

'But we must try to find him,' I continued. 'Shortly before his marriage you moved away to the town and then six months ago you came back here again?'

'I didn't like it there; I'd no need to work. I'm still sorry I was stupid enough to let myself be sent away!' And the girl's strong eyebrows drew close together.

'Hinrich Fehse,' I said, 'has often visited you in the evenings, then?'

'We couldn't keep him away.'

'It is said he came every evening in the end, then often stayed until midnight.'

'The women are liars!'

'But you've accepted gifts from him?'

A flush swept across her face. 'Who's said that?'

'It's being shouted from the rooftops; it's sown terrible discord in this married household.'

'Well, so if it is true!' she cried, defiantly pursing her red lips. 'Who told her to marry him!'

'And would you have married him, then?' I asked.

But before she could answer, the door to the room was thrown open and both the Fehse women, the younger with her child on her arm, entered the room. I noticed how the older farmer's wife and the midwife's daughter glared at each other with undisguised hatred; then the old woman stood in front of me and said, shaking:

'Herr Amtsvogt, what's that person there doing in our house? I don't believe I have to tolerate this!'

'That person,' I replied, quietly ushering both women out through the door, 'is under judicial enquiry and has been summoned here by me.'

We stood outside in the hallway. The gaunt old woman wrung her hands. 'Oh, the misery!' she cried. 'The misery!' The young farmer's wife dried the tears she was constantly weeping from the sleeping child's cheeks.

'Things were so good that first year,' she said, 'if only *she* hadn't come back; people like us simply don't understand such things, but he just had to fall for her! And all that money he recently got for the horses – we've searched the bureau and everything, but there's nothing to be found.'

Through the open doorway I saw a man outside pass by with a long pole and take the road down to the Moor. The old woman went outside and came back crying. But she suddenly wiped her eyes with her apron. 'He'll know up there where he is,' she said. 'He wasn't Godless, my Hinrich! – He'd fallen on his knees and he was pressing his poor head into my lap; for he was always my little boy! "Mother," he said, "you saw me ride off on the bay, and I told you I had to go to the north mill to the miller about the rent – that was a lie, mother; I deceived you, I drove around like mad for five hours; you yourself wiped the lather from the bay's flanks when I got home; I just didn't want to ride over to *her*; but it was as if I was being dragged there by the hair just the same – it got the better of me – I can't help it, mother!"'

'And he was a good man, my Hinrich!' continued the old woman, as though talking to herself. 'Especially after the baby was born! In our courtyard here, I once had to hand it up to him on the horse; the sun was shining so warm, the summer crop was standing so green over in the paddock. "What do you think, mother," he said, "I could take it on to the field for a little while!" He was so happy with his child; it was hard to separate him from it; and it was only just six weeks old!'

I left the women in the hallway while making it clear to them that they had to remain available for questioning too. When I returned to the room, the slanting rays of the evening sun were already pouring through the window. The girl was still standing in the same place as before; but she appeared to be calmer and even to have begun to feel trust in me, perhaps simply because I had supported her presence in the face of the other women. 'Yes, Herr Amtsvogt, I'll tell you about it,' she began, brushing back her shining black hair with both hands. 'Whether I would've married him if he hadn't needed that money from the other woman – I simply don't know, and there's no point asking about it now; I've been a good friend to him, we used to have a good dance together; but – and this is the truth, Herr Amtsvogt! – I never thought he'd take it all so seriously.'

'But you knew,' I said, 'he'd been running after you ever since he was a boy; and he didn't seem to me the sort to play at such things.'

She cast a rapid sidewards glance into the small mirror decorated with peacock feathers, and for a moment her dark eyes lit up with a wild zest for life. 'Well,' she said, 'in the end I couldn't help noticing; but then I couldn't get rid of him. I tried hard enough; because he drove me insane with his moods; especially when other young people came to see us, which of course they often did. He'd grind his teeth if I even brought one of them to the door, or even once when, just play-acting, Hans Ottsen tried to loosen my plaits; and he had his wife at home!'

I gave her a firm look. 'So Ottsen came to see you recently? Perhaps you're aware that his father made the farmstead over to him around St John's Day?'

She faltered for a moment as though confused; but then, as if she hadn't heard my comment, she continued: 'Many an evening, when the night watchman blew nine o'clock, my mother begged him to go home. But he didn't. "Neighbour," he'd say, "you'll surely not begrudge me a seat in your house; I'm not asking for anything more!" And so we'd remain seated, me at my sewing-stone in front of one of the table-drawers, he in front of the other. "Hinrich," I'd often say to him, "don't be so gloomy! You can dance with me on Sunday at the inn, if you like; bring your wife along too and let's all enjoy ourselves together." But he simply gave me a scornful grin and looked at me with his little eyes as if he wanted to hurt me with them.

'Just once,' she continued after a short pause, 'he stayed away for a while – when his child was born; and I really thought he'd regained his senses. Then, about a month later, his wife fell very ill; everyone thought it was the end with her, even my mother who had had to help with the birth. And then, Herr Amtsvogt – he came again.'

The girl took a deep breath. 'He'd completely changed, more like when he was still a young lad; he could talk freely again and spoke again of his farm; what he wanted to do and achieve. But once – when my mother wasn't at home – he suddenly grabbed hold of my shoulders and looked at me, beside himself with joy. "Margret!" he cried, "Just imagine it! If – oh, if!" Then he fell silent and let me go, but I knew very well what he meant and saw it for myself all too soon. So I tried to get him to change the subject. "Has the doctor been to your house today, then?" I asked. "How's Ann-Marieken?" At first it seemed as if he didn't want to answer. "She got something else to take with water from the doctor," he said in the end. "I don't know what for." At the same time he fished the geomancy book out of my mother's sewing box, sat down opposite me and began to make chalk marks on the table. He did it so hastily, and his face got so flushed, that I asked: "Hinrich, what are you making all those marks there for?"

' "Quiet, quiet!" he said. "Get on with your sewing!" But I leaned over the table without him noticing and read the number in the book his finger was resting on. It was at the question whether a sick person would get better. I said nothing and went back to my work; and he kept on making marks, counting "Even" or "Uneven" and then marking the figures with chalk on the table. "Well," I asked, "have you finished? Can we know what this is all about now?" He was resting his head in his hands and looking at me in silence, but so calmly and tenderly, as he hadn't done for some time. Then he stood up and offered me his hand. "Good night, Margret!" he said. "I must go home now." And so he left; it was still early in the evening. The figures were still on the table, and I looked them up in the little book. There stood the answer: "Comfort the soul of the sick and abandon all hope!" – But this time he was wrong; his wife recovered shortly afterwards; and then it was even worse with him than it ever was before. Believe me, Herr Amtsvogt, if I've ever treated him wrongly, it's been paid for with fear and suffering.'

At these words she broke into an uncontrollable fit of crying, and I let her sit down on a chair. But she soon lifted her head again, pressing it between her hands, and looked at me. The light of the setting sun, which was still in the room, fell on the girl's red lips, sharply setting them off against her pale face and dark eyes.

But I needed to question her further. 'Hinrich Fehse,' I said, 'did some horse-trading last week, and he should have brought home a lot of money. His mother and his wife, however, assure me they can find none anywhere.'

'We haven't got the money, Herr Amtsvogt!' she said gloomily.

'And you don't know where it's got to either?'

She nodded her head. 'Yes; I do know.'

'Some people are saying,' I continued, 'that he's gone to Hamburg to board an emigrant ship to America?'

'No, Herr Amtsvogt; where he's gone to I don't know, but he's not gone to America with *that* money. I'll tell you about that too, as truthfully as if I were standing before God! – It was last Sunday evening, it might have been around eight o'clock; my mother, who'd been up the night before, was sitting in the armchair nodding over her knitting; we were completely alone, and I was surprised that Hinrich Fehse hadn't come, for that morning in church he'd stared at me again, such a stare that all the women turned to look at me. Outside the storm was raging; but in between the blasts of wind I occasionally thought I heard footsteps going past our house. It was uncanny and I went outside to see what it might be. There was no moonlight, Herr Amtsvogt, but it was a bright night; through the bare elder hedge I could clearly make out the crosses in the churchyard that backs on to our garden; and I saw that there was someone standing down by the hedge; and as I walked towards it, it was Hinrich Fehse. "What are you standing out here for, letting yourself get chilled through?" I said. "Why don't you come in?" – "I must speak with you alone, Margret!" he replied. – "Well, go on, speak, we're alone; no one's going to come out here in this bad weather." But he didn't speak, till I said: "I'm cold; I'm going in to fetch my shawl." Then he grabbed me by the hand and said, very gravely: "It can't go on any more, Margret; I must put an end to it." – He looked so strange; I didn't know how to answer. "Hinrich," I said, "it would be best if I went away again, then everything would be much better!" – "We must both go, go away together, Margret!" he answered, and at the same time he pulled out a purse and clinked it several times on the edge of the well where we were standing at that moment. "Hear that?" he said,

"That's gold! The day before yesterday I sold my bays; I'm going to my cousin abroad in the New World; it's easy to earn a living there." – "You wouldn't do that to your wife!" I said. "Not do that to her, Margret? It'll be no blessing for her if I stay here; the few thousand thaler she brought to the business will soon be gone; I'm not a farmer any more, my only thoughts are for you!" He wanted to put his arms round me, but I sprang back.

' "A fine thing for me," I said, "to run away with you as your mistress into the wide world!" – "Just listen," he began again, "we'll leave secretly; my wife will then ask for a divorce; then we can get married there." – "No, Hinrich; I won't do it, I won't go away like that." When I said that he was beside himself; he threw himself on the ground, I don't know everything he said; and the storm was howling round the church so that I could hardly make his words out, and my clothes were flapping and I was frozen stiff. "Get off home, Hinrich," I begged. "You're not yourself today, let's talk about it tomorrow!"

'As I was saying this I heard loud voices behind us from down the churchyard path; Hans Ottsen's was among them, and I listened for the sound of our gate opening, for from time to time over the last few weeks he had come to see us. But they must have walked on past; I heard the handle turn in the large churchyard gate, and soon the voices were below in the village street. When I turned my head back, Hinrich was standing in front of me. "Margret," he said, and he was choking on his words, "will you go with me?" But before I could answer he put his hand over my mouth. "Don't answer too hastily!" he cried. "I'll not ask again – never again." I didn't reply; I was fighting for breath; how should I have answered him? "Look!" he said. "I knew it; you're deceitful, you're waiting for *him*!" He made a movement with his arm, and immediately afterwards I heard something clashing and splashing deep down in the well. "Your gold, Hinrich!" I cried. "What are you doing?" – "Let it go!" he said. "I don't need it any more now – but" – and he grasped hold of me with both hands and held me out in front of him as though he wanted to study me from a distance – "give me another kiss, Margret!" '

'And then what?' I asked, when the girl faltered.

'I won't lie to you, Herr Amtsvogt, I wouldn't have refused it to him; but he suddenly pushed me away. I began to run to the front door; then he angrily called my name, and when I didn't answer he ran after me and grabbed hold of me with arms like steel. My hair fell loose; he wound one of my plaits round his hand and pulled my head back with it. "Just a minute, Margret," he said, and through the darkness I saw his little eyes flashing above me; and with the storm almost tearing the clothes from my body he shouted into my ear: "I'll tell you a secret, Margret; but don't let it go any further! There's no room left for both of us on this earth; you will be damned, Margret!"

'I cried out; I believed he was going to strangle me. Then he let me go and ran off. I heard him closing the churchyard gate, and then my mother came to the front door and called for me. "He'll come to his senses in the morning," she said, after I had told her everything, as much as I was able to; "then he can fish the gold out of the well himself." She fetched a padlock and fastened it to the front of the well cover which my grandfather had once made in case of unwelcome guests; for someone else could have lifted the purse out in a bucket.

'When we returned indoors, my mother got into bed and I went on with my work. The storm raged on outside; occasionally I heard the watchman's horn down in the village, and the big clock striking in the church tower. An uncanny feeling came over me and I was on edge; all the time I was thinking he might have harmed himself. When I noticed that my mother had fallen asleep, I took my shawl and slipped out.

'I met no one on the road; most of the houses were already in darkness; only at the Fehses' could I see a light still shining through the crack between the window shutters. I took courage and went up the bank and in through the garden gate. As I stood close by the window I heard the whirring of the spinning-wheel inside, with an occasional word from the old woman. "What would they be talking about!" I thought to myself and put my ear to the shutter, but I couldn't make out a thing. Then I noticed an upturned wheelbarrow under the other window, and when I climbed on it and stood on my toes my eyes reached the heart-hole in the shutter. I could see the wall-bed from there; I saw too that someone was lying on it, and when the head tossed about on the pillow I recognised it was Hinrich. All of a sudden he raised his head from the pillow and stared in my direction. I was seized with dread, and jumped down from the barrow and ran off across the road and through the churchyard. The wind came whistling and howling round the corner of the church tower; one of those times when old Finkeljochim used to say the dead were screaming in their graves. I was terrified, I've no idea how I got home and into bed. The next morning they said Hinrich Fehse had disappeared in the night; I've seen nothing of him since.'

She fell silent. Dusk had settled in the meantime. When I cast a glance outside through the small windows, the last weak light of the sun still showed on the horizon; the trees in the garden stood in dark silhouette; across the Moor below, mist drifted like white veils. I had two tallow candles lit and placed on the table in front of me; then I called the Fehse women into the room.

'Should she be here with us?' asked the old farmer's wife, casting a half shy, half hate-filled glance at the girl who at my behest had sat down in one of the corners by the window.

'She won't be disturbing you, Frau Fehse!' I replied.

'Well, as far as I'm concerned, what I've got to say God and all the world can hear, but' – and she raised her withered finger threateningly – 'the wicked will get their reward!'

The girl appeared not to hear these words; as though exhausted, she had leaned her head so far back against the wall that her black hair had fallen back from her temples.

'Enough of that, Frau Fehse!' I said. 'Tell me what took place.'

She appeared to stir herself from deep thought.

'Yes,' she said, 'he was over there on *that* evening, there, with *her*! But he still came home early; for Ann-Marieken lay very ill – the doctor had just prescribed something new for her – then he sat up the whole night by her bed; yes, he did! And stroked her hand! "Ann-Marieken," he said, "it's not your fault; don't be too harsh on me up there; it'll be better for you there than here with me." '

The young woman, who had just laid her child in the cradle, burst into bitter tears.

'I meant, Frau Fehse,' I reminded her, 'what happened on that last evening when your son left the house.'

'Well, what happened?' she replied. 'It was last Sunday evening; we'd cleared away the meal and the maid had gone to her room – no, it must have been around ten o'clock already; Ann-Marieken and I were still sitting at our spinning wheels. My Hinrich had come home very disturbed; he'd been lying in the wall-bed there for some time. But he didn't sleep, he tossed and turned and even groaned to himself; we were quite used to that with him, Herr Amtsvogt. The weather was bad, as it often is in November; the north-west wind was in full fury and tearing the leaves from the trees; I was afraid as usual it might even topple the pear tree on to the barn, the tree my late father planted himself at Hinrich's christening. Then I heard the sound of faint footfalls outside the window, and I listened to it, and, Herr Amtsvogt, I didn't know if it was an animal or a human being. "Do you hear that, Ann-Marieken?" I asked. But she grasped her spinning wheel and said: "No, mother, I don't hear anything!" Then I pushed a chair up to the window and looked out through the eye-hole in the shutters, for we had fastened them to against the storm. The pear tree stood there against the grey night sky and groaned and fought pitifully against the storm; I could see too across the paddocks and the meadows below, and the pools glistening in the Moor beyond, for the night was clear at the time. No living thing was to be seen. But I noticed that something was huddled below the window, and it moved as though a shaggy coat was rubbing itself along the wall. As I got down from the chair there was a scratching at the other shutter, and immediately I heard the hand-strap creaking over in the wall-bed and my Hinrich was sitting bolt upright in his pillows and staring with completely lifeless eyes towards the window. When I cried out: "Good God, Hinrich! What's wrong?" the cattle in the stalls at the back of the house became restless too, and through the din of the storm I heard the bull bellowing and tearing at its chains with all its might. But my Hinrich went on sitting there deathly quiet and staring, so that I was quite afraid, and when I turned round myself – Oh, my Lord Jesus Christ! – an animal was looking through the window shutters! I clearly saw the pointed white teeth and the dark eyes!'

The old woman wiped the sweat from her brow with her apron and began murmuring quietly to herself.

'An animal, Frau Fehse?' I asked. 'Have you got such large dogs in the village then?'

She shook her head: 'It was no dog, Herr Amtsvogt!'

'But there are no wolves here any more!'

The old woman turned her head slowly towards the girl and then said in a sharp voice: 'It might not have been a real wolf!'

'Mother! Mother!' cried the young wife. 'But you've always told me it was the midwife's Margret looking in at the window!'

'Hm, Ann-Marieken, I'm not saying it wasn't her either.' And the old woman sank back again into her obscure complaining and murmuring.

'What nonsense is this, Frau Fehse!' I cried. But as I saw the girl sitting there so lifeless with her face as white as a sheet and her red lips – the white demon from her grandfather's homeland passed through my mind, and I almost added: 'You're wrong, you know. I know better, Frau Fehse, she's drunk his soul; perhaps he's gone to find it!' But I simply said: 'Just tell me quietly, what happened later with your Hinrich?'

'My Hinrich?' she repeated. 'He grasped the hand-strap and his feet were suddenly on the floor. "Let *me* do it, Hinrich!" I said. But he dressed quickly: "No, no, mother, you can't control the bull!" and all the while his eyes were on the window shutters. Then as he was leaving he knocked the cradle, which stood there next to the bed just as it does today, and the little one stretched out its arm in its sleep and snatched at the air with its tiny fingers. My Hinrich suddenly stood still and bent over the cradle, and I heard him say to himself: "The child! The child!" And just as he was stretching out his hand towards the little hand, the storm buffeted the shutters again and the noises in the stalls outside began once more. Then he sighed deeply and went out of the door as though he was in a daze.'

For some while I had observed that Margret had been holding her head towards the window as though listening to something; now I too heard the dull rumbling of a wagon that seemed to be coming up the road from the Moor.

'And since then,' I pressed the old woman, 'you've not seen your son at all?'

I received no answer. The living room door creaked, and a small grey dog squeezed itself through the opening, wet and bespattered; it ran to the old farmer's wife and looked questioningly at her for a moment, sniffed whining around the bed space, then ran out just as quickly through the door again. Both women, who had followed the dog with their eyes, holding their breaths, burst out into loud crying. This was, as far as I could gather, the missing person's dog which he had reared himself and which had always been around him; the animal had also been missing since that evening.

In the meantime the rumble of the wagon had been coming nearer. I noticed the girl at the window lift her head and stare out with wide-open eyes. I could hardly see her in the dim light cast by the tallow candles, but a bright moonlight fell through the windows. She rose slowly like a snake and then remained standing with wide-open mouth. At the same moment the wagon rumbled on to the threshing floor of the house.

For a while there was deathly silence, then loud men's voices came from the hallway, the living room door flew wide open, and a broad-shouldered man stepped into the room. 'We've come with the body,' he said, 'it was lying in the Dark Pool out there on the Moor.'

The women began to scream hysterically; the young wife flung herself over her baby's cradle with both arms and, disturbed from sleep, it added its shrill cries to the rest.

But something suddenly seized the old woman's mind; her bony hands trembled, and she walked up to the girl who, as if turned to stone, was still staring out into the empty night. 'Do you hear?' she cried. 'He's dead! Be off! There's nothing more for you here.'

The girl turned her head as though she had understood nothing; but despite the cover of her clothing I saw a shiver run through her body as she walked quietly out through the door. Through the window I saw her walking away across the yard; her head seemed to turn on her neck automatically, always facing the barn where the corpse lay. Suddenly, when she had reached the road, she began to run with raised arms, as if to escape from whatever it was behind her. Soon she disappeared into the white mist coming up from the Moor and shrouding the road.

I had the carriage made ready; my duties for the day were over. As I drove through the village the sexton came towards me from his farm and laid his hand on my carriage. 'I'm sorry about Hinrich, Herr Amtsvogt!' he said. 'But who knows if it's not for the best; we must just see to it now that we get an efficient farm manager who can marry the widow and run the place for little Hinrich Fehse. Everything will be dealt with, Herr Amtsvogt!' And with his old imperturbability he solemnly shook my hand in farewell. With these comforting words still in my ears, I drove out of the village and along the edge of the Moor, now lit by a dim moon.

To conclude my report: the next day the midwife's well was emptied, and the sunken treasure really did return to the light of day. A husband was even found for the young widow, after the child had followed its father into that unknown land within just a year through an attack of angina. Hans Ottsen, rather than attach himself to the midwife's disreputable daughter, preferred to add, by the simple means of marriage, the Fehses' holding to his father's. And so, in accordance with the sexton's wife's remedy, with some handfuls of churchyard earth everything was soon put to rights again.

Should anyone ask after the Slav girl, I am unable to give an answer; she is said to have moved to some large town, I do not know which, and must have disappeared into the tide of people there.

Paul the Puppeteer

I HAD SOME SKILL as a wood-turner in my youth, and concerned myself somewhat more with this occupation than was good for my studies; and so it was that one day the deputy headmaster strangely asked me, on returning a not exactly error-free piece of written homework to me, whether perhaps I had again been turning a wooden pin-cushion holder for my sister's birthday. Such minor setbacks, however, were more than outweighed by the resulting acquaintance with a fine man. He was the master turner and mechanicus Paul Paulsen, a member of our town council. At the request of my father, who expected a degree of thoroughness in everything he saw me undertake, he agreed to teach me the necessary tricks of the trade for my small tasks.

Paulsen possessed a wide range of knowledge not simply derived from a recognised competence in his own craft. He also had a deep insight into the future development of the crafts in general so that when I heard something that sounded like a new truth to most people, it would suddenly occur to me: your old Paulsen said that forty years ago. I soon won his affection and he looked pleased when I paid him evening visits outside the arranged times of instruction. Then we would either sit in his workshop, or during the summers – for our friendship lasted many years – on the bench beneath the tall linden tree in his little garden. From the conversations we held there, or rather, which my older friend conducted there with me, I learned and was led to think about things of which, however important they were in life, I was later to find no mention even in the school books of my final year.

Paulsen was of Frisian descent, and the character of this people was most finely revealed in his face; beneath smooth blond hair he had a thinker's brow and pensive blue eyes, and along with these features, inherited from his father, his voice had something of the soft tones of his native language.

The wife of this Nordic man was dark-complexioned and of slender build, her speech having an unmistakable south German ring. My mother used to say of her that her dark eyes could set a lake on fire, that in her youth she had been a rare beauty. In spite of the grey threads that already ran through her hair, the charm of her features had even now not disappeared, and youth's innate appreciation of beauty soon induced me to be helpful to her, whenever I could, with small favours.

'Just look at the fine lad,' she'd then say to her husband. 'Isn't it enough to make you just a little jealous, Paul?'

Paul smiled. And her joking remark and his smile expressed the most intense closeness.

Apart from a son, who was abroad at the time, they had no children, and it was partly perhaps for that reason that I was made so welcome by them, especially by Frau Paulsen who repeatedly assured me that I had just as funny a little nose as her Joseph. I will not conceal that she also knew how to prepare a most delicious pastry for me, which was completely unknown in our town, and she would invite me to their house from time to time. So there were attractions enough to make me go there. My father, however, had his own reasons for thoroughly approving of my visits to this worthy household. 'Take care, though, that you don't become a nuisance!' was the only thing he said to me about the matter from time to time. But I don't believe I really visited my friends too often.

Then one day in my parents' house my most recent and actually rather successful handiwork was shown to an old gentleman of our town.

When he expressed his amazement my father responded that I had been apprenticed to Paulsen, the master craftsman, for almost a year now.

'Well, well,' replied the old gentleman, 'to Paul the Puppeteer!'

I was not aware that my friend had such a nickname and asked, perhaps a little nosily, what it meant.

But the old gentleman simply gave an enigmatic smile and would say nothing more about it.

On the following Sunday the Paulsens invited me for the evening to celebrate their wedding anniversary with them. It was late summer, and as I had set out earlier than expected and found his wife still busy in the kitchen, Paulsen went with me into the garden where we sat together on the bench under the tall linden tree. The nickname 'Paul the Puppeteer' came back to me and kept going round in my head, so that I was hardly responding at all to what he was saying; until eventually, when he had almost seriously rebuked me for my lack of attention, I asked him directly what that name meant.

He became very angry. 'Who mentioned that ridiculous nickname to you?' he cried, leaping up from the bench. But before I could reply, he had sat down again beside me. 'Never mind! Never mind!' he said, collecting himself, 'it actually means the best that life has given me. I'll tell you all about it; we've time enough for it.

– 'I grew up in this house and garden, my good parents lived here and I hope my son too will live here one day. It's a long time ago now since I was a boy; but certain things from that time I can still see before my eyes, as though they'd been drawn in coloured pencil.

In those days a small white seat stood beside our front door with green wooden bars in its back and armrests, and from it you could see in one direction down the long street as far as the church, and in the other the open fields beyond the town. My parents would sit there on summer evenings, resting after work; but during the hours before this I would take over the seat and do my schoolwork there in the open air, refreshed by the views to the east and west.

Well, I was sitting there one afternoon – I remember clearly it was in September, just after our St Michael's fair – writing out my algebra homework for the mathematics teacher on my slate, when I saw a strange-looking horse-drawn vehicle coming up the road. It was a two-wheeled cart pulled by a scraggy little horse. Between two tall chests loaded on it sat a large blonde woman with stern expressionless features and a girl of about nine, who turned her black head of hair excitedly this way and that; alongside, reins in hand, walked a short man with a sprightly air, below whose green peaked cap short black hair stood out like spikes.

And so, to the tinkling of a tiny bell that hung below the horse's neck, they came up the road. When they had reached our house, the cart stopped. "Hey, you lad," the woman called down to me, "where's the tailors' hostel, then?"

My slate pencil had been idle for some time; I eagerly jumped up and went towards the cart. "You're in front of it," I said, and pointed towards the old house with the boxed linden tree, which as you know still stands opposite here today.

The pretty little girl had stood up between the tall chests, poked her head out of the hood of her short faded cloak, and was looking down at me with her large eyes; but the man, with a "Sit still, girl!" and a "Thanks, lad!", whipped the scraggy little horse on and led it to the door of the house I had indicated, from which the burly house-father in his green apron was already emerging to meet him.

That the new arrivals did not belong to those entitled to stay at the tailors' hostel as guests of the guild must have been perfectly clear to me; but there used to be others like them who would stop off there – which, when I now come to think of it, does not seem wholly in keeping with the reputation of that highly respectable craft, although in my view they were much more agreeable people. It used to be up there on the second floor, where instead of today's windows only simple wooden shutters gave on to the road, that all the travelling musicians, tightrope-walkers or animal trainers who performed in our town lodged.

And to be sure, the next morning, when I stood in front of the window up in my room fastening my school satchel, one of the shutters opposite was thrown open and the short man with the black spiky hair poked his head out and stretched both his arms in the air; then he turned his head back towards the dark room behind him, and I heard him call out: "Lisei! Lisei!" Then a small rosy face, the black hair falling round it like a mane, pushed its way forward under his arm. The father pointed across at me with his finger, laughed, and gave her silky locks a few tugs. What he said to her I couldn't catch; but one might have guessed it to be something like: "Look at him, Lisei! It's the boy from yesterday, isn't it? The poor thing, he's got to trot off to school now with his satchel! What a lucky girl you are, all you need do is travel up and down the land with our bay!" For the little girl looked sympathetically across at me, and when I dared to nod to her in a friendly way, she nodded back quite seriously.

But her father soon withdrew his head and disappeared into the rear of the attic room. In his place the large blonde woman now appeared beside the child; she seized her head and began to comb her hair. It appeared to be done in silence, and Lisei obviously wasn't allowed to move, although several times, when the comb went into the back of her neck, her little red mouth performed the most fitful contortions. She lifted her arm only once and let a long hair drift outside into the morning air over the linden tree. I could see it gleaming from my window; for the sun had just broken through the autumn fog and was shining on the upper storey of the tailors' hostel opposite.

I could now see into the previously impenetrably dark upper room. I clearly caught sight of the man sitting at a table in a gloomy corner; something in his hand glittered like silver or gold; then again it was like a face with a huge nose; but however much I strained my eyes, I was unable to make it out. Suddenly I heard what sounded like something wooden being thrown into a chest, and now the man stood up and leaned out of another shuttered window over the street again.

The woman meanwhile had dressed the little black-haired girl in a short faded red dress and braided her hair into a chaplet on her head.

I continued to look across at her. "She might even nod to me again," I thought.

"Paul, Paul!" I suddenly heard my mother's voice calling from downstairs.

"Yes, yes, mother!"

I felt a shock go through my whole body.

"Now," she called again, "your mathematics teacher will make sure you know the time all right! Don't you know it's long past seven?"

How rapidly I clattered down the stairs!

But I was lucky; the mathematics teacher was just about to inspect and approve his bergamots and half the school was to be found in his garden to help him with their hands and mouths. It was almost nine o'clock before we were all sitting at our desks with rosy cheeks and happy faces before our slates and exercise books.

When I came out of the schoolyard at eleven o'clock, pockets still bulging with pears, the stout town-crier was just coming up the road. He was banging his shining brass cymbal with his key and crying in his loud tavern voice:

"The mechanicus and puppeteer Herr *Joseph Tendler,* from the royal capital of Munich, arrived here yesterday, and will give his first performance this evening in the Schützenhof assembly room. He will present: 'Count Palatine Siegfried and Saint Genovieve', puppet play with songs in four acts."

He then cleared his throat and strode magisterially on in the opposite direction from my home. I followed him from street to street to hear the thrilling announcement over and over again; for I had never seen a play before, let alone a puppet play. When I turned back at last I saw a little red dress coming towards me; indeed, it was the puppeteer's daughter. In spite of her faded clothes she seemed to me to have a fairy-tale aura about her.

I plucked up courage and spoke to her: "Off for a walk, Lisei?"

There was a look of bewilderment in her dark eyes. "A walk?" she repeated slowly. "Oh, you *are* clever!"

"Where are you off to then?"

"The cloth shop!"

"Going to buy a new dress for yourself?" I asked rather foolishly.

She laughed out loud. " 'course not, silly! – No, just some odds 'n' ends!"

"Odds 'n' ends, Lisei?"

"Of course! Just bits 'n' pieces for the puppets' costumes; never costs much!"

A happy thought crossed my mind. An old uncle of mine had a draper's shop here in the market place at that time and his old shop assistant was a good friend of mine. "Come with me," I said boldly, "it won't cost you a thing, Lisei!"

"Really?" she responded; then together we went to the market place and into my uncle's shop. Old Gabriel stood as always behind the counter in his pepper-and-salt-patterned coat, and when I had explained our need to him, the kind man gathered together a pile of 'odds and ends' on the counter.

"Just look at that lovely fiery red!" said Lisei, nodding longingly across at a small piece of French cotton fabric.

"Can you use it?" asked Gabriel. Could she use it! The knight Siegfried would have a new waistcoat made for him that evening.

"And this strip of braid goes with it too," said the old man and brought out all kinds of small pieces of cloth adorned with gold and silver sequins. He presently added some small pieces of green and yellow silk and ribbons, and then a sizeable piece of brown plush. "Take it, child!" said Gabriel. "That'll make an animal hide for your Genovieve when the old one gets faded!" Then he wrapped up the whole bundle of treasure and laid it in the little girl's arms.

"And it costs nothing?" she asked anxiously.

No, it cost nothing. Her eyes lit up. "Thank you, you kind man! Oh, when father sees this!"

Hand in hand, Lisei with her package under her arm, we left the shop. But as we neared our house she let go and ran across the road to the tailors' hostel, her black braids flying down to the back of her neck.

After the midday meal I was standing by our front door and pondering, with a beating heart, whether I might venture to ask my father right away for the ticket money for the first performance; I was quite satisfied with the gallery, and it cost us children only two schillings. But before I had settled the matter in my mind, Lisei came dashing across the road to me. "From Father!" she said, and before I knew it she was gone again; but in my hand I held a red ticket bearing, in large letters, the words: FRONT ROW.

As I looked up, the short dark-haired man was waving across at me with both arms out of the attic window opposite. I nodded back to him; what fine people they must be, these puppeteers! "So, this evening," I said to myself, "this evening, and – front row!"

* *

You know our Schützenhof in the Süderstrasse; well, on the front door at that time there was a finely painted life-size figure of a rifleman in plumed hat complete with rifle; but as for the rest of it, the place was more dilapidated then than it is today. The guild had shrunk to just three members; the old silver goblets, powder horns and gold chains of honour presented centuries ago by the provincial dukes had been gradually disposed of; the long garden, as you know, that runs down to the footpath along by the river, was leased out for grazing sheep and goats. The old two-storeyed house was neither lived in nor used by anyone; wind-shaken and run-down, it stood there between the well-kept neighbouring houses; only in the sparse, white-washed assembly room, which occupied almost the entire upper floor, were there occasional performances by strong men or conjurers. The main door below with the painted rifleman on it opened at that time with a noisy creak.

Evening was slow to come; but what can't be cured must be endured – my father would not let me go until five minutes before the church clock struck the due hour; he thought an exercise in patience most necessary so that I would sit still in the theatre.

At last I was there outside the Schützenhof. The main door stood open, and all sorts of people were strolling in; for at that time such entertainment was eagerly attended; it was a long journey to Hamburg, and few people went to the grand spectacles there in preference to the modest shows put on in their home town. When I had climbed the oak spiral staircase I found Lisei's mother sitting at the ticket desk at the entrance to the assembly room. I approached her in a familiar manner and expected her to greet me as an old acquaintance; but she sat silent and motionless and took my ticket as though I had not the slightest connection with her family. Somewhat dispirited, I entered the room where the audience was waiting for something to happen and chatting in lowered voices, while our town's music director and three of his apprentices were playing violins. The first thing that caught my eye was a red curtain at the far end of the room above the musicians' stands. The design at its centre showed two long trumpets laid cross-wise over a golden lyre; and – something that I thought very peculiar at the time – hanging from their mouthpieces, as if the eyes had been punched out of them, was on one side a grim, and on the other a laughing mask.

The three front rows were already occupied; I pushed my way along the fourth row where I had noticed a school friend sitting beside his parents. Behind us the rows of seats climbed steeply so that the last row, the so-called gallery, where there was standing room only, must have been almost head-high above the floor. That appeared to be full too; I couldn't see it clearly, for the few tallow candles that burned in metal lanterns on both the side walls produced only a dim light; the heavy timbered ceiling also

darkened the room. My neighbour wanted to tell me something
about school; I couldn't imagine how he could think about such
things, and I just looked at the curtain, which was grandly illu-
minated by the lamps on the podium and the musicians' lecterns.
And now it began to billow in places, the mysterious world
behind it was already beginning to stir; the very next moment
came the ringing of a hand-bell, and as the drone of voices
among the audience instantly fell silent, the curtain flew up.

A glance at the stage took me back a thousand years. I was
looking into a medieval castle yard with tower and drawbridge;
two small persons, each about two foot tall, were standing in the
middle of the scene in lively conversation. The one with a black
beard, plumed silver helmet and gold-embroidered cloak over a
red undergarment was the Count Palatine Siegfried of Brabant;
he was going to ride to war against the infidel Moors, and
ordered his young castellan, Golo, who stood beside him in a
blue, silver-embroidered doublet, to remain in the castle to guard
the Countess Palatine Genovieve. The unfaithful Golo, however,
pretended to be wild with anger that he should have to let his
good master ride out alone to the grim battle. During this
exchange of words the two of them turned their heads this way
and that and threw their arms violently about.

Then faint, long-drawn-out trumpet calls sounded outside,
beyond the drawbridge, and at the same time the fair Genovieve
in a sky-blue dress with a long train came rushing out from
behind the tower and threw her arms round her husband's neck:
"Oh, my dearest Siegfried, if the terrible infidel should kill
you!" But it was to no avail; the trumpets sounded again, and the
count strode stiffly and with dignity out of the castle yard and
over the drawbridge; the armed troop could be clearly heard
setting off outside. The wicked Golo was now in charge of the
castle.

And so the play continued just as it is printed in your reading
book. I was spellbound in my seat; these remarkable movements,
these pure or rasping little puppet voices which actually came
out of their mouths – there was an uncanny life in these small

figures that at the same time drew my eyes to them as if by magnetic force.

The second act was even better. Among the servants of the castle there was one dressed in a yellow Nanking suit called Kasperl. If *this* boy wasn't alive, then nothing or nobody ever had been; he made the most outrageous jokes so that the whole room erupted with laughter; he must have had at least one joint in his nose, which was as long as a sausage, for when he let out his mock-stupid laugh, the tip of his nose swung from side to side, as though even it was unable to stop itself in the fun; at the same time the young fellow opened his huge mouth and snapped his lower jaw-bone like an old owl. "Whoops!" he would cry every time he came jumping on to the stage; then he would settle himself down and speak with just his large thumb, which he could move back and forth so expressively that it really went like: 'Here nix and there nix! You get nix, so you have nix!' And then his squint – it was so bewitching that the whole audience instantly squinted too. I was simply infatuated with the dear fellow!

At last the play came to an end and I was sitting at home again silently eating the roast dish that my dear mother had kept hot for me. My father sat in his armchair smoking his evening pipe. "Well, lad," he said, "were they alive?"

"Don't know, father," I said, and went on eating my dish; I was still in a state of bewilderment.

He looked at me for a while with his keen smile. "Listen, Paul," he then said, "you shouldn't go too often to see this puppet theatre; these things might end up running after you to school."

* *

My father wasn't altogether wrong. During the next few days my algebra homework was so poor that the mathematics teacher threatened to remove me from the top of the class. When I tried to calculate in my head: "a + b = x – c", I heard instead the fair

Genovieve's pure bird-like voice in my ears: "Oh, my dearest Siegfried, if the terrible infidel should kill you!" Once – but no one saw it – I even wrote "x + Genovieve " on my slate. One night there was a loud cry of "Whoops!" in my bedroom, and dear Kasperl in his Nanking suit in one bound jumped on to the bed beside me, pressed both his arms into the pillow on either side of my head and cried, grinning and nodding down to me: "Oh, my dear little brother! Oh, my *dearest* little brother!" At the same time he pecked at my nose with his long red one and woke me up. Then I realised that it had only been a dream.

I locked it all away inside me and hardly dared open my mouth at home about the puppet show. But when the town-crier went through the streets again the following Sunday, banging his cymbal and loudly proclaiming: "This evening, at the Schützenhof: 'Doctor Faust's Journey to Hell', puppet play in four acts!", I could hold out no longer. Like a cat circling a hot plate of food, I prowled round my father until at last he understood my silent pleading.

"Paul," he said, "you may lose some blood; but perhaps the best cure is for you to have your fill of it once and for all." And he reached into his waistcoat pocket and gave me a two-schilling piece.

I ran straight out of the house; in the street it became clear to me that there were still eight long hours to while away before the beginning of the play. I therefore ran along the footpath at the back of the gardens. When I came to the open garden of the Schützenhof, I couldn't help going in; perhaps there would be some puppets up there looking out of the windows; for the stage after all lay at the back of the house. But I had to go through the upper part of the garden first, which was dense with linden and chestnut trees. I felt uneasy and dared go no further. Suddenly I received a great butt in the back from a tethered he-goat, sending me flying forward about twenty paces. It helped; when I looked around I was standing among the trees.

It was an overcast autumn day; occasional golden leaves had already fallen; overhead a few shore-birds screeched in the sky as they flew out to sea over the tidal flats; there was no one to be seen or heard. I walked slowly through the weeds which grew rampant over the narrow paths until I reached a small paved courtyard that separated the garden from the house. I was right! Two large upper windows above looked down on to it; but behind the small leaded window-panes it was dark and empty, no puppet was to be seen. I stood for a while; it felt eerie in the surrounding stillness.

Then I saw the heavy back door being opened a hand's width from the inside, and at the same instant a small head of black hair peered out.

"Lisei!" I cried.

Her dark eyes opened wide at me in surprise. "God forbid!" she said, "I'd no idea who was rummaging about out here! Where've you come from?"

"Me? – I'm out for a walk, Lisei! – But tell me, is your play on at the moment?"

She shook her head, laughing.

"Then what are you doing here?" I asked, as I crossed the paved courtyard towards her.

"Waiting for father," she said. "he's gone to fetch some string and nails from the hostel; he's getting things ready for this evening."

"Then you're all on your own here, Lisei?"

"No – you're here too, silly!"

"I mean," I said, "is your mother up in the assembly room?"

No, her mother was still in the hostel mending the puppets' clothes; Lisei was here all alone.

"Listen," I went on, "you can do me a favour; there's a puppet called Kasperl in your collection; I'd just love to see him really close up."

"You mean little Hans Wurstl?" said Lisei, and appeared to be thinking it over for a while. "Well, all right; but you'll have to be gone before father gets back!"

We entered the house and quickly ran up the steep spiral staircase. It was almost dark in the large assembly room; for the

windows which all looked out on to the courtyard were blocked
by the stage; just a few rays of light fell through the gaps in the
curtain.

"Come on!" said Lisei, pulling aside a screen of old carpet
that hung from the wall; we slipped through, and there I stood in
the temple of wonders. Viewed from the rear, however, and now
in the light of day, it looked rather shabby; a framework of bars
and planks over which hung some pieces of canvas daubed with
paint; this was the set on which Saint Genovieve's life had so
vividly impressed me.

But I had been too readily disappointed; for there on a wire,
which stretched from a coulisse to the wall, I saw two of the
wonderful puppets hovering; but they hung with their backs
towards me so that I could not recognise them.

"Where are the others, Lisei?" I asked; I wanted see the
complete collection at the same time.

"Here in the chest," said Lisei, banging her small fist on a
large chest standing in a corner. "Those two there are ready for
the show; but go over and have a good look; he's there, your
friend Kasperl!"

And indeed, there was Kasperl himself. "Is he in the play
again this evening?" I asked.

" 'course, he's always in it!"

I stood with my arms folded and gazed at my dear jolly friend.
There he dangled, hanging by seven strings; his head looked
down so that his large eyes stared at the floor and his red nose
rested against his breast like a broad beak. "Kasperle, Kasperle,"
I said to myself, "how miserable you look hanging there." The
puppet answered in the same tone: "Just wait, my little brother,
just wait till this evening!" – Was this just in my mind too, or had
Kasperl really spoken to me?

I looked round. Lisei had gone; she was down by the front
door watching for her father's return. Then I heard her call from
the exit of the assembly room: "Promise me you won't touch the
puppets!" Yes – but I just couldn't resist it now. I climbed up
quietly on to a bench standing nearby and began to pull first one

string, then another; the jaws started to clap, the arms lifted, and now the wonderful thumb began to jerk this way and that. It was not at all difficult to do; I'd never thought that manipulating a puppet was so easy. But the arms moved only backwards and forwards; I was quite sure that in the last play Kasperl had also stretched them sideways, and yes, that he'd even clapped them together above his head! I pulled on every string, I tried to bend the arms with my hand; but all without success. All at once a dull crack sounded inside the figure. "Stop!" I thought. "Leave off! You might damage it!"

Quietly I got down from the bench again, and at the same moment heard Lisei coming back into the assembly room.

"Hurry, hide!" she cried, pulling me along in the darkness towards the spiral staircase. "It was wrong for me to leave you alone in there," she continued, "but it was fun for you, wasn't it?"

I thought about the dull crack of a moment ago. "Oh, it was nothing!" I said to myself. And with this assuring thought I ran down the stairs and out through the back door into the garden.

This much was certain, Kasperl was really just a wooden puppet after all; but Lisei – what an enchanting way of speaking she had! And how kind it had been of her to take me up to the puppets! Of course, it was quite wrong to do it behind her father's back, as she had said herself. But this secrecy, I must confess to my shame, was not unpleasant to me; on the contrary, the whole business took on a most piquant flavour because of it, and a self-satisfied smile must have settled on my face as I sauntered back through the linden and chestnut trees of the garden down to the footpath along the river again.

Among such flattering thoughts, however, I kept hearing in my head from time to time that dull crack inside the body of the puppet; whatever I was doing for the rest of the day, I could not silence this uncomfortable noise which now came out of my own soul.

* *

Seven o'clock had struck; all the seats in the Schützenhof were
full today, Sunday; I was standing at the back this time, some five
feet above the floor, in the two-schilling area. The tallow candles
were burning in the metal lanterns, the town's music director
and his three apprentices were playing their violins; the curtain
rose.

A high-vaulted gothic chamber appeared. Doctor Faust sat in
a dark ankle-length gown in front of an opened folio volume,
complaining bitterly that his learning earned him so little, not
even a decent coat to his back; at a loss what to do because of
debts, he was now going to join with the forces of Hell. – "Who
calls for me?" sounded a terrifying voice from the vault of the
room to his left. – "Faust, Faust, don't go!" came another,
gentler voice from the right. But Faust had conspired with the
powers of Hell. – "Woe, woe, unto your poor soul!" The angel's
voice sounded like a dying breath of wind; from his left a shriek
of laughter resounded across the chamber. – There was a knock
at the door. "Excuse me, Your Magnificence." Faust's famulus,
Wagner, entered. He asked to be allowed to engage the services
of a helper for the burdensome housework so that he could
better concentrate on his studies. "A young man came to see
me," he said, "by the name of Kasperl, who seemed to possess
excellent qualities." Faust graciously nodded his head and said:
"Very well, my dear Wagner, your request is granted." Then
they left the chamber together.

"Whoops!" came the cry; and there he was. With a leap he
jumped on to the stage, and his knapsack bounced on his back.

"God be praised!" I thought. "He's still all right; he jumps
just as he did last Sunday in the fair Genovieve's castle!" And it
was strange, however much he had appeared in my thoughts that
morning as just a pathetic wooden puppet, with the first word he
uttered, the whole magic was there again.

He bustled up and down the room. "If my father could see me
now," he cried, "he'd surely be pleased. He always used to say:
'Kasperl, see you put a swing into it!' And now it's got a swing; I
can swing it as high as the roof top!" With that he pulled a face

and slung his knapsack into the air; and it really flew, for it was pulled by wires, right up into the roof vaulting; but – Kasperl's arms were glued to his sides; there was pulling and tugging, but they didn't lift an inch. Kasperl just spoke and did nothing more. There was a commotion backstage, low but angry voices were heard, the flow of the play was obviously interrupted. My heart stood still; it just had to happen! I would willingly have run away, but I was ashamed. And if something should happen to Lisei because of me!

Then Kasperl, with his head and arms hanging limply down, suddenly let out a pitiful howl on the stage, at which Wagner reappeared and asked him what he was wailing about.

"Oh, my tooth, my tooth!" howled Kasperl.

"Good friend," said Wagner, "let me take a look in your mouth!" And as he seized him by his huge nose and peered between his jaws, Doctor Faust too came back into the chamber.

"Your humble pardon, Your Magnificence," said Wagner, "but I'm not able to take this young man into my service; he must be taken to an infirmary immediately!"

"Is that an inn?" asked Kasperl.

"No, good friend," replied Wagner, "it's a slaughterhouse. They'll cut a wisdom tooth out of your head there, then your pain will be gone."

"Oh, dear God!" moaned Kasperl. "Must such a terrible thing happen to a poor creature like me! A wisdom tooth, you said, Herr Wagner? No one's had that in the family before! Then it could even bring my Kasperlship to an end?"

"Certainly, my friend," said Wagner. "A servant with wisdom teeth I can well do without; these things are only for us learned folk. But you've got a nephew who's also applied for service with me. Perhaps," and he turned towards Doctor Faust, "you will permit it, Your Magnificence!"

Doctor Faust gave a dignified turn of the head.

"Do as you wish, my dear Wagner," he said, "but do not disturb me in my studies of magic any further with your trifles!"

"Just listen to that, my friend," said a tailor's journeyman,

who was leaning on the balustrade in front of me, to his neighbour. "Doesn't belong in the piece at all. I know it, saw it not so
long ago in Seifersdorf."

"Shut up, Leipziger!" the other replied, poking him in the
ribs.

On the stage, meanwhile, a second Kasperl had entered. He
bore an unmistakable likeness to his sick uncle, and even spoke
exactly like him; he was simply missing the moving thumb and
appeared to have no joint in his large nose.

When the play continued smoothly I felt as if a stone had been
lifted from my heart, and I soon forgot everything around me.
The diabolical Mephistopheles appeared in a fiery-red cloak, a
small horn on his forehead, and Faust signed the hellish pact
with his blood:

"You shall serve me for twenty-four years; then I will be yours,
body and soul."

Thereupon they both sped away through the air in the devil's
magic cloak. Then a huge toad with bat's wings came down out
of the air for Kasperl. "Am I supposed to ride to Parma on the
back of the sparrow from Hell?" he cried, and as the creature
wobbled, its head nodding, he climbed up on to it and the two
flew off together.

I had placed myself far back against the wall, where I could
see better over the heads of those in front of me. And now the
curtain lifted for the last act.

The hellish pact has come to an end at last. Faust and Kasperl
are back in their home town. Kasperl has become the night
watchman; he is walking through the dark streets calling the
hour:

> Listen, you men, and hear what I say,
> My wife, she beat me half-dead today;
> Defend yourselves from a woman's frock!
> Twelve is the hour! Twelve is the clock!

A clock is heard striking midnight a long way off. Faust staggers on to the stage; he tries to pray, but howling and chattering of teeth are the only sounds to come out of his mouth. A thunderous voice comes down from above:

"*Fauste, Fauste, in aeternum damnatus es!*"

And just as three dark-haired devils descended in a rain of fire to seize the poor man, I felt one of the boards under my feet move. As I bent down to straighten it, I was sure I heard a noise coming from the dark void beneath me; I listened more closely; it sounded like the sobbing of a child.

"Lisei!" I thought. "What if it's Lisei!" My whole misdeed fell again like a stone on my conscience; what did I care now about Doctor Faust and his journey to Hell!

With a heavily beating heart I pushed my way through the audience and slipped down the side of the stage scaffolding. I was quickly in the space beneath it where I could walk along fully upright against the wall; but it was almost dark, so that I knocked into the planks and pieces of wood lying everywhere. "Lisei!" I called out. The sobbing that I had just heard suddenly stopped; but in the furthest corner I saw something stir. I groped my way to the end of the space, and – there she sat, huddled up, her head pressed into her lap.

I tugged at her clothes. "Lisei!" I said softly, "is it you? What are you doing here?"

She didn't answer, but began sobbing to herself again.

"Lisei," I repeated, "what's wrong? Please say something!"

She lifted her head a little. "What can I say!" she said. "You know very well you damaged Hans Wurstl."

"Yes, Lisei," I answered, in a subdued voice. "I think it was me who did it."

"Yes, it was you! And I told you not to touch him!"

"Lisei, what can I do?"

"Nothing!"

"But what's going to happen?"

"Just nothing!" She began to sob loudly again. "But as for me – when I get home – I'll get the strap!"

"The strap, you, Lisei?" I felt devastated. "But is your father really so strict?"

"Oh, my dear father!" sobbed Lisei.

So it was the mother! Besides myself, how I hated this woman who always sat at the ticket desk with her stony face!

I heard Kasperl the second cry from the stage: "The play is over! Come, Gretl, let's have the last dance!" And from above our heads at that same moment came the scraping and trampling of feet and soon everyone got down from their benches with a rumbling and pressed towards the exit; the last to go, from his deep bass tones, was the town's music director with his apprentices as they all bumped against the walls on leaving. It grew quiet; only the two Tendlers could still be heard busying themselves and talking to each other at the back of the stage. After a while they too went into the auditorium; it seemed that they were snuffing out the candles, first on the music stands, then on the walls, for it grew gradually darker.

"If only I knew where Lisei's got to!" I heard Herr Tendler call over to his wife, who was busy with something at the opposite wall.

"Where do you think she is!" she called back. "She's an obstinate little thing, that one; she'll have run back to the lodgings!"

"You've been far too stern with that child," answered her husband, "she's got a sensitive nature, that's all!"

"Rubbish!" cried the woman. "She's got to take her punishment; she knows very well that that fine marionette was my dear father's! You'll never repair it again, and the second Kasperl is just for emergencies!"

The loud exchange echoed around the empty assembly room. I had crouched down beside Lisei; we grasped each other's hands and sat as quiet as mice.

"It serves me right," the woman continued, who was standing just above our heads. "Why did I allow you to put on that godforsaken piece again today! My father never wanted to in his last years!"

"Now, now, Resel!" called Herr Tendler from the other wall.

"Your father was an exceptional man. Anyway, the piece always brings the money in; and it's a good lesson and an example for all the godless in the world!"

"Well, today's the last time we're going to do it. And don't mention it to me again!" the woman retorted.

Herr Tendler fell silent. There appeared to be only one candle burning now as the couple went towards the exit.

"Lisei," I whispered, "we're going to be locked in."

"Doesn't matter!" she said. "Can't go; I'm not leaving!"

"Then I'm staying too!"

"But what about your father and mother!"

"I'm staying here with you!"

The assembly room door now closed; then footsteps receded down the stairs and we heard the heavy front door being closed from the street outside.

So we sat there. We sat for a good quarter of an hour without exchanging a word. Luckily I remembered I still had two pastries in my pocket which I had bought on the way to the assembly room with a schilling I had wheedled from my mother; in all the excitement of the show I had completely forgotten about them. I put one of them into Lisei's tiny hands; she took it without a word as if it went without saying that I should provide the supper, and we feasted for a while. Then that too came to an end.

I stood up and said: "Let's go behind the stage; it'll be lighter there; I think the moon's shining outside!" And Lisei patiently let me lead her into the assembly room over the planks of wood that were scattered about everywhere.

When we had slipped backstage behind the screen, bright moonlight was shining in through the window from the garden.

On the wire from which only two of the puppets had hung that morning, I now saw all those that had appeared in the performance a short while before. There hung Doctor Faust with his severe pale face, the horned Mephistopheles, the three small dark-haired devils, and there beside the winged toad were both the Kasperls. They hung there completely still in the pale moonlight; almost like the dead, it seemed to me. Fortunately the principal Kasperl had his broad beak of a nose lying on his chest again, otherwise I was certain that his gaze would have been following me about.

After Lisei and I had spent some time climbing and standing about on the staging, not knowing what to do with ourselves, we propped ourselves up against each other on the window seat. The weather had worsened; in the sky a bank of cloud rose up against the moon, below in the garden the leaves could be seen being blown from the trees in heaps.

"Look," said Lisei pensively, "how the storm's getting up! Dear old Auntie can't look down from the sky any more."

"What old Auntie, Lisei?" I asked.

"Oh, where I used to be before she died."

We looked out into the night again.

As the wind blew against the house and the small draughty windows, the silent company on the wire behind me began to clatter with their wooden arms and legs. I instinctively turned round and saw their heads waggling and their stiff arms and legs swaying about in all directions in the strong draught. When the injured Kasperl suddenly tossed his head back and stared at me with his white eyes, I thought it better to move a little to one side.

Not far from the window, but far enough for the scenery there to block the swaying dancers from view, stood the large chest; it was open; a few woollen blankets, presumably for packing the puppets, lay carelessly thrown over it.

Just as I was moving towards it, I heard Lisei by the window let out a huge yawn.

"Are you tired, Lisei?" I asked.

"Oh, no," she replied, folding her arms tightly about herself, "but I'm cold!"

It had grown really cold in the large empty room, and I was freezing too. "Come over here!" I said. "We'll wrap ourselves up in the blankets."

Lisei came at once to stand beside me and patiently let me wrap her in one of the blankets; she looked like a chrysalis, except that her lovely little face peeped out from the top. "Know what," she said, looking at me with two large tired eyes, "I'm getting into the chest, it'll be warm in there!"

That seemed a good idea to me too. Compared to the bare surroundings, here was a cosy space, almost like a compact little room. And soon we poor foolish children were sitting well wrapped up and huddled together inside the tall chest. We had our backs and feet pressed against the sides; we heard the far-off sound of the heavy assembly room door banging in its frame; but we were sitting secure and comfortable.

"Are you still cold, Lisei?" I asked.

"Not a bit!"

She had let her head drop on to my shoulder; her eyes were already closed. "What will dear father . . . " she went on murmuring; then I could hear from her regular breathing that she had fallen asleep.

From my position I could see the upper panes of one of the windows. The moon had drifted out of the bank of cloud in which it had been concealed for some time; old Auntie could look down from the sky again, and I am sure she was pleased to do so. A streak of moonlight fell on the face that rested close to mine; the black lashes lay like silk fringes on the cheeks, the small red mouth breathed softly, only occasionally would a short sobbing break from her breast; but even that subsided. Old Auntie looked down so kindly from the sky.

I dared not stir. "How wonderful it would be," I thought, "if Lisei were your sister, and she could always be with you!" For I didn't have any brothers or sisters, and even though I had no longing for brothers, I had often pictured a life with a sister to myself, and could never understand when my friends who actually had them started squabbling and fighting with them.

I must have fallen fast asleep over these thoughts; for I still remember the many wild things I dreamed of. I dreamed I was sitting in the middle of the auditorium; the candles burned in the sconces on the walls, but no one sat on the empty benches except me. Above my head, under the timbered ceiling of the room, Kasperl rode around in the air on the infernal sparrow, crying over and over again: "Bad little boy! Bad little boy!" or else in a pitiful voice: "My arm! My arm!"

Then I was woken by a laugh that resounded above my head, perhaps also by the gleam of light that suddenly fell on my eyelids. "Just look at this for a bird's nest!" I heard my father's voice say, and then somewhat more brusquely: "Out you get, my boy!"

That was the tone that always automatically made me sit up. I opened my eyes wide and saw my father and the Tendler couple standing by our chest; Herr Tendler carried a lighted lantern in his hand. My efforts to lift myself up, however, were hindered by Lisei, who, still sleeping, was resting all her small weight on my chest. But when two bony arms stretched out to lift her out of the chest, and I saw the stony face of Frau Tendler bent down over us, I threw my arms round my little friend so impetuously that I almost knocked the good lady's old Italian straw hat off her head.

"Now, now, my lad!" she cried, stepping back; but I, from inside our chest, hurriedly explained, without sparing myself, what had happened that morning.

"Well, Madame Tendler," said my father when I was at the end of my story, with a hand movement that made his meaning clear, "you can leave it entirely to me to sort out this affair with my son."

"Oh, yes, yes!" I cried eagerly, as if the most pleasant amusement was in store for me.

Lisei in the meanwhile had also woken up, and her father lifted her into his arms. I saw her flinging her arms round his neck and earnestly whispering in his ear, now tenderly looking into his eyes, now persuasively nodding her head. Presently the puppeteer grasped my father's hand. "My dear sir," he said, "the children are pleading for each other. Mother, you're not as unfeeling as all that! We'll let it pass this time!"

Madame Tendler, however, still looked wholly unmoved beneath her large straw hat. "You just see how you get on without Kasperl!" she said, casting a severe look at her husband.

I saw an amused twinkle in my father's eye which gave me hope that the storm would pass me by this time; and when he promised to use his skill to repair the invalid next day, thereby setting Madame Tendler's Italian straw hat in the sweetest motion, I was certain that we were both safely out of it.

We were soon walking along the dark narrow streets, Herr Tendler in front with the lantern, we children following the grown-ups hand in hand. Then: "Good night, Paul! Oh, how I'll sleep!"

And Lisei was gone; I hadn't even noticed that we had arrived at our house.

* *

The next morning when I came home from school I found Herr Tendler with his daughter in our workshop. "Now my friend," said my father, who was examining the inner parts of the puppet, "what would we two mechanici say for ourselves if we couldn't set this young fellow here back on his feet!"

"Yes, father," cried Lisei, "and mother won't be grumpy any more either."

Herr Tendler tenderly stroked the child's black hair; then he turned to my father as he explained how he would go about the repair. "But, sir," he said, "I'm not a mechanicus, I simply took on the title with the puppets; I'm actually a wood carver by trade from Berchtesgaden. But my late father-in-law – you're bound to have heard of him – he certainly was one, and my Reserl, of course, is always just a little proud that she's the daughter of the famous puppeteer Geisselbrecht. He made Kasperl's mechanisms; I simply carved out his face."

"But Herr Tendler," replied my father, "that's an art in itself. And then – tell me, how could you possibly have known what to do when my son's disgraceful behaviour came to light like that in the middle of the play?"

The conversation began to grow somewhat uncomfortable for

me; but the whole prankish character of the puppeteer suddenly
shone out of Herr Tendler's good-natured face.

"Oh well, sir," he said, "there's always a joker in the pack, just
in case! There's another nephew as well, Hans Wurstl Number
Two, he's got a voice just like this one's here!"

Meanwhile, I had tugged at Lisei's clothes and happily
escaped with her into our garden. We were sitting here under
this linden tree, which now spreads its green canopy over both of
us; only then the red carnations were no longer in bloom over
there in the flowerbeds; but I still remember very well it was a
sunny September afternoon. My mother came out of her kitchen
and began talking to the puppeteer's daughter; now she too was
becoming a little curious.

What was the child's name, she wanted to know, and had she
always been travelling from town to town? Her name was Lisei –
I had told my mother that often enough – but this was her first
journey; that was why she couldn't speak High German properly yet. Had she been to school? Of course she'd been to school,
but she'd learnt to sew and knit from her old aunt; she'd also had
a garden like ours, they'd sat together on a bench in it; she was
taught by her mother now, but she was very strict!

My mother nodded approvingly. How long would her parents
be staying here? she asked Lisei further. She didn't know, that
would depend on her mother; but they usually stayed in a place
about four weeks. Did she have a warm coat for the winter's
journey, for it would be really cold on the open cart in October?
Well, said Lisei, she did have a coat, but only a thin one; she had
frozen in it on the journey here.

Now my dear mother had reached the point towards which I
had seen her steering for some time. "Listen, my little Lisei,"
she said, "I have a good coat hanging in my wardrobe, from
earlier times when I was a slim girl; I've now grown out of it and
don't have a daughter for whom I could have it altered. Come
again tomorrow, Lisei, there'll be a warm coat in it for you."

Lisei flushed with joy and without hesitation kissed my
mother's hand, which embarrassed her greatly; for as you know,

we find it hard to understand such strange antics in these parts! Luckily both the men came out of the workshop at that moment. "Saved this time," cried my father, "but —!" His warning finger shaking at me signalled the end of my reprieve.

At my mother's request I gladly ran into the house to fetch her large shawl, so that the scarcely recovered puppet could be carefully wrapped up now to save him from the cheers of the street urchins which, however well-meaning, had been so trying on his way here; then Lisei took him on her arm, Herr Tendler took Lisei by the hand, and so, with expressions of gratitude, the two happily set off down the street to the Schützenhof.

* *

And now began the happiest of times for us children. Lisei came not only the next morning, but on the following days too; she would not give up until she herself was allowed to help alter her new coat. Admittedly, it was probably just token work that my mother put into her small hands; nevertheless, she meant the child to be properly taught. I sat beside her sometimes and read aloud from a volume of *The Children's Friend* which my father had once bought for me at a sale, to the great delight of Lisei, to whom publications designed purely for entertainment were still unknown. "That's wonderful!" – "To think – what things there are in the world!" She would often come out with such exclamations while working, laying her hands with her sewing on her lap. Now and then she would look up at me cannily and remark: "Yes, but if only it's not made up!" I can still hear her today.'

– The narrator paused, and in his fine manly face I saw an expression of deep happiness, as if everything he was telling me, although in the past, was in no way forgotten. After a while he began again.

'My homework was never done as well as at that time; for I clearly felt my father's eyes on me more sharply than ever before, and that my association with the puppeteer's family could only be the reward for hard work. "They're respectable people, the Tendlers," I once heard my father say. "The landlord of the tailors' hostel opposite even offered them a proper room today; they pay him every morning; only, according to the old man, what they are prepared to pay is unfortunately extremely little. – And that," my father added, "pleases me more than it does the house-father; they may be putting money aside for a rainy day, which is not usually the case with those people." How happy I was to hear my friends praised! For the whole family were my friends now; even Madame Tendler gave a most friendly nod beneath her straw hat when (an admission ticket being no longer needed) I slipped by her ticket desk into the assembly room in the evenings. And how I raced out of school now! I was certain I would meet Lisei at home, either with my mother in the kitchen, where she had learnt how to do all kinds of small jobs for her, or sitting on the bench in the garden, with a book or sewing in her hands. And I was soon to involve her in my activities too, for after I felt sufficiently initiated into the essential nature of the business, I had formed no lesser plan than that of building my own marionette theatre.

I began with carving the puppets. Herr Tendler, not without a good-natured twinkle in his small eyes, lent me a hand with advice and help in the choice of wood and knives; and soon an enormous Kasperl-nose rose out of the wood block into the world. But Hans Wurstl's Nanking suit, on the other hand, held little interest for me; so it was Lisei who set about making, out of the 'odds 'n' ends' that old Gabriel had been obliged to provide again, gold- and silver-trimmed cloaks and doublets for God knows what other future puppets. Old Heinrich, with his short pipe, also stepped out of the workshop now and then to join us; he was a journeyman of my father's who had been with the family for as long as I could remember. He would take the knife out of my hand and with a few cuts here and there give the figure the right shape and look. But even my imagination was already dissatisfied with Tendler's principal figure, Kasperl; I wanted to create something quite different. I devised three further, completely original and highly effective joints for my puppet: the chin would waggle sideways; the ears would move to and fro, and the lower lip would be able to swing open and shut. And in every respect he would have been a splendid and remarkable fellow too, had not all these joints been his undoing at birth. Unfortunately, however, neither Count Palatine Siegfried nor any other of the puppet plays' heroes was to achieve blissful resurrection by my hand. I had better luck with the creation of an underground cave in which, on cold days, I sat next to Lisei on a small bench and, by the sparse light that fell through a conveniently placed window pane above us, read her stories from *The Children's Friend*, which she always liked to listen to over and over again. My friends teased me a lot and called me a girl's boy because I now spent my time with the puppeteer's daughter instead of with them. It didn't bother me; I knew it was just jealous talk, and once when it became too much I put my fists to good use.

But everything in life lasts only for a short time. The Tendlers had performed their repertoire; the puppet stage in the Schützenhof was taken down; they prepared to move on.

So there I stood one stormy October afternoon on the high ridge of heathland outside our town, one minute looking sadly at the wide sandy track that ran eastwards into the barren land-scape, the next longingly back at the town that lay on the low ground in haze and fog. And then it came rolling up, the cart with the two tall chests on it and the little lively bay in the shafts. Herr Tendler sat in front on a short plank, and behind him Lisei in the new warm coat next to her mother. I had already said goodbye to them outside the tailors' hostel; but then I had run ahead to see them all once again and to give Lisei – I had obtained my father's permission for this – the volume of *The Children's Friend* as a memento; I had also spent some savings from my Sunday pocket money on a bag of cakes for them. "Stop! Stop!" I now cried, and rushed down the hill towards the vehicle. Herr Tendler pulled on the reins, the bay halted, and I handed my small present up to Lisei, which she laid beside her on the seat. But when we grasped each other's hands, without exchanging a word, we poor children burst into tears. At that moment Herr Tendler applied the whip to the horse. "Bye, me lad! Be good, and our thanks to your father and mother!"

"Goodbye!" cried Lisei; the horse moved on, the bell round its neck tinkled; I felt the tiny hands slip out of mine, and on they travelled into the wide world beyond. I climbed again up the bank at the side of the road and stood with my eyes fixed on the little cart as it rolled on through the soft sand. The tinkling of the bell grew weaker and weaker in my ears, and once I saw a white handkerchief fluttering among the chests; then gradually they became more and more indistinct in the grey autumn fog. Suddenly something like a deadly fear seized my heart: you'll never see her again, never again! "Lisei!" I shouted. "Lisei!" And when despite my cry the blurred image in the fog, perhaps because of a bend in the road, now disappeared completely from view, I ran after it as if I were insane. The storm ripped the cap from my head, my boots filled with sand; but however far I ran, I saw nothing but the sparse treeless landscape and the cold grey sky that hung over it. When I arrived home at last in the gathering darkness, I had the feeling that the whole town had passed away in the meantime. It was the first parting of my life.

With the return of autumn each year that followed, when the fieldfares flew through the gardens of our town and the first yellow leaves of the linden trees in front of the tailors' hostel opposite our house blew in the wind, I would sit on the seat in front of our house and wonder whether the cart with the little bay would ever again come tinkling up the street.

But I waited in vain; Lisei did not return.

* *

It was about twelve years later. After elementary school I had also completed the third year of grammar school, as was the habit of most craftsmen's sons in those days, and had then been taken on by my father as an apprentice. This period, during which in addition to working at my craft I devoted much of my spare time to reading good books, was also over. Now, after three years travelling as a journeyman, I found myself in a town in central Germany. The people here were strongly and most strictly Catholic: if one's hat was not removed in front of their processions, which moved through the streets with singing and pictures of saints, it was likely to be knocked off by someone; otherwise they were fine people.

I was employed by the widow of a master craftsman whose son, like myself, as required by the statutes of the guild, was working away from his home town to complete his years of travel and training in order to meet the requirements of the master craftsman's certificate. I was well looked after in this house; the widow, the good Frau Meisterin, treated me as she would have liked others to treat her son, and soon such a trust grew up between us that the business in all but name rested in my hands. – Our Joseph now works for her son, and the old woman, so he often writes, pampers him as though she were the boy's own grandmother. – Well, one Sunday afternoon I was sitting with Frau Meisterin in the living room whose windows faced the entrance of the large prison opposite. It was January; the thermometer stood at twenty degrees below zero; no one was to be seen outside in the street; now and then the wind whistled down from the nearby hills and drove small lumps of ice tinkling over the cobblestones.

"Makes one glad of a warm room and a bowl of hot coffee," said Frau Meisterin, filling my cup for the third time.

I had gone to the window. My thoughts were of home, not of loved ones, for they were no more; I had now been well schooled in leave-taking. I had been permitted to close my mother's eyes myself, and a few weeks before I had also lost my father, and because of the tedious length of the journey at that time I could not even accompany him to his resting place. But the paternal workshop awaited the return of its late craftsman's son.

However, old Heinrich was still there, and with the permission of the masters of the guild could run the business for a short while; and so I had promised the good Frau Meisterin to stay with her for a few weeks more until her son's return. But there was no peace for me; my father's fresh grave no longer tolerated my absence.

I was interrupted in these thoughts by a sharp scolding voice from across the street. When I looked up I saw the prison warder's consumptive face leaning out from behind the half-open door of the prison; his raised fist was threatening a young woman who appeared to be trying to force her way into this usually feared place.

"She'll have a loved one inside," said Frau Meisterin, who had also witnessed the incident from her armchair, "but that old sinner over there's got no heart for anyone."

"The man is probably just doing his duty," I replied, still buried in my thoughts.

"I'd hate to have duty like that," she answered, settling back almost angrily in her chair.

The prison door opposite had slammed shut in the meanwhile and the young woman, with just a short fluttering cloak round her shoulders and a small black scarf knotted round her head, was walking slowly down the ice-covered street. We both remained quietly in our places; but my sympathy was now aroused, and I believe we both felt we should help in some way but simply didn't know how.

As I was about to turn away from the window, the woman came up the street again. She stopped in front of the prison door and hesitantly put a foot on the stone step below the entrance; then she looked round and I saw a young face whose dark eyes wandered over the empty street with the most helpless and forsaken expression; she appeared simply not to have the courage to face the official's threatening fist yet again. Slowly, and continually looking back at the closed door, she went on her way; it was evident that she did not know where she was going. When she now turned into the narrow lane at the corner of the prison that led up to the church, I instinctively grabbed my cap from the door hook to go after her.

"Yes, of course, Paulsen; it's the right thing to do!" said the good-hearted Frau Meisterin. "Go after her; I'll heat up the coffee in the meantime!"

It was fiercely cold when I stepped outside the house; the town seemed deserted; from the high hill that reared up at the end of the street the dark fir forest looked down almost threateningly; white curtains of ice hung in front of the window-panes of most houses; for not everyone, like my old Frau Meisterin, had a rightful claim to five bundles of wood for domestic use. I went up the narrow lane to the church square; and there on the frozen ground at the foot of the tall wooden crucifix knelt the young woman, head bowed, hands folded in her lap. I quietly stepped closer; but when she looked up at the bloodied face of the crucified figure, I said: "Excuse me if I'm interrupting your prayers, but you're a stranger to this town, aren't you?"

She simply nodded without shifting her position.

"I'd like to help!" I continued. "Where is it you want to go?"

"Don't know any more," she said without expression, letting her head sink lower on to her chest.

"But it'll be dark in an hour; you won't be able to stay out much longer on the open street in this deathly weather!"

"The good Lord will help me," I heard her say quietly.

"Yes, yes, I'm sure," I said, "and I almost believe He's sent me to you!"

It was as though the firmer tone of my voice had woken her, for she rose and walked hesitantly towards me; with her neck straining forward she brought her face nearer and nearer to mine, and her gaze fixed itself on my face as though she wanted to seize me by it. "Paul!" she cried suddenly, and like a cry of joy the word flew from her breast. "Paul! Yes, the good Lord's sent you to me!"

Where had my eyes been! I had her here again, my childhood friend, Lisei the little puppeteer! Of course, the child had become a beautiful slim young woman, and on the child's face once so radiant, after the first ray of joy had spread over it, now lay an expression of deep sorrow.

"How is it you're here all alone, Lisei?" I asked. "What's happened? Where's your father?"

"In the prison, Paul."

"Your father, that fine man! – Come with me; I'm working here for a good woman; she knows all about you, I've often told her about you."

And hand in hand, as we had been as children, we walked to the old Frau Meisterin's house. She was watching us approach from the window. "It's Lisei!" I called out as we entered the room. "Just think of it – little Lisei!"

The good woman clasped her hands to her breast. "O Holy Mother of God, pray for us! Little Lisei! – so that's how she looked! – But," she continued, "what've you got to do with that old sinner?" – and she pointed her finger towards the prison opposite. "Paulsen has been telling me you're from honest folk!"

But she had soon drawn the girl further into the room and set her down in her armchair, and as Lisei now began to answer her questions she was already holding a steaming cup of coffee to her lips.

"Now drink up," she said, "and recover yourself first; those hands of yours look frozen stiff."

And Lisei had first to drink, while two bright tears rolled down into the cup, before being allowed to talk any further.

She didn't speak in the dialect of her homeland now, as she had once and a short while ago in the isolation of her sorrow, only a slight trace of it was left; for her parents had never come as far north as our coast again, but had remained mostly in central Germany. Her mother had died some years earlier. "Don't leave father!" her mother had whispered in her ear in her last hour. "His child's heart is too good for this world."

Lisei burst into heavy sobbing at this memory; she would drink no more from the cup Frau Meisterin had refilled thinking that it might still her tears, and it was some time before she could continue with her story.

It had been her first task after her mother's death to study the female roles in the puppet plays with her father. Meanwhile, the funeral had been dealt with and the first requiems celebrated for the deceased; then, leaving the fresh grave behind them, father and daughter had set out once again across the country and performed their shows as before: *The Prodigal Son*, *Saint Genovieve*, and the rest.

And so in the course of their travels they had arrived the previous day at a large village where they made their midday halt. Her father had fallen sound asleep for half an hour or so on the hard bench at the table where they had eaten a modest meal, while Lisei saw to the feeding of their horse outside. Shortly afterwards, well wrapped up in woollen blankets, they had set out on their way again in the fierce winter cold.

"But we didn't get very far," explained Lisei, "for just beyond the village a mounted policeman came riding up to us, ranting and raving. He said the innkeeper's purse with money in it had been stolen from the table drawer, and my dear innocent father had been all alone in the parlour! Oh, we haven't any home, any friends, any honour; no one knows us!"

"Child, child," said Frau Meisterin, giving me a glance, "don't fall into sin too!"

But I kept quiet, for Lisei was quite right to complain. They had had to return to the village; the cart, with everything that was loaded on it, had been sequestered by the village magistrate; old Tendler had been ordered to trot beside the policeman's horse all the way to the town. Lisei, repeatedly turned back by the policeman, had followed at a distance, confident that at least, until the good Lord cleared the matter up, she would be able to share the prison with her father. But no suspicion rested on her, so it was with some justification that the warder had driven her away from the prison door as an intruder who didn't have the slightest claim to a room in his house.

But Lisei still refused to accept the situation; she thought it far harsher than any punishment that would be sure to catch up with the real villain, though she commented at the same time that she wouldn't wish such a harsh punishment on him either – if only the innocence of her good father could be proved; oh, he would certainly not survive it!

It suddenly struck me that I was as much an indispensable party to the old corporal opposite as to the Criminal Commissioner himself; for the one I kept his spinning-machine in order, for the other I sharpened his precious quill-pen knife; through the one I could at least gain access to the prisoner, for the other I could provide a character reference for Herr Tendler and perhaps expedite matters for him. I begged Lisei to be patient and immediately went across to the prison.

The consumptive warder complained bitterly about the shameless women who constantly wanted to join their villainous husbands or fathers in the cells. But I refused to accept such descriptions as applying to my friend, as long as they were not bestowed upon him 'by law', which I knew for sure would never happen; and in the end, after some further exchange of words, we climbed the wide stairs together to the upper part of the building.

In the old prison even the air was held prisoner, and a repulsive smell hit us as we walked along the long upper corridor with cell doors on either side. At one of these, almost at the end of the passage, we stopped; the warder shook his large bunch of keys to find the right one; then the door creaked open and we entered.

In the middle of the cell, with his back to us, stood a small, lean figure who appeared to be looking up at the small piece of sky which shone down on him in the gathering darkness, grey and gloomy, through a window set high in the wall. I immediately noticed the short spiky hair on his head; only like nature outside, it had taken on the colour of winter. The little man turned round as we entered.

"You don't recognise me any more, Herr Tendler?" I asked. He looked briefly at me. "No, my dear sir," he replied, "I've not had the honour."

I gave him the name of my home town and said: "I'm the good-for-nothing lad who twisted your very special Kasperl's arm that time!"

"Oh, that was nothing, really nothing!" he replied in embarrassment, making a slight bow. "That's long forgotten."

He had obviously been only half-listening; for his lips moved as though he were speaking to himself about many other things.

I then explained to him how I had just discovered Lisei, and only then did he fully look at me. "Thank God! Thank God!" he said, clasping his hands together. "Yes, of course, little Lisei and young Paul, they played together! Young Paul! You're young Paul, then? Oh, I do believe you now; that young lad's honest little face, I can see it all!" He nodded so warmly to me that the grey spikes of hair on his head shook. "Yes, yes, down there by the sea with you; we never went there again, you know; they were good times then, they were; my wife was there too, daughter of the great Geisselbrecht! 'Joseph!' she used to say, 'if only people too had wires attached to their heads, then you could control them as well!' If she'd been alive today they couldn't have had me locked up. Oh, dear God; I'm no thief, Herr Paulsen."

The warder, who was walking up and down outside in the corridor in front of the slightly open door, had already rattled his bunch of keys several times. I tried to calm the old man and asked him to mention my name at the first hearing, for I was known and well respected here.

When I returned to Frau Meisterin in the living room, she said to me as I went in: "She's a stubborn girl that, Paulsen; there's little to be done with her; I've offered her the small room to sleep in; but she wants to be off, to the beggars' inn or God knows where!"

I asked Lisei if she had her passes with her.

"My God, the village magistrate took them from us!"

"So no landlord will open his door to you," I said. "You know that well enough."

She knew it all too well, and Frau Meisterin warmly shook her hands. "I think you've got a good head on your shoulders," she said. "Paul here has told me all about how you both sat together in the chest; but you won't escape from me so easily!"

Lisei looked at the ground somewhat embarrassed; but then eagerly asked after her father. After I had given her my news, I asked Frau Meisterin for some bedding, added some of my own, and carried it over to the prisoner's cell myself, having received permission to do this from the warder a short time before. And so as night fell we could but hope that our old friend in his bleak cell, in a warm bed and on the best pillow there is in the world, would have a serene and refreshing night's sleep.

* *

The next morning, as I was about to step into the street on my way to the Criminal Commissioner, the warder came shuffling towards me from across the way in his slippers. "You were right, Paulsen," he said in his brittle voice. "It wasn't one of those rascals this time; they've just caught the right man; your old man will be released today."

And indeed, after a few hours the prison door opened and old Tendler was directed over to us by the authoritative voice of the warder. As lunch was just about to be served, Frau Meisterin would not rest until he too had taken his place at the table; but he hardly touched the good food, and however much she tried to encourage him, he said little; he sat withdrawn next to his daughter, and only occasionally I noticed how he took the girl's hand and fondly caressed it. Then I heard the tinkling of a little bell outside the door; I recognised it at once, albeit it rang to me from far away in my childhood.

"Lisei!" I said quietly.

"Yes, Paul, I can hear it too."

And we were soon both standing outside the front door. It was there, coming down the street, the little cart with the two tall chests, just as at home where I had so often longed to see it again. A farmer's lad walked beside it with reins and a whip in his hand; but the little bell now tinkled round the neck of a small grey.

"What happened to the bay?" I asked Lisei.

"The bay?" she replied. "It collapsed in front of the cart one day; father fetched the vet from the village at once, but it didn't survive."

With these words her eyes filled with tears.

"What's the matter, Lisei?" I asked. "Everything's all right now!"

She shook her head. "My father's a worry! He's so quiet; the shame, he can't get over it."

Lisei, with her devoted daughter's eyes, had noticed it. Hardly had they both been settled at a small inn, with the old man already outlining his plans for moving on – as he didn't want to appear before the public here now – when a fever forced him to stay in bed. We soon had to call a doctor and it developed into a lengthy illness. Anxious that they might fall into need because of it, I offered Lisei my financial support; but she said: "I'd gladly accept it from you; but don't worry, we're not so poor." There remained nothing more I could do other than share the night-watch with her or, as the patient got better, chat with him for a few moments at his bedside in the evenings.

And so the time for my departure drew nearer, and my heart grew heavier and heavier. It almost hurt to look at Lisei; for she too would soon be going away from here out into the wide world again. If only she had a home! Where could they be found when I wanted to send them greetings and news! I thought of the twelve years since our first parting – would such a long time pass again, or in the end, a whole lifetime?

"And my greetings, too, to your home when you return there!" said Lisei; she had accompanied me to Frau Meisterin's door on the last evening. "I can still see it before my eyes, the little white seat by the door, the linden tree in the garden; oh, I'll never forget it; I've never found anything like it again in the world!"

As she spoke, it was as though my home flashed before me from out of dark depths; I saw the gentle eyes of my mother, the firm honest face of my father. "Oh, Lisei," I said, "where is my real home now! That one is all empty and deserted."

Lisei said nothing; she simply gave me her hand and looked at me with her kind eyes.

Then I seemed to hear my mother's voice saying: "Hold this hand firmly and go back with her, then you'll have your home again!" – and I held that hand firmly and said: "Come back with me, Lisei, and let's try to breathe new life together into the empty house, one as good as they led, who once meant a lot to you too!"

"Paul," she cried, "what are you saying? I don't understand."

But her hand trembled strongly in mine, and I said: "Oh, Lisei, understand me!"

She paused for a moment. "Paul," she said, "I can't leave my father."

"But he must come with us, Lisei! At the back of the house, the two small rooms that are empty at the moment – he can live and work there; old Heinrich's got his small room quite close by."

Lisei nodded. "But Paul, we're travelling folk. What will they say about it in your town?"

"They'll have a lot to say about it, Lisei!"

"And it doesn't worry you?"

I simply laughed in response.

"Well," said Lisei, and her voice sounded like a peal of bells, "if *you've* got the courage, I have too!"

"But, do you really want to?"

"Yes, Paul, if I didn't want to" – and she shook her small dark head at me – "I never would!"

– 'And, my lad,' the narrator interrupted himself at this point, 'how a girl's dark eyes look into yours as she says that, you'll learn when you're a good deal older!'

'Yes, of course,' I thought, 'especially a pair of eyes that could set a lake on fire!'

'And so,' continued Paulsen, 'you've guessed by now who Lisei is.'

'Frau Paulsen,' I replied. 'As if I hadn't realised that long ago! She still says "nit" as they say in Bavaria and she still has those dark eyes beneath her delicate eyebrows.'

My friend laughed, while I secretly decided to take a good look at Frau Paulsen on our return to the house to see whether I could still recognise the puppeteer Lisei in her. 'But,' I asked, 'what happened to old Herr Tendler?'

'My dear boy,' replied my friend, 'he went where we all go in the end. He's resting over there in the churchyard next to our old Heinrich; but there's someone else buried there with him; the other little friend from my childhood. I'll tell you all about it; only let's go out to the back, just a little way, my wife may be calling us soon, and she mustn't hear this story again.'

Paulsen stood up and we went on to the footpath that runs behind the gardens of the town. We met few people; for it was already late in the afternoon.

– 'Well,' Paulsen began again, 'old Tendler was very happy with our decision; he thought of my parents whom he had once known, and he began to have confidence in me too. Moreover, he was tired of travelling; indeed, since it had exposed him to the danger of being confused with the worst vagabonds, his longing for a settled home had only grown stronger. My good Frau Meisterin, however, wasn't so enthusiastic; she voiced her fear that the child of a travelling puppet player, with the best will in the world, might still not make the right wife for an established master craftsman. – Well, she has been converted for some time now!

And so, hardly a week later I was back here again, from the hills to the North Sea coast, in our old home town. I eagerly took charge of the business with Heinrich, and at the same time furnished both the empty rooms at the rear of the house for Lisei's father Joseph. Two weeks later – the scent of the first spring flowers had just begun to drift across the gardens – a tinkling was heard from the street. "Master! Master!" shouted old Heinrich, "they're coming, they're coming!" And the little cart with the two tall chests stopped outside our door. There were Lisei and her father Joseph, both with flushed cheeks and excited eyes; the whole puppet cast then moved in with them; for it was an express condition that they should accompany Joseph to his place of retirement. The cart, on the other hand, was quickly sold.

Then we had our wedding; a very quiet one; for we had no blood relatives in the district any more; only my old school friend the harbour-master was present, as a witness. Lisei was a Catholic like her parents; that this could have been an obstacle to our marriage never occurred to us. During the early years of our marriage she travelled readily to the neighbouring town to Easter confession; as you know, there's a Catholic community there. After that she confessed her worries only to her husband.

On the morning of the wedding Joseph laid two bags in front of me on the table, a large one filled with old silver coins and a small one with Kremnitz ducats.

"You've not asked for it, Paul!" he said. "But my Lisei is not so poor that she's brought you nothing. Take it! I've no further need of it."

It was the savings my father had once spoken about, and the money now came to his son at a most opportune time at the outset of his business. With it Lisei's father had given away his whole fortune and entrusted his own welfare to his children; but he did not become idle; he took up his woodcarver's knife again and knew how to make himself useful around the workshop.

The puppets together with the theatre apparatus were stored in the loft of the house next door. On Sunday afternoons, however, Joseph would fetch first one puppet, then another down into his living room, check the wires and joints, and clean or improve this or that on them. Old Heinrich with his short pipe would stand beside him and listen to the puppets' past fortunes, almost every one having its own story; indeed, as it now emerged, the masterfully carved Kasperl had once even served as the matchmaker between its young creator and Lisei's mother.

Occasionally, in order to make a particular scene come alive, the wires were even manipulated; Lisei and I often stood outside peering in at the windows, which looked out on to the yard from their snug frame of vine leaves; but the old children inside were so deeply engrossed in their play that the presence of an audience was only noticed from our applause.

As the year progressed, Joseph found another occupation; he took the garden under his care, he planted and harvested, and on Sundays, smartly dressed, he would wander up and down between the beds, trimming the rose bushes or binding the carnations and stocks to thin stakes he had cut himself.

So we lived contentedly and as one family; my business steadily improved. For a few weeks strong opinions were expressed in our good town about my marriage; but since almost everyone was agreed on the folly of my conduct, so the debate was denied the nourishment of contradiction and soon starved itself out.

With the return of winter, Joseph would once more fetch the puppets down from their place in the loft on Sundays, and I had no reason not to think that he would pass his remaining years in these quietly alternating occupations. But one morning, when I was sitting alone at breakfast in the living room, he came to see me with a most serious expression on his face. "Son," he said, after he had run his hand through his spiky white hair a few times as though embarrassed, "I simply can't go on always accepting charity at your good table."

I didn't know where this was leading, but I asked him what made him think such a thing; he worked well in the workshop, and if my business was now making a larger profit, this was essentially the return on his own money which he had placed in my hands on the morning of our wedding.

He shook his head. He did not consider this enough. He had once, however, earned a part of that little fortune in our town; he still had the theatre and he still had all the plays in his head.

I saw clearly that the old puppeteer in him would not let him rest; his friend Heinrich no longer sufficed as his public, he had to perform his plays again before an assembled audience.

I tried to talk him out of it; but he always returned to the subject. I spoke to Lisei, and in the end we couldn't help giving in to him. The old man, of course, would have preferred to see Lisei speaking the female parts in his plays as she had before our marriage; but we were agreed not to understand his hints at this; it would certainly not be fitting for the wife of a burgher of the town and master craftsman.

Luckily – or, it could be said, unfortunately – there was a woman of very good repute in the town at the time who had once served as a prompter with a theatre troupe and hence was not inexperienced in such matters. This woman, Cripple-Lieschen people called her because of her hunched back, accepted our offer immediately, and soon there was the most lively activity in Joseph's room in the evenings and on Sunday afternoons. While old Heinrich carpentered sections of the theatre in front of one window, the old puppeteer stood in front of the other and rehearsed one scene after another with Cripple-Lieschen amongst freshly painted scenery which hung down from the ceiling. She was a very clever woman, he continually assured her after such sessions; not even Lisei had mastered things so quickly; it was just that her singing was not so good; she sang in a deep throaty voice not suitable for the beautiful Susanna who had to sing the song.

The day of the performance was finally settled. It needed to be as respectable as possible, and took place not in the Schützenhof but in the main assembly room of the town hall where school-leavers gave their speeches around Michaelmas; and when one Saturday afternoon our good citizens unfolded their fresh weekly newspapers, an advertisement in large letters immediately met their eyes:

Tomorrow Sunday evening 7 o'clock here in the town hall.
Mechanicus JOSEPH TENDLER & his MARIONETTE-THEATRE
THE BEAUTIFUL SUSANNA, play with singing in four acts.

But by this time the innocent, curious youths of my school years had disappeared from our town; the Cossack Winter lay in between, and a terrible thuggishness had spread among the apprentice craftsmen particularly; the formerly enthusiastic audience from among the respected burghers of the town now had its thoughts fixed on other things. However, everything might have gone well if only Black Schmidt and his sons hadn't been involved.'

– I asked Paulsen who that was, for I had never heard of such a person in our town.

'That I can believe,' he replied, 'Black Schmidt died years ago in the poorhouse; but at that time he was a master craftsman like me; he didn't lack skill, but he was slovenly in his work as in his life; he wasted the day's meagre earnings on drink and cards in the evenings. He always hated my father, not only because my father had far more customers, but also from back in his youth when he had been a fellow apprentice with my father and been dismissed by the master craftsman because of a bad trick he played on him. Since the summer of the year I'm talking about he had found every opportunity to take this dislike out on me in every possible way; for work on the machines in the newly built calico factory, in spite of his constant efforts to obtain it, had been given only to me, and because of this, he and his two sons, who were employed by their father and whose appetite for spiteful activities if anything exceeded his, had never failed to show me their annoyance through every kind of trick. These people however were far from my thoughts at this time.

So the evening of the performance arrived. I still needed to work on my books, so it wasn't until later that I learned what happened from my wife and Heinrich who had gone to the town hall with father.

The first row was almost empty, the second only partially occupied; but in the gallery the audience stood closely packed. When the play began in front of this audience, everything went well; old Lieschen knew her part thoroughly and spoke without prompting. But then came that unfortunate song! In vain she tried to give her voice a softer tone; as Joseph had said, it had a deep throaty sound. Suddenly a voice called from the gallery: "Higher, Cripple-Lieschen! Higher!" And when she responded by trying to climb to the unreachable treble key, a roar of laugher burst through the room.

The play on the stage came to a halt and the trembling voice of the old puppeteer called out from between the wings: "Ladies and gentlemen, I implore you, please be quiet!" Kasperl, who was in the middle of a scene with the beautiful Susanna, and whose wires he was holding at the time, waggled his magnificent nose convulsively.

Fresh laughter was the answer. "Kasperl should sing!" – "A Russian song! 'Beautiful Minka, I must away!'" – "Hurrah for Kasperl!" – "No, Kasperl's daughter must sing!" – "Mind what you say! She's now the Frau Meisterin, she doesn't do it any more!"

The uproar continued for a while. All of a sudden, a large well-aimed cobblestone landed on the stage. It had struck Kasperl's wires; the puppet slipped out of its master's hand and fell to the floor.

Joseph couldn't restrain himself any longer. In spite of Lisei's pleading, he immediately stepped on to the puppet stage. Thunderous clapping, laughter, foot-stamping greeted him, and it must have been a very strange spectacle, the old man, his head in the flies above the set, trying to give vent to his righteous anger with vigorous motions of his hands. But suddenly, amidst the tumult, the curtain fell, old Heinrich had brought it down.

In the meantime, at home with my accounts, I felt a certain disquiet; I will not say I sensed disaster, but I felt an urge to follow after my family. As I was about to climb the steps to the assembly room in the town hall, what seemed like the entire audience came rushing down them to meet me. Everyone was laughing and shouting at once. "Hurrah! Kasperl is dead! Lott is dead! The comedy's over!" As I looked up I caught sight of the swarthy faces of the Schmidt boys above me. They halted for a moment, then ran past me out of the door; but I was now certain where the source of this mischief was to be found.

Arriving upstairs I found the room almost empty. My father-in-law sat on a chair behind the stage like a broken man, his hands covering his face. Lisei, on her knees before him, slowly stood up as she became aware of my presence. "Well, Paul," she asked, looking sadly at me, "do you still have the courage?"

She certainly must have read in my eyes that I still did; for before I could answer, her head was already resting on my shoulders. "Let's just stick firmly together, Paul!" she said quietly.

– And just look! With that and honest work we came through it all.

When we got up the next morning we found those insulting words "Paul the Puppeteer" – a term of abuse they undoubtedly were – scrawled in chalk on our front door, but I quickly wiped them off, and when they later reappeared a few times in public places I played my trump card; when it became known I wasn't going to stand any nonsense, things returned to normal. – Anyone who has said these words to you now will not have meant ill by it; and I don't want to know their name.

But after that evening old Joseph was no longer the man he had been. In vain I pointed out to him the despicable cause of the whole mischief, and that it had been directed more against me than against him. Soon afterwards, without our knowledge, he put all his marionettes up for public auction where, to the joy of the children and rag-and-bone women, they were auctioned for just a few schillings; he never wanted to see them again. But it was an unfortunate way to get rid of them; for when the spring sunshine filled the streets again, the puppets he had sold came out of the dark houses one after the other into the light of day. Here sat a girl on a front doorstep with Saint Genovieve, there a boy had Doctor Faust riding on his black tom; in a garden near the Schützenhof one day Count Palatine Siegfried was seen hanging in a cherry tree beside the Sparrow from Hell as a scarecrow. The desecration of his favourites so hurt Joseph that at first he would hardly leave our house and garden. I could plainly see that this hasty sale was gnawing at his heart, and I managed to buy back one or two of the puppets; but when I brought them to him, they gave him no joy; the whole thing had been destroyed. And, most strangely, despite every effort I could not discover where the most valuable figure of all, the magnificent Kasperl, was being hidden. And what was the whole puppet world without him!

But the curtain was about to go up on another, more serious play. An old chest complaint of Joseph's had recurred, his life appeared to be drawing to its close. Patiently he lay on his bed, full of gratitude for every small act of kindness. "Yes, yes," he said smiling, and raising his eyes so serenely towards the ceiling beams that he seemed already to be looking through them into the eternal hereafter, "she was right, after all: I wasn't always able to cope with people; it'll be far better with the angels up there; and – in any event, Lisei, I'll find your mother there."

The good child-like man died; Lisei and I, we missed him terribly; and old Heinrich, who followed him a few years later, wandered about on his remaining Sunday afternoons as if he didn't know what to do with himself, as if he was looking for someone he couldn't find.

We decked father's coffin with all the flowers from the garden that he had tended; it was carried out laden with wreaths to the churchyard where the grave had been dug not far from the wall. When the coffin had been lowered into the grave, our old priest stepped up to its edge and spoke a word of comfort and promise; he had been a constant true friend and counsellor to my parents; I had been confirmed, and Lisei and I married, by him. The churchyard was thick with people; from the burial of the old puppeteer it seemed that a final, special performance was expected.

And something special actually did happen; but it was noticed only by those of us standing close to the grave. Lisei, who had come out of the church holding on to my arm, had just convulsively clasped my hand as the old priest, in accordance with custom, grasped the waiting spade and tipped the first soil on to the coffin. A dull thud sounded from the bottom of the grave. "For out of the ground wast thou taken!" rang the words of the priest; but hardly were they spoken when I saw something flying towards us from the churchyard wall above the heads of the people. I thought at first it was a large bird; but it dropped and fell straight into the grave. Glancing quickly behind me – for I was standing a little above ground level on the dug-out earth – I had seen one of the Schmidt boys duck behind the churchyard wall and run away, and I knew at once what had happened. Lisei had let out a cry at my side, our old priest held the spade undecidedly in his hands for the second cast of earth. A glance into the grave confirmed my suspicion: on top of the coffin, between the flowers and the soil, which had already partly covered them, there he had seated himself, my old childhood companion, Kasperl, my little jolly friend. But he didn't look at all jolly now; he had let his great beak of a nose fall sadly on to his chest; the arm with the elaborately crafted thumb was stretched up at the sky, as though he were saying that when all puppet plays had ended here, another one would begin up there.

I saw it all in a brief moment, for the priest had already cast the second spadeful of earth into the grave: "And unto dust shalt thou return!" And as the earth slid off the coffin, so Kasperl too rolled off its flowers into the bottom of the grave and was covered.

Then with the last pitch of earth the comforting promise rang out: "And together with my dead body thou shalt arise!"

When the Lord's Prayer had been said and the people had dispersed, the old priest came over to us as we remained staring into the grave. "It was meant to be a wicked act," he said, as he kind-heartedly grasped our hands. "But let us take it another way! As you've described it to me, the deceased carved the little figure in his youth, and it brought him a happy marriage; later, and throughout his life, by means of it he brightened many a human heart after a day's work, and in the mouth of the little jester he placed many a word of truth agreeable both to God and the people – I watched it once myself, when you were still children. – Let the little puppet simply follow his master; that will be entirely in the spirit of the words of our Holy Scripture! And be of good cheer; for the Blessed may rest from their labours."

And so it was over. Quietly and at peace we went home, never to see old father Joseph or the magnificent Kasperl again.

'It all caused us much pain,' added my friend after a while, 'but it did us young ones no serious harm. Not long afterwards our Joseph was born, and then we had everything that makes for complete human happiness. But year after year I am still reminded of those events by Black Schmidt's eldest son. He became one of those eternally wandering journeymen, in rags and gone to ruin, who eke out their miserable existence from alms which, as laid down by the guild rules, the master craftsmen have to give them at their asking. He doesn't even give my house a miss.'

My friend paused and gazed at the sun that was setting behind the trees in the churchyard before us; but for some time I had been observing the friendly face of Frau Paulsen looking out for us over the garden gate which we were now nearing. 'I'd never have thought it,' she cried, as we walked towards her. 'What have you two got so much to talk about? Come along inside! God's good food is standing on the table; the harbourmaster's there too; and there's a letter from Joseph and the old Frau Meisterin! – But why are you looking at me like that, my lad?'

Master Paulsen laughed. 'I've told him a few things, mother. Now he wants to see if you really are the little puppeteer Lisei!'

'Of course!' she answered, casting a loving glance at her husband. 'Just take a good look, my lad! And if you can't see it – that one there, he knows all about it!'

And Master Paulsen quietly put his arm round her. Then we went indoors to celebrate their wedding anniversary.

They were fine folk, Paulsen and his puppeteer Lisei.

Renate

SOME DISTANCE from my home town, yet not too far for a day's outing, lies the village of Schwabstedt, whose name according to some chroniclers is said to mean 'Suavestätte', or 'delightful place'. And high above the rich meadows of the Treene Valley, through which the river winds its beautiful way, is its old parish inn, whose landlord always used to be called Peter Behrens, until recent times when all tradition ended, and where a 'Mother Behrens', a new one in each generation but always of fine character, young or old, always took good care of the necessities of life for her guests like a true mother. The long arbour of linden trees with the 'snow-white' covered coffee table beneath, the steep granite steps under the ancient white poplars that led down to the river, the boat trips among the floating water-lilies, these things will recreate for many older people a charming remote corner of the paradise of their youth.

But to the youthful imagination Schwabstedt offered something quite different; for legend and half-faded history twine their dark ivy round this place. It is true that if visible traces are being looked for, the searcher must be content with few; for where there is said once to have been a harbour east of the village, used by the feared Vitalien brothers, of the original river valley there exists only a gully in the land today; and of the fortress-like residence of the bishops of Schleswig, which once rose high above the river close by the village, nothing more is to be seen than the depressions of dry moats and scant remains of walls showing here and there out of the grass; if, that is, the many wild boar tusks are excluded which as boys we used to dig out of the turf to hold in our own hands as evidence of the great wealth of flora and fauna said to have once existed here.

But something else aroused my curiosity far more than these places. To one side of the bishop's rise, nearly hidden among ancient lofty oaks, lay a farmstead that had evidently been left to fall into ruin. This house, clearly distinguishable from the usual farmhouses by its two storeys, gradually took on a mysterious force of attraction for me, but the timidity of youth prevented me from going nearer to it. I must have been a degree taller by the time I dared to do so; I still remember the event well and all the circumstances surrounding it.

While I was cautiously walking round the lonely farmhouse, first looking up at its begrimed windows, then up into the branches of the old trees where a pair of magpies screeched from their nest, an old woman came round the corner gathering fallen twigs in her apron. When I peered under the rough straw bonnet I recognised the sharp brown face of the well-known 'Mother Pottsacksch' who went from door to door in the town selling lilies of the valley and posies of woodruff or nuts and bilberries according to the season.

'Mother Pottsacksch!' I cried, 'do you live here in this big house?'

'Aye, young man,' the old woman replied in her broad dialect. 'I keep an eye on things around here!'

And on further questioning I learned the house had once been attached to a large farm, but that the land had been separated from it some hundred years ago, and before long, it was said, the farmstead itself – as it was still called then – was also to be sold for demolition and the trees felled.

I was sorry for the poor magpies which had carefully built their nest up in the trees. Then I asked her: 'And who was it who lived here then, a hundred years ago?'

'Then?' exclaimed the old woman, pressing her free hand against her hip. 'The witch, she lived here then!'

'The witch?' I repeated. 'Were there witches here then?'

The old woman waved a hand at me. 'Oho! The gentleman should mind his words.' By which she implied that I should tread carefully, that there was still something sinister about the place even today.

When I asked if the witch had been burned, she shook her old head violently. 'Oho! Oho!' she cried again and gave me to understand that the Amtmann and the Landvogt had simply wanted to avoid the issue; for – well, I was sure to understand; and amid meaningful nods of the head, she now made the gesture of counting money. The estate, in fact, had not been broken up until after the witch's death; she had run it herself with a firm hand, and had been a capable farmer.

How this witch had actually practised witchcraft, Mother Pottsacksch appeared not to know. 'The Devil's work, sir!' she said. 'What such-a-folk do!' This much however was certain: on Sundays, when other Christian folk had sat down in church to hear the Word of God, she had mounted a horse and ridden north into the heath and moorland; what she might have done there had given rise to many a dark speculation. But suddenly this had ceased, and she never again left her large gloomy room on Sundays; Mother Pottsacksch's great-grandmother had seen her pale face with large burning eyes as she sat behind the small window panes.

More I could not get out of the old woman.

'And was the horse she rode black?' I eventually asked, to complete the rapidly sketched picture in my mind.

'Black?' shrieked Mother Pottsacksch, as though indignant at such a needless question. 'Black as pitch! The gentleman can be sure of it!'

The Schwabstedt witch occupied my thoughts for some time; I made a number of inquiries in various quarters about her precise fate, but what Mother Pottsacksch had not been able to tell me, no one else could either. I certainly had no idea that I should have sought the answer so near by, in the loft of my parental home.

Many years later, when I had long forgotten these things, I was sitting in front of a chest of drawers that was stowed away up there with the rest of my grandfather's furniture and rummaging among its drawers for his love-letters to my grandmother. While doing so I came upon a notebook that was clearly in much older handwriting, and its contents, with an addition discovered later, as will be described, I shall now set before the reader.

In regard to the style of writing and presentation, I have changed only as much as appeared necessary for a livelier rendering of the content, perhaps in a few places hardly enough for a number of readers, but of the content itself nothing at all has been altered by me.

And so let the writer of this old memoir speak for himself.

* *

1700. At about this time my dear father, now resting in peace, was chaplain or deacon in the village of Schwesen, where he collected his meagre income from house to house, for the most part in butter, corn and meat, and where in addition to his ministry he also had the duty of running the school. My dear parents forwent everything for my sake, and kindly people did not begrudge me a place at their mid-day meal, and so it was made possible for me to enter the Latin school in Husum, of which the excellent Nicolaus Rudlof was then headmaster, and I lodged there with a devout tailor's widow. Also with God's help I had moved to an upper class when I underwent a perilous ordeal which could quite easily have put a sudden end to all my studies.

On the afternoon of the last Sunday in October I was walking back to the town after the usual Saturday visit to my parents' house in the village. I had quite tired myself out earlier, however, for since the village folk had not kept a swineherd, a 'Gergesene' as my late father used to say, for some years, our pigs had broken out of the pasturage outside the village so that we had been obliged to make a desperate hunt for them on this last hot day of the year. Nevertheless I had hurried on my way as my departure had been delayed, and the setting sun was already casting a red mist over the heathland; all kinds of vagabonds roamed about and committed robbery and theft after the only recently ended war with the King of Denmark, and it was also said that the previous evening, over by the wood where the old women gather their cranberries, the wild dancing of the jack-o'-lantern had been seen, which is best avoided at all times.

When at last I entered the town and reached the market place, the gables of the houses were already dark against the evening sky, and since it was Sunday a profound stillness hung over the streets; only from the old church behind the linden trees came the soft strains of organ music.

I knew full well it was the organist Georg Bruhn, brother and successor to the still more celebrated Nicolaus Bruhn, who for himself and his God alone loved to practise his masterly art at the twilight hour; and realising that the church door beneath the so-called 'Mother-Linden' stood open, I made my way inside and sat down quietly in one of the old monks' pews on the north side. Although the trees outside had already shed most of their leaves, there was a dimness here within in which I was hardly able to recognise the scenes and figures on the memorial plaques which adorn this massive church. Nonetheless, the incomparable master continued with his playing aloft; and as I sat in my corner of the church below, completely alone and increasingly engulfed in darkness, in which the lovely melodies of flutes and oboes played like soft lights, it was as though both the angels on the crucifix of the altarpiece had flown down and were covering me with their golden wings. How long I rested in such safe keeping I do not know; but then the resounding chime of the bell in the tower, reverberating in the immense space below, startled me out of it. Through the well-nigh leafless trees the moon shone in through the lofty windows; in particular, the mighty equestrian statue of St George and the dragon, which actually belonged to the nearby home for the poor but for the present had been placed here next to the altar, was bathed in such a bright light that from where I was sitting I could clearly recognise the rider's stern face and also, under the hoofs of the rearing stallion, the dragon's gaping mouth.

But the music from the organ above had ceased and over on the altarpiece the angels again hovered at the side of Christ on the Cross. An immense stillness surrounded me. When I opened the old monk's pew door and made to leave, only the sound of my steps echoed far into the nave. In haste I ran first to the north door, then to the tower door, then to the south door of the church, but found them all firmly locked, and all the banging that I now performed with my fists appeared to reach no one's ears. As I wandered helplessly about my eyes fell on the large memorial plaque which appeared in front of me on the pillar at the base of which the old mayor Aegidius Herfort lay buried. On it Death was shown as a realistic complete skeleton carved in wood crawling like a huge spider up the likeness of the deceased. This now greatly disturbed me; for through the shadows cast by the branches swaying in front of the windows and playing with the moonlight across the figure, it almost appeared to me as though the loathsome thing jerked its head and stretched its pointed bony fingers up towards the deceased's face. It then further crossed my mind that it could equally well climb down the pillar or turn round completely and jump on to the nearest pew. I knew of course this was simply a foolish figment of my imagination, but nevertheless I squeezed myself through the narrow space to the tall equestrian statue of the saint, imagining instinctively that I should find protection and help from it. It certainly occurred to me that these were papist thoughts and the wooden statue should simply be regarded as a symbol; however, my hand still gripped the spurred foot of the rider. I then heard the large key rattling in the main door of the church, and was about to rush there to get out when I saw the heavy door opening and at the same moment closing again. I could see nothing inside the church or make out any person's footsteps, yet I felt as though there was something there with me in the church, and as I listened almost afraid to draw breath, I clearly heard the sound of panting and trotting approaching the nave. Trembling, I placed my foot on the knight's so as to swing myself up on to the wooden horse. Some noise may have resulted as I was doing so, for a prolonged howl broke out and I saw a truly massive black hound bounding towards me. But I was already standing on the horse's shoulder; one hand I had placed round the knight's neck, while with the other – at the inspiration of our most merciful God – I pulled out his lance which was inserted loosely through the gauntlet.

A fight then ensued between a fourteen-year-old boy and an extremely strong and ferocious beast. With flashing eyes the brute sprang up at me, tearing at my shoes with its paws, and I stared into the open jaws with the red steaming tongue; just a few more inches and the white teeth bared towards me would have fastened hold and pulled me to the ground. But I protected my body and jabbed the beast in its shaggy coat with my lance, so that it fell away to one side howling several times.

I am not aware of having called for human help at such a time of need, only a silent and fervent prayer to God and His angels rose from my breast; I even thought of my dear parents, should they find me here so miserably torn to pieces at God's altar. For as the heavily panting animal constantly sprang at me, it was clear I had to fall prey to it in the end. My senses had already begun to leave me, for it appeared as if it were no longer the hound but Death itself that had climbed down from the epitaph and was springing at me from one of the pews. The bony hands were already seizing my lance when I heard a call and a loud noise in the church below, and suddenly it was as though one of the angels had again flown down to me from the crucifix and its arms were tearing the loathsome figure of Death away from my young body.

'Türk, Türk, you brute!' came the words of a small, brave voice below me, and as I glanced dizzily down I saw, next to the shaggy head of the monster, a most pretty face staring anxiously up at me with two dark eyes. Whimpering, the monster still tried to reach me, but two small brown arms had clasped themselves round its neck and would not let it go; the animal even licked at

the pretty face a few times with its tongue as if to caress it. I took
all this in at a single glance, as the moon was still shining brightly
through the church windows. I even heard a man's voice calling:
'A child, a boy, the pastor's son from Schwesen!' Then I lost
consciousness and fell from the wooden horse.

When I recovered I found myself lying in my bed in my lodgings and my old tailor's widow was sitting on the chair next to
me, with her small green flask of restorative in her lap. I acted
nevertheless as though I still lay in a faint, for as soon as I closed
my eyes the small face next to the fierce animal's head pleasantly
dominated my mind; I also wondered to myself if it might have
been an angel that had had its hair smoothed back under a small
glittering gold cap such as the girls in the villages hereabouts
wear on Sundays; indeed, I was almost overcome with a desire to
climb back on to St George's horse. It was not until the dear soul
had passed the smoking lamp under my nose that I raised myself
on my pillows. Then she loudly praised God again and again,
poured the liquid out for me from her green flask, and said: 'It is
well you listened to God's word in your father's church this
morning, Josias, for 'tis said there are times when the Devil sits
by the old font beneath the tower, and it bodes ill for anyone to
walk by with worldly thoughts on his mind.'

But I inquired anxiously if they had then carried me away
from there.

'Of course they did, Josias,' she replied. 'It was the sexton,
though; those in the office of the church have nothing to fear.'

I was glad that I had not been in my senses; for whether my
angel-thoughts, which I took with me out of the church, were
spiritual or secular, was not at all clear to me. Besides, it occurred
to me that the dreadful quadruped I had fought with must have
been the sexton's, Albert Carstens'. It had, as I knew, belonged
to a Danish captain who had once been quartered on him, but
who had lost his life in the storming of the Finkenhaus redoubt.
And the dear lady also told me that because of the high number
of break-ins they had been letting the dog loose into the church

as a guard. But from whence the angel came who protected me from it, I was not able to learn; nor afterwards, for reasons unknown to me, was I able to question others about her. And for the rest of my schooldays, however much I looked for it on market days thereafter, I was never again to meet that pretty face under the small glittering cap.

* *

Anno Dom. 1705. Now during the time of the Administrator, His Serene Highness Christian August, there were strange dealings with those in ecclesiastical office. The powerful Councillor von Goertz had even sold the parsonage at Böel in Angeln on the Hamburg Exchange to the highest bidder; a reveller and gambler, before whose eyes, when later he was on his death-bed, cards were held up to see if he was still able to recognise the suits. My father, however, managed to move from his miserable deaconry in Schwesen to the more lucrative parsonage at Schwabstätte and was confirmed in his post there. As I was already registered at the University of Kiel, the now considerably more generous support from my dear parents put me in high spirits for a while, and I strutted about in high boots and a red Rockelor, with a sword at my side; and indeed, I had even had an affair of honour with a nobleman who had proclaimed my landlord's virtuous daughter, a girl of otherwise no interest to me, a students' whore. For the rest, I was not behind in my studies, neither in theology nor in philosophy. Regarding the former I attached myself mostly to the older professors, for there were those, especially among the readers, who, contrary to the teachings of Paul and our Dr Martin Luther, strove to minimise the power of Satan, and to deny his kingdom among the children of this world. Such opinions, however, were not to my and my dear father's way of thinking.

Since, according to the old saying, repetition is the mother of study, it was agreed among us that at the end of my two-year period of study, I would spend the summer of the above

recorded year at my parents' house to such purpose, and thereafter should deepen my learning by studying for a time at the
famous University of Halle. And so eventually, after a safe
carriage journey, I arrived one afternoon in Husum, and for the
remaining eight miles conveyed myself in the manner of the
Holy Apostles.

I had never before been to Schwabstätte, and was unfamiliar
with the way there. The path led first across the marsh where it
followed the line of the former sea dyke, and then where it rose
into sand and heathland, a small cottage would appear here and
there, so that I had no difficulty in further asking the way.
Suddenly, as the path wound up a hill and evening began to cast
its shadows, I saw the village below me, with its smoking roofs,
lying stretched out amid the bushes and trees along the shore of
the charming river Treene. Then my heart began to race, since I
would soon be with my dear parents, and I hardly cast a glance at
the tower of the bishop's old residence which rose up at the
water's edge glittering like gold in the evening light, but waved
my stick and sang heartily:

> Down the path from the hill
> Here comes your student son!
> Father, oh dear Mother,
> Now greet me by the hand!

So singing, I was soon below in the village. The dogs barked as
they darted for my high boots, and the women, standing in front
of their doors, gaped at my red travelling cloak and nudged one
another with their elbows. As I strode past the small cottages of
the village, behind them, in the direction of the river, I caught
sight of a large two-storey building which appeared isolated and
well-nigh hidden among huge trees; and no living creature was
to be seen there, neither around the house nor the barn which lay
behind it; only large birds rose from the tops of the trees and
flew back and forth above them.

I asked an old man: 'Who lives down there?'

'Do you not know?'

'Why, no; that is why I have asked you.'

'The farmer, the Hofbauer,* lives there,' he replied, stroking his stubble beard and retreating inside his cottage.

With such information I proceeded on my way, but repeatedly turned my head round, almost involuntarily, to look back at the windows glittering so darkly and mysteriously down there among the dark trees. Then, as I walked on for a while almost lost in thought, I suddenly heard a call, 'Josias, Josias!' as though from out of the sky. And it was my dear mother standing above the churchyard on the high barrow on which the belfry stood; she had been looking out for me all evening. I was swiftly at her side, holding her to my breast, and asking the whereabouts of our home; and when she simply pointed to a pleasant-looking house and garden on the other side of the road, I gathered the slight woman into my arms and carried her down the hill.

And then came a further shout, but this time from the house: 'Josias, Josias!' And with hearty laughter: 'Is that the way to treat his mother?' It was my dear father. He had come to the door and taken the mother from her son's arms; he was one of those who knew full well the meaning of a jest born out of pure heartfelt joy. But when my mother urged him, in her eager way, to express admiration for their fine figure of a son in words as she had done, he answered cautiously: 'Yes, yes, mother; I can see our studiosus has turned out very well; we will just have to see if the theologus is none the worse for it.'

My parents then led me to my room; it was well located, facing the wood, and the rustling of the trees often used to lull me to sleep there after my evening prayers. The floor was laid with bricks, but my mother had spread matting over it, which the village folk here make from the rushes by the river.

I soon arranged my books and the well-stitched lecture notes on the large table, and to my father's joy set to work with great zeal. But my mother would forever be interrupting me, trying to

---

*An influential owner of a farmstead on a grander scale than usual, here the farmstead belonging to the former bishop's residence.

get me out into the open air, saying: 'What are the people here going to think if those full cheeks become hollow while your mother is looking after you!' And then one evening, when it had just struck nine from the belfry, she cried out: 'There you are still sitting there, Josias, knowing full well that the church elder's daughter is getting married! It is fitting that the pastor's son has a dance with the bride!' Then she lifted my cloak off the peg, brushed it clean, and put a silver coin as a wedding gift in my pocket. I could now make out the fiddles and trumpets in the distance, and it was not long before I was in the midst of the wedding.

The houses here are built in the old Saxon style, that is, the cattle, which in those days grazed in summer in the paddocks or out on the fens, in wintertime were housed indoors on either side of the large threshing floor, while the living quarters of the farmer's family and his employees, which they call the 'Döns', lay at the far end of the large floor directly opposite the main doorway.

As I went in from the stillness of the summer evening outside, I felt at first as if I were witnessing a strange and shifting shadow-play; for the tallow candles on the wooden beams cast only a dim, ruddy light over the heads of those who pushed past one another, or danced the two-step in pairs and encouraged the musicians with shouts and stamping. And as the large floor was almost filled with guests, it was some time before I saw the bride's gold-sequined crown emerge from among them; I made my reverence to her, and although it called for a particular rustic skill, managed to take a dozen turns with her on the crowded floor. Afterwards I joined a tradesman from the town who was known to me from my schooldays, or one or other of the older villagers who sat with their beer tankards among the musicians' barrels or in the farmer's living room.

Time may have passed in this way until midnight, when I saw a young girl standing on the step to one of the rooms at the rear, away from the others, as if she did not wish to lose herself in the crowd; and as I drew closer behind her I noticed that although she was traditionally dressed for the occasion, her skirt was made from stiff, black shiny silk material and the small cap on her brown hair was of red velvet and richly embroidered with gold sequins. As the musicians struck up a new dance, she was approached by a young farmhand; he shouted with excitement and beckoned her to join him in the dance. But she only moved her head slightly as if she hardly noticed him and did not stir from her place. The lad then cursed and stamped angrily on the floor, but it was not long before I saw him disappear into the crowd with another girl.

The slender young girl, however, remained standing by the doorway, and as she turned her head I noticed she had not long left her childhood behind, for her tanned cheeks were still covered with soft peachy down.

'Tell me,' I asked an old woman, about to go past me with a small keg of beer, 'who is the pretty young girl over there?'

'That one, Jungherr? It's Renate from the farmstead.'

'From the farmstead? Just north of the village?'

'Why, yes, sir! Oh, a proud one, that! Always want something better, them from the farmstead, but they're only farmers like us!'

'And who was the young farmhand,' I asked again, 'the one she sent away just now?'

'Didn't see, sir. But wouldn't have been good enough, for sure.'

After such a comment I looked at my red cloak and my high boots with some pleasure, saying to myself: 'You will be all right!' And so I approached and gently touched her arm, saying: 'If you'll allow me this dance!' But in response to this polite request I received a blow from her small elbow that almost caused me to tumble. 'What does that stupid boy want now!' she cried, and as she turned her head towards me, a pair of large dark eyes looked angrily into mine.

But when I answered: 'That was not right, Jungfer, although I must have startled you,' suddenly the scales seemed to fall from my eyes – the angel from St George, it was she, it was she who had just greeted me so roughly! And as she continued to stare at me, mute and open-mouthed, I cried: 'Yes, yes, Jungfer, go on looking; it's me, and I have not forgotten the angel!'

At these words a lovely blush spread across her young face; but just when I was thinking of a way to get her to come down from the step on which she stood and to dance, the musicians suddenly laid down their fiddles and trumpets and a wild commotion broke out across the barn floor; it appeared as if the wedding gifts were now to be presented. A table was soon set up; behind it sat the bride and bridegroom with an earthenware bowl in front of each. Everyone then pressed forward and, as was the custom, one brought a Krontaler, another a Lübeck Mark piece, or those of the wealthier class, even a piece of silverware; and the one in whose bowl the gift was laid drank with the giver from a glass which, together with a flask of wine, stood in front of each of them. I too reached into my pocket and without difficulty found the fine silver piece; but my thoughts were on the young girl, whom I could not see anywhere. So I stood on the step on which she had been standing, and there was the little golden cap glittering in the middle of the crowd; I also caught sight of a silver soup-ladle which was being held aloft in a small clenched hand. But strutting in front of her was the young farmhand whom she had refused a dance; he gestured to his companions who then packed close together to prevent the girl from moving forward.

I was down from the step in an instant and used my arms until I was by her side. 'Renate,' I asked, 'can I help you?'

She nodded almost shyly at me; but I searched for her free hand in the thick of the crowd where we stood, and said to her: 'And now I can give you my heartfelt thanks for that time at the statue of St George.'

She lowered her eyes and replied: 'Oh, yes, you stabbed at my poor Türk's coat most dreadfully!'

'Would you have preferred the ferocious animal to have torn me to pieces?'

She gave a quiet laugh, but then said sadly: 'That really was not a ferocious animal at all; it was the friendliest dog in the whole village!'

'I would rather not have met him, though!' I said.

'No one will meet him here again,' she answered. 'The gypsies lured him away in the night; he will probably have to drag their carts around now or let their grubby children ride on his back.'

While she was saying this, the youths in front of us pushed towards the bride's table. I grasped her small hand firmly in mine. 'Now!' I whispered in her ear, and with one vigorous shove made way for both of us; but I noticed how Renate turned up her little nose as if to avoid seeing any of the youths who, as they stepped aside, cursed or laughed scornfully at her. Then together we went up to the married couple. I tossed my silver coin into the groom's bowl and downed the glass with which he had drunk my health in a single draught; but when I turned to the girl I saw her hand back the full glass to the bride, untouched by her lips.

When we forced ourselves back through the crowd, the same jeering remarks followed us again. I said: 'You have made some bitter enemies, Renate. Was the young farmhand not good enough to dance with then?'

She cast me a haughty look with her dark eyes. 'You don't know him at all, Herr Studiosi. He is the Bauernvogt's son; he's a conceited fool. He glories in his father's moneybags and thinks he has just got to nod.'

I could well believe what she said, for at that time barley cost four thalers a tonne and wheat more than six; which had made the farmers overbearing, the young ones even more so than their elders.

We were again standing by the open doorway leading to the rear rooms where the guests from the town sat at card tables with the wealthier farmers, and where many candles burned. I could therefore study her face at my leisure.

And study it I did, so that from that moment on I have never been able to forget it; I lament to God for having done so, yet thank Him for it. It was delicately oval in shape, the forehead somewhat narrow and the upper lip of her small mouth slightly raised as if on the point of saying: 'Now, believe me, no one beckons to me in that fashion!'

The bride's table was soon cleared away and in their raised places the musicians were tuning up their instruments again. I was just about to ask, 'What do you say, Renate, shall we dance now?' when I heard the girl's name being called from the room close by; and as I turned my head I saw her already standing there beside the chair of a lean figure of a man with long dark eyelashes just like hers, and I was sure it was her father. She had put her arm round the man's neck and he his arm round her waist, so that he held his cards carelessly in his hand as he looked into his child's face, unaware that the others wanted trumps and the jack of hearts from him. But when Renate mentioned my father's name to him, I approached and introduced myself.

He cast a keen look at my splendid attire and said: 'You look quite a picture, Herr Studiosi, but quite soon your plumage will have grown black!'

Whereupon I responded in the same jocular vein; that it must surely be growing black already, for indeed the plumage of no full-grown raven could be otherwise, the species being, as was well known, the pastor among birds.

At this he gave me another of his keen looks, hinting that he also knew something of university life: 'for,' he said, 'you know, of course, that my brother-in-law's son in Husum also belongs to your order.'

When I politely asked him what the name was, I received the answer: 'He is the sexton, Albert Carstens. My Renate stayed at his house last year so that she could learn a little more than what is on offer at the village school here.'

I was deeply shocked at hearing this and thought to myself: 'Woe to your poor angel, to be under the roof of such an atheist!' For I knew that this same Carstens, while still a student, had preached vehemently against exorcism here in the village, and had also unearthed an old mandate promulgated by the Gottorf Calvinists in the last century by which the godparents had been given the option whether they wanted to exorcise the Antichrist in their child or not. This had caused my father great difficulty when he took up the post here, particularly as the glib-tongued innovator had also led the deacon and most of the otherwise devout Christians astray by his fanaticism.

While such repugnant thoughts were passing through my mind, I suddenly felt my hand grasped. 'But, Herr Studiosi,' said Renate, 'you wanted to dance with the Hofbauer's daughter!'

'Why, of course,' added her father, 'dance with one another. Renate learnt to in the town. And do visit us, Herr Studiosi, the Hofbauer still has a bottle of Rhenish in his cellar.'

All serious thoughts then vanished. With the pretty young girl on my arm I plunged into the dark crowd of people so that we seemed completely lost in it. From the barrels above us the musicians blew and fiddled, and all around us the young farmhands and girls stamped their feet and shouted. But all this was of little concern to us; as soon as a free space appeared I clasped the slender child round the waist and whirled her in my arms, and when she did not want to go on we stood still, and full of joy and curiosity gazed into each other's eyes. And when I think back on it today, I am unable to say what it was that most captivated my heart, nor how the night slipped by us in such a delightful succession of events; for when I glanced for a moment over the dancers' heads towards the open door, the stars in the sky had almost faded away and a faint light shone on the roof timbers. 'Look, Renate,' I said, 'our pleasure is coming to an end.'

I then felt her press gently against me, but she made no reply nor looked up. But when I noticed how her cheeks glowed, I asked: 'Are you thirsty too, Renate? Then let us go over to the table.'

She nodded, we walked to the table, and I took the glass out of the hand of a sprightly young girl who had just been drinking and filled it again from a beer-jug. But Renate took hold of another standing on the table and stooped with it to a bucket of water.

'Ah,' I cried with a laugh, 'you drink with the birds, what the good Lord Himself has brewed?' But she had simply rinsed the glass.

'Oh no, Herr Studiosi,' she replied, bashfully. 'Fill it up; I drink what the men drink!'

But as she raised her head and drank thirstily, a very old lady with a dark cap on her grey hair came hurrying up, pulled at her silk skirt and whispered: 'The Hofbauer's away home; the Hofbauer's away home!'

And by the time Renate had set down her glass and was calling: 'Marik, I'm coming, Marik!' the old woman was nowhere to be seen.

But I grabbed the girl's hand and said: 'You'll not be running away from me, will you? If you leave, Renate, I shall come with you!'

And so we left the wedding celebration silently together. And as we came to the rise in front of the bishop's residence where the path crosses over it, we remained standing under the tower, looking down on to the lowlands before us; for there in the early dawn of the day, in the deep red glow, the river flowed away into the still half-darkened land. At the same time, however, a sharp breeze blew from the east, and as Renate shivered, I put my arm round her bare neck and drew her cheek close to me. She resisted gently. 'Let be, Herr Studiosi,' she said, 'I must go home now!' and pointed down to her father's house which lay to one side among the dark trees. And as a shrill cock-crow now rose from there, I saw her already running down the hill; but then she turned and looked up at me openly with her dark eyes.

'Renate!' I called.

Then she gave me a last look before hurrying over the dew-covered meadows towards the farmstead. But I stood for a while longer up there in the sharp morning air and gazed down on the dark oaks out of whose leafless tops a pair of magpies now flew up and, chattering, shook the sleep from their heavy wings.

* *

Next day the high sun was already shining into my room when my mother brought breakfast to my bedside; and when she questioned me in her sweet way about the celebration, she was not displeased to hear about my acquaintance with the daughter of the wealthy Hofbauer and, as mothers do, was already spinning her firm web for the future. In the afternoon, however, when the web was almost complete, and when she jubilantly began to spread it out before my father, he appeared to be not entirely of the same mind, but, as he usually did in cases of doubt, thoughtfully stroked his nose with his finger and silently shook his head at the same time.

'Why, father!' exclaimed my mother. 'Are God's gifts of money and property likely to be a burden? Do you honestly believe that a future servant of the Lord must always live in poverty, just because, unfortunately, such has been our portion in life?'

'No, oh no, mother!' he replied. 'No, most certainly not!'

'Well, praise be for that!' cried my mother. 'What is there, then, to be doubtful about?'

'Well, mother, you women love to play the matchmaker even with your own sons; but – I think Josias has plans of his own.'

With that he went to his room and settled down to his next day's Sunday sermon; and I, who had stood by almost ashamed, clearly observed that my dear father wished to have nothing more said about the matter; – not least because he always regarded those at the farmstead with a certain reservation.

But I had been quite unsettled by all this. I ran out of the house and across the road on to the Glockenberg and looked across to the tower of the bishop's residence from where, in the early morning, I had gazed at the silent landscape with Renate; then I ran back home and plunged myself into my work, but achieved little except to write the letter R some hundred times in my notebooks, as if this were a letter I still needed to learn from my schooldays.

When evening came I set off for the village inn that lay above the Treene, to see whether I might learn something there; I spoke with various persons and from time to time directed the conversation towards the Hofbauer. I perceived that he had very few admirers. It was said that although he was fundamentally no farmer, yet everything had gone very well for him; for when there had been an epidemic among the livestock a few years ago not a single animal in his stalls had been affected by it, and when the mice and rats had devoured the corn in others' lofts, one bright autumn moonlit night the field-watchman had seen with his own eyes shrill swarms of the vermin, a loathsome sight, scurry down to the Treene from the Hofbauer's barn, and squeaking and squealing, throw themselves into the river. I was even buttonholed in a corner by the pale-faced village tailor, who said mysteriously: 'Jungherr, Jungherr! Do you know what the black art is?' He then put a hand to his lips and pointed in the direction of the farmstead.

I was all too aware that even priests concerned themselves with such art, as the previous pastor in Medelbye had done, who was said to have been especially knowledgeable in the subject; also that such a thing, even though not a definite pact with the enemy of souls, was nevertheless an evil gamble with the soul and eternal salvation which, given human weakness, could easily lead to everlasting damnation. But at the same time I saw that these people envied the Hofbauer his wealth, were hostile towards him because of his overweening pride, and could not forget how his father had once succeeded, against the will of the community, in getting a pew for himself up in the church gallery.

The next afternoon, therefore, as I had promised the Hofbauer, I made my way after the sermon along the path that led over the bishop's rise down to the farmstead. As I approached, the large building lay in perfect silence among its ancient oaks; not even a dog barked from the hall; only from the tree-tops above came the calls of the magpies, as if they kept watch here over the house. At that moment I heard footsteps from within, and the old peasant woman, who had called Renate away from the wedding the previous night, came to the door; in her hands she held a long woollen stocking which she immediately continued to knit.

'Are you the priest's son?' she asked, and when I said I was, she opened the door to a room and said: 'Go in; there's an easy chair there; I shall call the Hofbauer.'

It was a wide and high-ceilinged room I entered, and a gloomy one; for branches hung down all over the windows to the north and the east, so that from the latter it was hardly possible to see down to the river. Among the chairs was a sofa; for the rest, along the whitewashed walls stood a couple of linen-chests and other farmhouse items; but resplendent on a bureau stood a teapot with half-a-dozen cups, the like of which I had only ever seen before in the large and prosperous farmsteads in the marshland. Beside it, however, and I thought this a most strange ornament, I noticed a crude and ghastly-looking image, almost a foot high, which appeared to me to be made of red clay. As I was looking at the dreadful object with reluctant curiosity, the Hofbauer entered the room. 'Yes, yes, Herr Studiosi,' he said, offering me his hand, 'go on, examine it! People worship all kinds of things in this world! This red thing here, it's a pagan's idol. My uncle, who used to be a helmsman, brought it back with him from overseas.'

I saw now for the first time what a well-built man it was who had just spoken. His face was somewhat pale; but he carried his head with its black beard and dark, close-cropped hair erect on his shoulders.

The old woman, who had entered the room with the Hofbauer and was walking up and down with the stocking she was knitting, pointed to the idol with it and whispered in my ear: 'That's the Fingaholi! The pastor shouldn't know about it, but believe me, it's really good against mice and rats.'

I recalled the tailor's words; but the Hofbauer, who had overheard, laughed and said: 'I thought it was you who drove them away, Marike!'

The old woman cast him a dark look, then grumbling to herself while continuing to knit, began to wander up and down the room again.

Outside in the trees the magpies screeched; I suddenly felt very lonely in the large, gloomy room.

I felt some unease as the door now opened again, but the room suddenly seemed to grow lighter; for Renate had entered, and as she turned her small head towards me I saw a fleeting blush dull her bright eyes. She carried a tray with a bottle and glasses, setting it down on the table in front of the sofa.

The Hofbauer exclaimed: 'The Rhenish has arrived, Herr Studiosi; here, take a seat and let's talk.'

Renate, now looking anxiously towards the old woman, held her arm and speaking quietly to her walked up and down with her for a while. The old woman became calm again and soon left the room. 'She was my father's nursery maid, Herr Studiosi,' said the girl, 'and still thinks she is the only one who can knit his stockings. But otherwise she is a little weak – you know, up here!' And she tapped her finger against her forehead. Then she stepped towards the Hofbauer, who was already pouring the clear wine into the glasses, and threatening him playfully with her little fist, said: 'Father, what have you been up to again with Marike?'

But he looked crossly at her and said: 'Let it be, Renate. The old fool's loose talk could have me before a court! Come, Herr Studiosi,' he continued, 'try it! I am doubtful if there is better to be had at the parsonage.'

I drank to that, and replied there was seldom wine at the parsonage; that even the beer went off in the musty cellar, much to the dismay of my father.

The man laughed and grasped the silver buttons on his doublet. 'Just let the pastor speak to the Hofbauer; he will soon get him a better cellar for his beer.'

I looked over at Renate who sat by the window embroidering a small sampler. I kept thinking she would turn her large eyes towards me once again, but she looked only at her work, and I, unversed in the ways of a young girl's heart, grew almost indignant that she might be denying our acquaintance. But thinking that I should first respond to the Hofbauer's polite offer, I therefore began to express my admiration for the fine situation of his farm above the river Treene, which he seemed well pleased to hear.

'You might well say that, Herr Studiosi,' he began, 'and thereby hangs a tale. It dates from Catholic times, from the ancient Gottorp Bishop Schondeleff, whose residence was over there in the ruined tower-building where the King's administrator later had his seat. I should tell you too that before they built the town down there and the great sluice-gate on the Eider in 1621, the flood tides came up as far as here, and what you saw below through that window then would have been a wide and mighty river with its inlets running into the forest. But a wild and dangerous band of pirates roamed the seas at that time, the Likedeler they called themselves – you know, the 'Vitalien brothers', led by Gödeke Michels and Störtebeker, the ones they beheaded on the Grasbrooke in Hamburg.'

I had certainly heard about them. Not least because when pursued by the Hanseatic towns or the Mecklenburgers they would often retreat up the river Treene in their ships, where they had the dense forest at their backs. This I mentioned, and added: 'I have heard too that the bishop himself provided a haven for them up here.'

The Hofbauer laughed and felt his beard. 'You mean according to the saying that where the marten has his nest, there the chickens will be safe! But it's an old wives' tale. Old Schondeleff was on extremely bad terms with them and they would certainly have killed him if my mother's old ancestor hadn't hacked a way out for him with his trusty axe. The bishop therefore bequeathed him this farmstead as well as the wood and grounds, and dubbed him "Ohm" because he had behaved towards him, not as a servant, but as a friend and "uncle".'

And when I asked where this exploit had occurred, the Hofbauer answered: 'Just a quarter of an hour east of the village, by the Vitalien harbour, though there is nothing to be seen there now but an empty hollow, which is why they call the place "Holbek"; but the forest still stands close behind it as it used to, and from the high hill you can see far and wide across Dithmarschen .'

I must confess that my thoughts were only half fixed on this conversation; they had drifted over to the window where Renate was sitting, still bent over her embroidery. Inside the room it had grown even gloomier; but outside the light of the afternoon sun played behind the trees, so that the outline of her lovely face was set like a silhouette against a golden-green background.

'Now then, Herr Studiosi,' said the Hofbauer, for I had fallen well-nigh silent as I constantly glanced away from him, 'why do you keep peering at the window? Perhaps you are thinking I should chop a fathom of wood for the fire from my old trees?'

I hastily put down my glass; it was almost as if I had been caught trespassing; though equally it was as if the Hofbauer himself had kept me captive here at the table with his Rhenish wine. I therefore rose quickly from my chair and said: 'Well, what do you think, sir; it is still light outside; come with your daughter and show me where your "uncle" hacked the bishop free!'

The Hofbauer replied that he would accompany us through the village, but thereafter had to go across the moor to where his farm workers had been cutting peat during the week; his daughter, however, would show me the way.

And as I looked at her, Renate nodded to her father and rose from her chair; but the Hofbauer first took me on to his farm and through the stalls and barn, and I saw many things that seemed to me different from and also more enlightened than what farmers usually pass down to their sons.

'Just have a look at this, Herr Studiosi,' said the Hofbauer. 'You must believe me, the fellows hereabouts would most dearly love to tear me to pieces because of this guttering, simply because I didn't want to repeat the same old mistakes when I renovated recently. But it's true, there's none so blind as those who will not see.' He took a fork which lay in the way and flung it into a corner with a hefty swing.

As we left the stalls Renate came up to meet us and we walked together through the village. At a rifle-shot's distance, not far from the wood, the Hofbauer took his leave. 'You know the farm now,' he said, 'so do not forget to come again; I must go north from here. Senator Feddersen in Husum needs twelve days' cutting of peat delivered for his brewery, I must see to it there's the right amount in the stacks.'

And the two of us continued on our own.

* *

Only the moor lies between here and Schwabstedt, a bird would soon wing its way across it; but some thirty years have passed into eternity since that day – without increasing it; for man alone exists in time. I am sitting here in the village of Ostenfeld, as an all too prematurely disabled emeritus and wretched boarder with the local parish priest, with my dear, thoroughly able-bodied cousin Christian Mercacus. I should therefore have time enough to record, like the other details of my life, the events of that afternoon as well. They still lie within me, an exuberant sweet memory in the soul. I have even prepared a whole sheet of paper for it and had my quills cut by the sexton, and now my mind's eye sees nothing before me but a lonely path between green hedgerows that gradually winds its way up into the forest. I am certain, though, that this was the way we took that afternoon, and the summer scent of honeysuckle and dog-roses still seems to hang here in the air about me.

'Renate!' I said, after we had walked on in silence for some time.

'Yes, Herr Studiosi?' She turned her head and fastened her dark eyes on me.

But I did not know at all what to say, and thought to myself: 'It will never do for a learned person and a future man of the pulpit to be seen losing his place in the text in front of a Hofbauer's girl.' But this same girl was the angel of St George, so it occurred to me to ask her: 'Renate, have you no dog at your farm any more?'

'A dog? No, Herr Studiosi; it wasn't possible for us to keep one. I don't want one either, since they stole my Türk.'

'But I thought Türk belonged to the sexton in Husum?'

'Yes, he did, but he became attached to me and he would run after me; so my cousin let me keep him.'

'And now,' I said, 'all you have are the crows in your old trees.'

'You may joke, Herr Studiosi,' she replied, 'but we really have no need of a dog at home; my poor father suffers from asthma and is a very light sleeper. When he has a bad attack he calls for me; then we walk together for hours at a time, up and down the room and across the hall into the guests' room; where that picture of the residence and the old bishop hangs. People outside are never quite sure if a pair of eyes is not looking out of the window into the night.'

She looked most troubled as she spoke these words, and I said: 'But you're still so very young, Renate!'

'Yes, but my father has no one else at all; my mother died long ago.'

By this time we had walked under the broad beeches into the forest; a song thrush sang from the top of a tree and in the distance we heard something crashing through the bushes. 'Deer,' said the girl. 'There were herds of them here in Duke Adolf's time, so they say.'

Then she brushed the branches aside with her hands and said: 'Here, Herr Studiosi!' – We stood above Störtebeker's harbour and saw the broad Treene Valley below us. But the 'harbour' here was simply a ravine cut into the sandy high ground, with the water flowing far away from it in its beautiful serpentine course through the meadows. Renate led me to a broad, scarred oak and pointed to an almost healed gash in its trunk. 'Look,

Herr Studiosi, this is where my ancestor drove his axe in when the fighting had ended and the robbers had run down there back to their ships. He too had a daughter called Renate like me, and because her father had vowed it in battle, it was intended that she should enter a convent; but when she grew up she refused to go, and then she became my ancestor.'

She was leaning against the tree, her hands folded in her lap, and was looking at the red glow of sunset that now rose steadily above the horizon. I studied this young, serious face and asked myself almost anxiously what her attitude would have been in similar circumstances; and quietly I praised our father, Dr Martin Luther, for having put an end to the dreadful business of convents in our land.

While I was thinking of these things, she suddenly stood free of the tree. 'Please don't think it impolite of me, 'she said hurriedly, 'but would you mind going on with me now through the forest; there is a short cut from here across to the moor.'

And as I discerned disquiet in her face, I asked if she might be worrying about her father.

She shook herself as though out of a dream and said: 'It really is nothing, Herr Studiosi, but if you will, let's hurry; perhaps he'll meet us on the way.'

So we entered the thick forest. It grew increasingly quiet about us and the darkness grew thicker; I barely recognised the graceful figure of Renate as she walked ahead of me so rapidly amid the tall tree-trunks. From time to time I felt as though my happiness were flickering there before me, and that I should grasp it if I didn't want to lose it. But I knew full well that the girl's thoughts now excluded everything and everyone but her father.

Eventually, what seemed like grey twilight broke through the trees, the forest came to an end, and there it lay before us – wide open and misty; here and there shimmered a pool of water, with dark round piles of peat rising up beside it; a large dark bird, as though it had lost something, was quartering the ground with slow wing beats. Renate stood at my side; I heard her breathing and noticed her eyes looking anxiously in all directions into the night that stretched out before us; for at our backs behind the deep shades of the forest lay the last light of day. I had then to say with the psalmist: 'Lord, Thou makest darkness, and it is night; the heavens are Thine, the earth also is Thine: as for the world and the fulness thereof, Thou hast founded them.'

Touching my shoulder with one hand, Renate pointed to the moor with the other.

'What is it, Renate?'

'Can't you see? Over there?'

And as I strained my eyes I thought I saw a shadowy figure in the far distance striding about in the mist; but only for a brief moment. 'Was that your father?' I asked again.

She nodded and said: 'Forgive me, I was silly to be afraid; he is already on the firm uplands on the other side of moor.'

'Let us hurry, then,' I cried, 'we might still be able to catch him!'

But she grasped my arm with both hands: 'The moor, Herr Studiosi, do you know the moor? We can't possibly cross it!' Then, as if seized by a sudden terror, she held me back and said: 'Come, the path here leads down by the forest!' and she did not let go of my hand so long as we had the dark unsure ground about us . . .

* *

Here the manuscript is fragmented. The following pages are missing completely, and the next ones almost ruined by water stains. But it emerges that the student Josias was fond of music and like his father shared the view of Dr Martin Luther that the Latin language is much more musical and fitting for song, and should certainly not be excluded from divine service. As a boy he had been one of the pupils chosen to assist Petrus Steinbrecher, the Husum choirmaster and organist at that time, before the morning sermon and, 'to the glory of God and the awakening of reverence in every Christian soul', had joined in the singing of the *Te Deum laudamus* from the organ loft of the then huge church. Here in Schwabstedt some of the Latin hymnal is still preserved to this day; for he succeeded in gathering round him – where from is not apparent – a number of young choir boys and girls, 'for the better practising of familiar hymns, as well as the learning of some recently added.' Renate's voice, which 'floated like a silver light above all the rest', appeared to have further strengthened the spell cast so unconsciously by the Hofbauer's daughter upon our learned man of God. How far the relationship between the two young people extended that summer we cannot know; not until the end of that time do the preserved parts of the manuscript resume the narrative up to a certain point, so now it shall be left to continue as before.

* *

. . . it was one evening at the end of September as I sat with my late father in his study drafting a petition to our most gracious duke; for as my dear father had weakened his eyes through excessive study in his youth he was well pleased when I took up the pen for him. The matter of our cellar was making no progress. In truth, the Hofbauer himself had brought the matter up again with the parish, simply because of my earlier conversation with him – for my father had no wish to enlist his services – but the farmers had told him that as the previous pastor could preach well enough on his beer, so his cellar should be good enough for the new one.

The weather was exceptionally wild that evening, and the roar from the forest outside so great that here inside it was often difficult to catch a word that was said.

'Write this down,' said my father, moving towards me: 'Although the majority of my parishioners would be most pleased for me to have a better cellar, there are those who have stubbornly argued against it. From the middle of May until the present time I have had no fresh, cool beer, only stale stuff, and

God knows best what a torment that has been to me. How much of God's good gift, *salvo honore,* has had to be poured away into the pig-trough, I will sadly refrain from mentioning here.'

I can still remember all these words of my dear father; for I put my pen down when doubt overcame me about making such an appeal to His Grace's sympathy over the pastor's stale beer. But just as I was about to express this doubt, outside in the hall I heard a loud conversation with our old Margreth. The study door was then violently thrown open and a man appeared in noticeably soiled travelling clothes, seemingly of my father's age and also of clerical status, but with a round, ruddy face from which a pair of small bright eyes rapidly looked us up and down. '*Salve, Christiane, confrater dilectissime!*' he cried. 'I come late under your hospitable roof! But the Devil, he is always at my heels seeing I am his keen adversary, by his hellish craft lured my horse straight off the road into the moor, so that I needed the help of some cottagers to dig it out from between the patches of firm ground; indeed, the foul fiend had scented that beneath my jacket I carried on my person a newly forged weapon against him.' Upon which this vehement man, tapping his breast, pulled out a thick manuscript from under his mantle and threw it down on the table in front of us among my papers. 'There, you see,' he cried, 'my *Devilish Morpheus* gave a stern lesson to that Dutch fanatic, that disgraceful Doctor Balthasar Becker and his *Bewitched World*; but there are ever more depraved defenders of wizards and witches rising up among us! *Nitimur in vetitum*, dear brother! There is much need to resist this irrational reason!'

From these words I realised that a most learned man had entered our house: Herr Petrus Goldschmidt, present pastor of Sterup, born in Husum, who had been a school-fellow of my dear father there and later been with him at university. After his celebrated *Morpheus* he had prepared a second work, in this case rebutting the Halle professor Thomasius, who in his book *De crimine magiae*, which had just appeared in German translation, maintained that all alliances with the Devil were pure fantasy, and who as a clever advocate strove in this way to snatch

accursed witches and sorceresses from worldly justice. All that
Herr Petrus now needed to publish his new work was simply to
examine a few texts which he himself did not possess, but knew
to be among my father's books; for example, Remigii's
Daemonologia, Christian Kortholt's tract on the witches' fiery
circles, and a few others.

'I have a sound head on my shoulders, Christian,' he cried,
'but I have the wisdom to mistrust human weakness; and it
would certainly ill become the pastor of Sterup to be caught
misquoting by the father of lies!'

As my father now warmly welcomed him, he cheerfully threw
off his hat and mantle, and I listened attentively to the conversation in which both learned men soon became actively engaged. I
must confess that owing to my studies and certain youthful
distractions which had occupied my time, I had read neither
Goldschmidt's *Morpheus* nor his opponent's writings, but as the
learned man expounded on the latter, I very soon began to
regard them with the utmost distaste; and on making my feelings
known, was heartily praised by him and warned henceforth
never to associate myself with such atheists and fanatics.

The conversation even continued over the rice soup which my
dear mother brought to the supper-table in honour of our guest;
she would dearly have heard a different subject, and she soon
began to make a long apology for the weak beer and to complain
of the wretched condition of the cellar.

But the man of God grasped hold of the full mug standing in
front of him, downed it in one go and said with a dignified bow
of the head: 'Frau Pastor, one should never scorn God's gift in
such a way!' Then he brushed the droplets from his beard with
his hand and began a new conversation about exorcism, and all
that my dear mother could do was to take the emptied mug back
to the barrel to be filled again.

Herr Petrus now asked my father what formula was in general
use here for baptisms, and when he replied that he said to the
infant: 'Do you renounce the evil spirit and his works?', the
passionate man sprang from his chair, sending his spoon flying

across the table. 'Christian, oh Christian!' he cried. 'How does a
suckling know whether it has the Antichrist in its tender insides
or not? *Exi immunde spiritus*! Get thee hence, unclean spirit! That
is what you should say! Then, if you are lucky, you will see the
evil issue forth as a foul-smelling odour from the infant's little
mouth!' Here he took up his spoon again, which my mother had
returned to its place, and paid further respect to my dear
parents' generous hospitality. But when my father politely
suggested that the child would give its answer through the
mouth of the godfather, Herr Petrus simply shook his leonine
head and said: 'Yes, but only if the blockheads don't have the
unclean spirit in their own bodies!'

In discussion of such matters, midnight had passed before we
showed the revered man to his room for the night.

'Should you hear anything, Petrus, do not worry,' said my
father, setting the night light on the table beside him, 'it will just
be the rats that live in our loft.'

A word now sprang to my mind and I said jokingly: 'We had
best ask the Hofbauer for his Fingaholi!'

At this word our guest started and asked: 'What is this about a
Fingaholi?'

And when I had told him, he pinched his strong lips between
thumb and forefinger and said: 'The Fingaholi, as you call it,
young man, is simply a fetish; but the one granted authority by
God over the vermin is altogether different, and no lifeless and
impotent image like this pagan god or the popish saints.'

I responded by saying it was just an old and simple-minded
woman who had said these things without thinking. But he
turned to my father and cried repeatedly: 'Christian, Christian!
Watch your flock! And when you find the evil deceiving fool,
seize him firmly by the ears and destroy him completely, every
bit of him, including his swinish tail!'

I lay awake for some while that night, looking through the
windows at the dark clouds scurrying across the clear sky and
listening to the roar of the wind coming from the forest. I

regretted having mentioned the Fingaholi in front of our guest; for being used to my father's pleasant manner, I was not altogether taken with his strong language, although his spiritual wisdom and zeal for God's Kingdom commanded my just respect.

He himself, however, appeared to be enjoying a very sound sleep; for towards morning, when the raging wind had abated outside, I heard his heavy and regular snoring coming up through the floors and walls from the guests' room.

* *

During the two days Herr Petrus Goldschmidt stayed with us, he sat busying himself in the mornings among my father's books, and when visiting him I never ceased to wonder at his ready knowledge of the most obscure passages in them. He declined my offer to assist him in his work with a calm wave of his hand: 'Pursue your own studies, young man! What one can do should not take the work of two!'

But in the afternoon when my father rested, he would take his walking stick and three-cornered hat and wander about the village talking to the women and old men and patting the children on their blond heads, so that next day almost everyone ran to their front doors even when, loudly clearing his throat, he was striding towards them from some distance.

On the third day, when this remarkable man had mounted his horse and ridden away, it was extremely quiet in our house. My dear father looked rather tired, and my mother said jokingly: 'I need to look after you, Christian; such weighty and solid theology is not for everyone's constitution!'

The village, however, was like a hive about to swarm; everywhere people whispered, not wanting to be heard, yet unable to remain silent; the older villagers spoke once more of the witch they said they had seen burnt to ashes in Husum twenty years before, but who had had her neck broken the night before by her lord and master while in the prison dungeon awaiting execution;

someone came from Flensburg who had heard in the Südermarkt there that witches had again poisoned all the fish in the fiord; and in the village itself fingers were pointed at one person or another for strange behaviour, so that I was rather apprehensive, but I noticed that the Hofbauer's name was not among those mentioned.

And so the time approached when I too was to take my leave, and this for a considerable period. For some days now Renate had been staying at the sexton's house in Husum, and when I went to the farm on the evening before my departure she had still not returned. 'I expected her back today,' said the Hofbauer, 'but it will be tomorrow now; you might meet her on the way or go yourself to the sexton's in Husum!'

At this old Marike came to the door with the long stocking she was knitting, looked with a troubled expression at the Hofbauer, then made to leave again. But he called to her to fetch another bottle of Rhenish from the cellar as a farewell drink; and the old woman mumbled something to herself and hurried out of the room. After a while the servant girl came in and set a bottle on the table, but the good wine did not taste good in my mouth that day, for we sat quite alone in the large room. For that reason I soon took my leave, and it felt exceedingly strange as I left the house under the ancient oaks, which had already littered the ground with their yellow autumn leaves.

Standing by the door, the Hofbauer grasped my hand. 'Farewell, Herr Studiosi,' he said, 'keep your wits about you out there; and when you come back, I think you'll manage to find your way to the Hofbauer's door again!'

He looked at me with his dark eyes as if he wanted to detain me or still had something more to say. But he said nothing further, and I went away with no idea that I would never see this man again.

After I had said good night to my parents that evening, I opened my bedroom window and looked out on to the village. For a while I studied a single light over in the deacon's house until it too went out; but my mind was full of unrest, and at last, as the eleventh hour sounded from the belfry, I was already outside in the clear night and soon making my way over the bishop's rise and down the familiar path leading from it.

It was the beginning of October and clear moonlight stood over God's beautiful world; the farmstead lay among its dark trees as though it slept in a world filled with soft light. It was so quiet that I heard only the falling of leaves and occasionally the call of a deer from the forest. I listened in the direction of the house, but no sound came from it; then I walked beneath the trees and looked through a window into the large room. Straight before me I saw the back of Renate's chair; otherwise it was silent and dark inside. Nonetheless, I could find no reason to leave, and went along the wall and round the corner to the entrance to the house. There, in the deep shadow, something stirred, and my heart was filled with joy, for although I could not make it out, I knew I had heard the rustling of her clothes.

'Renate!' I cried.

A warm pair of hands then lay in mine. 'I was sure you would come, Josias!'

She continued to listen at the door, then I drew her out into the bright moonlight, for I longed to see her.

We clasped each other's hands and walked together across the farmstead towards the river. What we said might not have been very much; yet I still remember how we looked at our shadows together, how they merged in front of us on the grass, and when the moonlight was about to come between them we would lean silently towards each other and watch as they joined together again. Then we stood on the river bank and without speaking looked across at the landscape beyond, listening to the flow of the river below as it carried its waters down to the sea.

Then midnight struck from the village, and with every stroke, which we heard with bated breath, we clasped our hands together more firmly. 'Renate,' I said quietly, 'that was the last day.'

'Yes, Josias!' she replied in the same tone.

'And will I still find you here when I come back?'

'I think so; who else will come for me?'

'Who else, Renate? Just mind you don't drive them all away in future!'

I do not know what impelled me to say such things, but a jealous fear had suddenly attacked me like a vulture. She threw back her head, and the gold on her cap glittered.

'What are you talking about, Josias!' she said. 'I have nothing to do with those louts; they can come or go as they like!'

These were vainglorious words, yet I would be lying to say that they were not like balsam to my heart.

But something else now occurred that instantly drove such thoughts from my mind.

We were standing as we spoke in front of the huge barn door which was bathed by the moon in what almost seemed daylight. Some weeks previously I had seen heavy loads of God's harvest being driven in there amid the crack of whips; now everything lay in deep tranquillity.

And yet – or had my ears deceived me? Something stirred there inside the barn; Renate's hand quivered in mine, and her eyes opened wide; and now, like a broad grey shadow, a billowing came out from beneath the barn door, more and more of it, as though being driven by an inaudible crack of a whip. It moved swiftly by us, so that we could hardly protect our feet, and across the dew-covered fields down towards the river; and I never knew where it disappeared to in the night.

I noticed Renate's whole body shaking; but I said nothing for a long while, for what my eyes had just seen I could henceforth never disavow. At last I said: 'That was extraordinary, Renate; how it frightened you!'

She straightened up and said: 'The rats do not frighten me; they run here, there and everywhere; I know very well what they say about my father; I know it all too well! But I hate them all, those stupid zealots! I only wish he would possess them, the one they constantly drivel about with their venomous tongues!'

Such talk completely horrified me, for the girl had raised her small fist threateningly towards the sky. 'Renate!' I cried, 'Renate!'

'Yes, yes; that is what I want!' she repeated. 'But he is power-less, he can't come!'

I pulled down her raised hand. 'Do not invoke him, Renate,' I cried, 'pray to God and our Redeemer that they will keep him from you! It is the Husum atheist's spirit that speaks from your young mouth.'

'Atheist?' she asked. 'I do not know the word; who are you reprimanding?'

What kind of explanation I gave her, I can no longer recall. But she simply shook her head and said sadly: 'And our poor old Marike, they have now completely confused her, so that it is quite impossible to live with her any more! It will be very lonely when you stop coming, Josias.'

I took her face in both my hands, and as I turned it towards the full light of the moon I saw it was very pale and the eyes full of tears. I could not help drawing her towards me; she did not resist, but laid her head on my arm as though she were tired and looked up at me as if she wanted to rest there.

At the same moment, however, from deep inside the house, so that I was quite startled by it, came the repeated call of her name in an anguished, groaning voice.

'My father! My poor, dear father!' she cried. Then I felt her arms round my neck and a warm kiss on my lips. 'Farewell, Josias! Dear Josias, farewell!'

And as the front door closed from within, I stood alone in the farmstead and once again heard nothing but the falling of the leaves and the soft nightly melody of the waters. But the strange phenomenon I had just witnessed still made me shudder and strove against the bliss in my young heart.

The next morning, when I had taken leave of my dear parents and was about to get into the carriage, the pale-faced tailor came rushing up asking if he might take the opportunity to accom-pany the young gentleman since he had to visit the cloth merchant in the town. I therefore had a travelling companion, and one whose tongue constantly wagged, while I should have much preferred to travel alone with my heavy heart. I wrapped myself in my cloak and only half-listened in a dream as his busy tongue rummaged through every demonic rumour that had recently been about among the villagers.

But just as we were descending from the sandy uplands into the marsh, he started afresh, sensing he might gain my attention: 'Indeed, Jungherr, you know him, the visiting pastor, much better than I do; but quite a fellow, that, a devil of a fellow! He even made old Marike at the farm open her mouth. I am sure you will have seen, Jungherr, how the Hofbauer always wears one stocking round his ankle! It has always been known he dares wear only one garter, otherwise he and all his wealth will come to a bad end. But I would advise you to let the matter rest; for when my curiosity got the better of me one day, he told me to mind my tongue. "Yes, tailor," he said, "the cat took one of them; do you want the other round your scrawny neck to hang yourself with?"'

When I replied that I had never seen such a thing round the Hofbauer's stockings, he said: 'But of course, you only visit the farm on Sundays; then he wears his high-boots!'

As this was indeed the case, I said nothing. The tailor thrust a plug of tobacco behind a lean cheek and said, inclining his face towards my ear: 'A pair of garters often lies at the foot of his bed; but the Hofbauer is on his guard; he knows all too well who laid out the second one! Old Marike has indeed tried to knit the stockings narrower so that they won't fall down; but when she starts to knit them – she told me this herself only yesterday – it's as if flies are dancing before her eyes, or vermin swarming over her old body. It appears the game might well have lasted too long for him – and you know who, Jungherr – for the Hofbauer often has to resist strong temptations in the night, so that he cannot remain in his bed; something rolls over him and chokes the breath out of him; then he jumps out of bed and wanders around his dark room crying out for his child.'

When I started in my seat at these words, the tailor said: 'I know, Jungherr, you've had many dealings with the girl, and I know of nothing against her except her complete contempt for the likes of us; she might, though, be much better suited to your kind!'

The man went on for some time in this vein, although I gave him no further word of encouragement. He was simply a burden I had inherited for the journey. Indeed, I told myself a hundred times that he was just a gossip who passed on these things; one of those people who plucked floating scraps of rumours out of the air simply to fill their empty heads with them; I was left nevertheless with a most bitter taste in my mouth.

* *

1706. Regarding my studies in Halle, I will simply note here that I listened to many celebrated theologians and other learned men there in my subjects, and diligently attended their lectures in the hope of acquiring a sound systematic education for myself in the shortest time. At the same time I had no desire for my black attire, for which I had been measured by the pale-faced tailor before my departure, to be exchanged for red.

Only occasionally, especially when I took an evening walk along the banks of the river Saale when the waters reddened and their gentle flow sounded in my ears, was I overcome with feelings of the most intense longing for my homeland; and when the moon rose in the south-east and filled the landscape with its pale light, I would see in every dark corner the farm by the distant river Treene, and my heart would cry out for the girl whom I had left behind there.

After one such walk, when a year had already passed and autumn had again scattered its red leaves, I arrived home one evening to find in my room, on lighting the lamp, a thick letter in my dear father's handwriting lying on my table. I broke the seal, and my hands trembled with joy; for my mother too would always add a few lines, and even if it were to slip in only a brief

word or two about Renate, I could still read it a hundred times
over. But this particular letter, which I faithfully preserved like
the few I was still to receive from this deeply respected hand, was
from my father alone and, after many affectionate words,
continued as follows:

But what has thrown the community into such disorder, in
which even my words of admonishment are scarcely heeded,
should not remain concealed from you either, my Josias.

Last Saturday afternoon, as I sat preparing my sermon,
Hansen, a member of the parish committee, rushed hurriedly
into my room. 'What is the matter, Hansen?' I said. 'You know
I don't like being disturbed at this time.'

'Yes, of course, Herr Pastor,' he said. 'But have you not
heard? He's gone and won't be coming back!'

And when I asked, startled: 'Who's gone?' he replied:
'Who else but the Hofbauer! I always thought it must come to
this!'

'So tell me, Hansen,' I said, thrusting my paperwork aside,
'what has happened to him?'

'I don't know, Herr Pastor, the servant girls heard groaning
and raging coming from his room in the night; but as the
daughter was not at home no one dared go in; then when old
Marike got up they clung to her skirts. There was great
screaming when they entered the room; it was as if the whole
bedstead had been tipped over, the pillows and cushions,
everything, lay strewn across the floor; but the old woman
went down on her knees rummaging amid the disorder, carefully lifting every handful of straw bedding as though
searching for her Hofbauer beneath it, but there was no trace
of him to be found.'

'It's still early in the day, though, Hansen,' I said cautiously.
'The Hofbauer will soon be home.'

He shook his head: 'Herr Pastor, it's already well past
mid-day.'

On learning that the daughter was staying in Husum again

with Carstens, the sexton and preacher at the 'Monastery' nearby, I was able to send Hansen to the town in her father's wagon with a message for her. But by three o'clock she had returned to the farm of her own accord, and the women who had gathered there were amazed that this girl, barely eighteen, had gone among them neither crying nor lamenting her father's disappearance; only her eyes stood out much darker against her pale face. The birds in the old trees – so it was said – made a great noise that day as though all the magpies in the forest had been summoned there.

The girl said that she thought her father must have met with an accident while out peat-cutting on the moor where he had spent these last few days; but when she tried to enlist the help of others in the village besides their own two farmhands, very few joined her, for they did not believe what she said, and even the few who did go returned well before dark, as there had been no trace at all of the Hofbauer at the peat workings, and the moor was far too vast a place to search all its swamps and ponds.

Now when the Almighty God covered the forest and fields and the desolate moor too with darkness, Held Carstens, the blacksmith, was skirting the edge of the forest around midnight, returning home after taking his mother-in-law back to Ostenfeld after she had been helping her daughter during confinement. The man had his old and trusty carriage team in harness and was beginning to doze when the otherwise quiet horses suddenly became restless and edged over, snorting, to the side of the forest. He roused himself, now struck with fear, for out on the moor a light wavered about like a lamp in the darkness; one minute it was still, the next swaying to and fro. He thought at first it might be jack-o'-lanterns about to dance – being the courageous man he is he had frequently observed them in the past during his journeys – but when it came nearer he made out a dark figure close to the wavering light wandering about on the firm ground between the dark ditches. Saying a quiet prayer, he whipped up his horses and

made straight for home. But early next morning people saw
the Hofbauer's daughter in the street below without her cap,
with hair dishevelled and a smashed lantern in her hand,
making her way slowly towards her father's farm.

When I went there that morning, as the duties of my office
demanded, I learned she had gone out on the moor again with
the farmhands; but when I returned late in the afternoon, she
came towards me in torn and soiled clothes and gave me an
almost black look with her dark eyes. I wanted to direct her to
Him, without whose help and will all our strength is just vain
weakness; but she said: 'Thank you, Herr Pastor, for the good
intention, but there is no time for that. Just find me some
people if you want to help!' She did not listen to my reply, for
she went straight off to the barn with her farmhands to fetch
ladders and ropes. I had need to return home, and on the way
I succeeded in sending her a couple of young fellows, and
persuaded by your mother, who thought it would comfort the
young girl, as she put it, our Margreth also decided to join
them. This sensible and, as you well know, in no way easily
frightened person nevertheless returned home late that
evening with shaking knees and horror-stricken face. The
search for the missing man – so she said, as soon as she had
recovered her breath – had all been for nothing. But when all
the weary young farmhands had departed and Margreth was
left completely alone with the girl, who could not be induced
to leave the moor, one jack–o'–lantern after the other had
emerged out of the moor with the onset of darkness, and
whisperings and flickering of lights began, so that she was able
to see the shining surface of the pool round which this abom-
inable dance took place. – But let that be as it may. Something
else happened, and I will first remind you that we have never
yet caught our Margreth lying.

When the jack–o'–lanterns were performing their dance, the
Hofbauer's daughter watched them like a mute statue; but
when Margreth drew her by the hand to hurry her home, she
suddenly uttered a loud wail for her father and cried out into

the vast space, as if beseeching tidings of him. And not long afterwards, as though in answer, a dreadful howling came down from out of the dark sky which was like a hundred confused voices calling, each anxious to tell her more than the other.

Then old Margreth called on God and His heavenly hosts, but even with her strong arms she was unable to drag the girl away from the spot, it was as though she were chained to it, until the raging noise above them, just as it had come, subsided in the darkness.

If it causes you pain, my Josias, what I have been compelled to write to you here, for I am fully aware that this girl's earthly beauty has captivated your inexperienced heart, then remember and build on Him who said: 'He that loseth his life for my sake shall find it.' And weigh this carefully, so that you may choose the right way!

I will just mention in closing that our house guest Petrus Goldschmidt, whom I often wished to be here during my spiritual distress over the above matters, was lately appointed Superintendent in the city of Güstrow, and an honorary doctorate was also conferred on him for his learning and services to the Kingdom of God by the . . . [the writing here is illegible] Faculty.

So read my dear father's letter. I will not record here the heavy heart it gave me, how I wrestled with myself and with my God for many sleepless nights, and even thought I could do no other than go straight home to save the poor girl's body and soul, but then with the dawn of each new day it became ever clearer to me how impossible such an undertaking would be.

But, as the saying goes, one sorrow breeds another, and so it happened with me. For just before Christmas I received a letter from my mother to say that my dear father was stricken with an unexpected illness, and that in spite of all earthly remedies, it had almost completely exhausted him, and then a second letter followed a few weeks later urging me to complete my studies, since the dear and faithful man would be unable to attend to his duties himself for much longer.

This latest news, which brought further anguish to my heart, drove me to intense work from morning till night, for I was aware that only such work could hasten my return home.

* *

1707. It was well towards March, however, in this recorded year before I entered my dear parents' house as my father's solemnly ordained assistant. But simply to comfort, not gladden; for I found my father upon his sick-bed, and I clearly saw that, in accordance with the all-wise will of God, he would never rise from it again. And as he now wished not to be without his only child during these days, which he recognised as his last, so I had still not seen anyone from the village; not even Renate. I properly avoided asking my parents about her, so I simply listened to our old Margreth repeat what I had already read in my father's letter.

It was the second Sunday in Lent on which I was to take the service for my dear father for the first time. He had not been able to administer Holy Communion for some while, and so many had registered their intention of receiving it from his son. I even thought Renate would be among them; but she was not.

The night before, during which I shared the nursing of my sick father with my dear mother, the storm had raged with fury; but now everything lay in the bright morning sun, and just as I entered the churchyard a thrush over in the forest burst into song like an Easter greeting. And it was not long before I was in the church standing in front of the altar and saying from a fervent heart: *O Lord, shew thy mercy upon us*; and the congregation devoutly responding: *And grant us thy salvation!* – 'Yes, O Lord,' I repeated quietly, 'grant us Thy salvation; and her also for whom I here humbly plead at Thy feet!' And when the canticle *Let us Sing Praises unto the Lord* began, with the men's rough voices joining in, a sound like a pale silver light floated among them which shone down into my troubled heart; and I knew whose voice I had heard.

In almost joyful spirits, therefore, I climbed the steps to the pulpit, and as I raised my eyes I saw in a pew in the gallery opposite a pale face which was easily recognisable in spite of the balusters. I then began my sermon:

And, behold, a woman of Canaan . . . cried unto him, saying: Have mercy on me, O Lord, thou son of David; my daughter is grievously vexed with a devil.

But he answered her not a word. And his disciples came and besought him, saying: Send her away; for she crieth after us.

But he answered and said: I am not sent but unto the lost sheep of the house of Israel.

And my heart swelled up inside me, and the Word was upon my lips; what I had noted down at home for my sermon was simply dust above which rose my soul, and my words flowed like a stream from holy springs. There was hardly so much as a breath in the full church; young men and old looked up at me, and the women sat in their pews with devotion on their faces. Beside me the sand in the hour-glass seeped away; but I did not notice it, nor did I know how I reached the end of my sermon:

Lord, Lord! Call her forth with Thy loving voice: for a table stands prepared, where she might receive Thee, Thy salvation and Thy grace. Amen.

And as I glanced across at the balustrade after the Lord's Prayer, I saw the large dark eyes in the pale face staring fixedly towards me.

'Call her forth, O Lord, with Thy voice!' I prayed again, and then went down to the vestry to dress myself in the Communion vestments that were still in use at that time.

When I stood in front of the altar, the candles in the tall candelabra on it were already burning and members of the congregation were pushing forward from the pews; men and women, young and old; yet while I divided the body of our Lord and offered up the Communion cup to each mouth, there was a constant cry in my heart: 'Lord, bring her too, her too to Your table!' But her silvery voice still constantly floated above the singing of the congregation. Then it fell silent as the last Communicants neared the altar, and I heard a light step come down the stairs from the gallery. But there were still others who desired Salvation; an old man and woman, supported by their grandchildren, came feebly forward and looked up at me with dull eyes; and when I offered them the Communion cup their trembling lips could hardly hold its rim.

They were led away; then there she stood, Renate, before me; pale, with lowered eyes and in a black dress, a small black cap on her brown hair. I was seeing her for the first time in almost two years; I hesitated, for my heart was in a ferment, and as I took the Host from the paten and laid it between her lips, I prayed: 'Lord, sanctify my soul!' Then I said: 'Take! Eat! This is my Body which is given for you . . .'

I turned to the altar and took the Communion cup. But as I brought it to her lips, I saw a grimace on her lovely face and how she shuddered at the wine in it. I then spoke the sacramental words: 'This is my Blood . . . which is shed for you . . .' And she lowered her face over the almost empty cup; whether her lips touched it I was not able to see. But as I looked to one side – for what reason, I could not say – I noticed the Host lying in the dirt on the floor; her lips had rejected it and the toe of her shoe trod upon the bread she had received as our Lord's Body.

My whole body trembled and the cup almost slipped out of my hand. 'Renate!' I cried softly; in deathly fear this cry broke free of my lips: 'Renate!'

I clearly saw a shiver pass through the girl's lovely figure, but then, without looking up, her white handkerchief clasped in her hand, she turned away, and during the congregation's closing hymn I saw her walk slowly down the long aisle.

How I took off my vestments and returned to my parents'

house I hardly know how to tell; I only knew, standing at home by my desk, that even a young preacher such as I was should not have hurried down the church path in such unseemly haste. I was unable to approach my father's sick-bed now; I held my head in my hands and closing my eyes carefully considered the course that duty impelled me to take.

But only for a short while; then I took the familiar steep foot-path down to the farmstead. Again, as in former times, the magpies chattered in the trees above; and as I entered the room on the left of the hall, it appeared to be larger and emptier than when I had last seen it. Nonetheless, I immediately caught sight of Renate; she was sitting at her place over by the window, her head bent, her hands folded in front of her. Then as I approached she rose slowly to her feet as though tired; and in the long black dress which she now wore she appeared to me to be taller and almost like a stranger. But when I stopped and addressed her by name, she cried: 'Josias!' and stretched out her arms towards me.

Whether it was love, which God creates between a man and a woman, that rang in her voice or a cry for help, I really could not tell; however, I did not take her to my breast where my heart pounded heavily, but remained standing where I was and said: 'You are wrong, Renate; it is not Josias, it is the priest who stands here before you.'

She let her arms drop and said in a dull tone: 'So speak! What is it you want to say to me?'

And as she looked at me now with her grave face and large eyes, something cried out within me: 'You can never leave her; in this woman is all your worldly happiness!' But I called to my God and He helped me in my holy office to banish these earthly thoughts.

'Renate!' I said, 'who was it who tempted you to the deadly sin of spitting out the Lord's Body? Speak his name so that we can defeat him with God's angels!'

But she simply shook her head. 'Oh those poor old folk!' she cried, 'I know it was a sin! But when I saw their faces so completely disfigured by the afflictions of old age, I shuddered at the thought that I should drink with them out of the same Communion cup, and the sacred Host fell from my lips into the dust. Pray for me, Josias, that I shall be pardoned for this sin!'

I did not believe her words. 'So,' I thought to myself, 'this is how the Tempter tries to escape you,' and said aloud: 'You might well shrink from the wedding glass, but the Lord's Communion cup is pure for all to whom it is offered! An evil trap deceived your eye; and it came from him whom even your father played his wretched game with, until his body and soul were lost as a result.'

At these words she fell to her knees, raised her arms and cried: 'My father, O my poor father!'

'Yes, weep for him, Renate!' I said. 'And may God's mercy cast its light down into his deep pit!'

She looked up at me and said in a firm voice: 'It will shine on him, Josias, as well as on any other person overtaken by sudden death!'

But I exclaimed: 'It is the Devil's arrogance that speaks from your mouth! Submit yourself to Him who alone is salvation and pour out your heart to me who stands here in His place!' And as she remained silent, I continued: 'When you went out in the night with our old Margreth on to the moor, whom were you calling who might have brought you news of your father, and what was it that answered you with such terrible howling out of the empty sky?'

'I know of no howling,' she replied, 'but, priest of God' – and a defiant flame burnt in her beautiful eyes – 'if I knew there were information there, I would go this very minute and cry out my need across the moor, and I would not ask too closely where my answer came from!'

'Renate!' I cried, '*Exi immunde spiritus*!' and spread my hands out towards her. 'Confess! Confess! What evil spirits have you too been dealing with?'

She had risen from the floor, and as I looked at her there was a cold look in her eyes. She brushed her dress with her hands and said: 'I do not understand what you are talking about; but this large room feels gloomier to me than it has ever been.' And when at this moment there came a knock at the door, to which my back was turned, and it opened, she added: 'Come in, Margreth! Your master is here!'

I turned round and saw our old Margreth standing there in front of me; she looked at me gravely, then said at length: 'Come home, Herr Josias; your dear father is ready to die, he wants to speak to you for the last time.'

It felt as if the ground were about to give way beneath my feet, and I left Renate and hurried to my father's deathbed. When I entered the room he was propped up, talking loudly, among his pillows, but I thought his voice strange, as though I had never heard it before.

'He is talking about your grandfather,' whispered my mother.

'He does not see me, mother!' I quietly replied.

'No, Josias, he is with those who have gone on already to God's throne.'

And with glowing eyes and staring in front of him my father continued: 'Long, long ago I used to preach in his place – Josias would gladly do the same for me too – for he was very old; his natural sight had gone and worldly sounds were confusion to his ears. But as he felt his hour approaching he bade me and my sisters take him to the church, and we led him to the pulpit. He looked about him in every direction and beckoned slightly with his hand; and his silvery hair hung down over his blind eyes. He thought it was Sunday, and the congregation assembled. He erred; my sisters were up there by his side, and I alone was below. But the old man raised his voice in the pulpit and it sounded strong in the empty church; then he took his leave and spoke in a deeply moving way to all those who were not present.'

The sick man had stretched his arms out over the bedcovers, and his emaciated face shone as though by an inner light. 'Yes, father,' he cried, 'I hear your voice from Eternity, I hear you saying: "And as Thy hand once led me up to this place, so let it now lead me down from it! But, my God and Lord, Thou lightest the darkness before me, and, like my forefathers, my son and grandsons will pronounce Thy word from Thy pulpit. Let them be Thine, O Lord! Gather their weak spirits under the protection of Thy grace!'"

After these words my dear father fell silent; and as my mother folded her arms round him, his head sank back on to her shoulder. But he raised it again; and when she said to him: 'Christian, spare your strength and rest,' he gently shook his head and simply said: 'Later, later, Maria!' Then he looked up at me, lovingly, but with an almost imploring look in his eyes, and spoke slowly and with great effort. 'You have come from the farmstead, Josias; I know it. The Hofbauer is gone, and may God be a merciful judge of him – but his daughter lives! Josias, the only true life is that to which Death has already opened the gates for me!'

The dying man's hand searched in the air for mine, and when I had given it to him, he held it firmly with his wasted fingers.

Then he began to speak again: 'We are a long line of preachers; the first of us sat at the feet of Dr Martin Luther and Melanchthon. Josias!' – he called my name so that it cut through my soul like a sword – 'do not forget our holy calling! – The Hofbauer's house is not one from which a servant of God should take that woman in marriage!'

The dying man's breathing became heavier, but his voice sank to a whisper, and as we listened in silence there came the fading words as though from afar: 'Promise – earthly things are vanity – '

Whereupon he became completely silent; his fingers released my hand and the Lord's peace spread over his blanching face. But I leaned forward to the dead man's ear and said: 'I solemnly promise, father! May your departing soul still hear your son's word!'

My mother looked at me full of compassion; she drew the sheet over the beloved dead face, knelt down beside the bed, and said: 'May God grant us blessed successors and gather us together again in eternal joy.'

* *

When my dear father's grave was closed, the first days of spring
came once again; the snow dripped from the thatched roof of
our house and the birds carried the sunlight on their wings; but
the words of the Creation: 'Let there be light!' had yet to hold
good for me. On the following Sunday, in the afternoon, I
happened to be returning from the village of Hude along the
footpath to Schwabstedt; I was in clerical dress, for I had given
the comfort of our holy religion to a sick man. The first days of
my office had been difficult and I was walking along deep in
thought.

Not far from the village, the path was crossed by a stream
which flowed out of the forest down towards the river Treene.
Water-loving birds gather here, and the joyful song of finches
and blackbirds now rang out as if they were already announcing
the arrival of May. I was so enthralled by the charm of the spot
that I did not cross the little bridge over the stream, but walked
a few paces on this side of it up towards the forest and sat down
on a bank where the stream broadens out into a small pond. The
water, as was usual at this time of year, was so clear that I could
quite easily make out the tangled stalks of the water-lilies deep at
the bottom and the budding leaves on them, and so was able to
admire God's wisdom even in these small things which are
usually hidden from our eyes.

All at once I was startled – and even the birds which, interrupted by my arrival, had just resumed their singing, rose up and
flew off in sudden commotion – by shouts coming from the
other side of the stream: *Hoido! hoido!*, like the calls of country
lads at a battue in a stag hunt. When I turned my head I saw a
band of youths rushing out from among the fir trees on the other
side of the stream. 'Swim! Swim!' they shouted. 'Into the water
with the witch!' And now for the first time I noticed the fleeing
figure of a woman among them who, harried by first one of them
then the other, was trying to escape to the bridge. But one of the
youths darted ahead of her, blocking her way. I knew him well,

from the time of the great wedding, for he was the Bauernvogt's son; and the game here being hunted was Renate.

I scrambled to my feet, ran down to the bridge, and called across: 'You there, what do you think you're doing?'

'A witch! A witch!' they shouted back.

But I asked them: 'So you want to act as judge, do you? Who appointed you as judges?'

And when they fell silent at this, one of them stepped from their midst and said: 'Firewood is expensive, the demons run about freely and the Amtmann and the Landvogt do nothing about it.' And they all shouted again: '*Hoido! hoido*! Into the water with the witch!'

I then set my foot on the bridge and cried: 'Let her be! In God's name, I command you!'

But the youth who was on the bridge pushed me away. 'You rely on your priest's clothes,' he said, 'otherwise you would spare us the sermon; but I advise you, don't be so sure!' And with that he stood in front of me with clenched fists, and his small eyes flashed beneath his curly hair.

Something then took hold of me and I undid my priestly attire and threw it on to the ground; for young blood was still in my veins at that time. As I glanced across at the youths I saw that one of them had seized Renate and was holding her hands behind her back; but her eyes, shining brilliantly in her pale face, rested on me.

'Out of my way!' I cried, and hit the youth hard with both my fists; and I am still certain today that I would have knocked him into the deepest abyss if I had been able and if there had been one beneath us.

For a moment there was deathly silence, then he attacked me too and we faced each other as though cast in bronze. I then noticed the others trying to drag Renate down to the stream; and without uttering a sound I fought tooth and nail with my adversary. 'Patience, you witches' priest,' he shouted in a hoarse voice. 'First she's got to float, before the Devil lays her beside you in the bridal bed!'

A loud ring of laughter and '*Hoido*' came in response from across the stream; I tried in vain to make out Renate. But I had already forced the youth back on to the bridge, and was grabbing his neck to bring him down when I received a blow in the chest from him, and with a cry caused by the sudden pain I sank to the ground.

This may have frightened the whole band, for I ceased to feel a stranger's hand on me and heard them all making off on the other side of the water.

But when I had struggled to my feet, I felt a woman's arms folding round my neck, and the voice which I have never forgotten softly spoke my name: 'Josias, oh, Josias!' And as I brushed the girl's hair back with my hand, for it fell in disorder over her eyes and brow, I saw around her mouth what even now I must call a beatific smile, and her face appeared to me to be of indescribable beauty.

'Renate!' I said quietly, and my eyes were fixed longingly on her lips.

They moved again as though about to answer me, but I listened in vain; the girl's arms sank from my neck, her lips trembled for a moment, and her eyes closed.

I stared anxiously at her and did not know what to do. But when I saw life actually passing into death in the beautiful face, I suddenly felt as if my eyes were looking far out over the edge of the earth, and in my ears I heard my father's dying voice: 'Do not forget our holy calling! – earthly things are vanity!'

And while I was still holding the unconscious figure in my arms, I noticed our neighbour, Held Carstens the blacksmith, with his wife walking up the path on our side of the stream towards us. I explained to them how the girl had been frightened by the young farmhands, and asked if they might look after her as there was another duty that called me away from here.

But the smith approached somewhat hesitantly, and looking at the unconscious girl, said: 'Her there? – Well, if that's your wish, Herr Josias.'

I repeated my request and now the woman too, who was

known by the whole village to be a sensible person, also drew closer. But when I lifted the girl's body up into her arms, a sudden pain pierced my chest which very nearly brought me to my knees again.

And so, doubly wounded, I went home and cast no further glance behind me. But in the room in which my father had died I spent the long night in fervent prayer.

Whatever my dear mother might have said against it, and although the succession to my father's living was as good as promised, I knew full well that my place was no longer in this village. And so I journeyed the very next day to Schleswig to look for another appointment. On my arrival, however, I was overcome with sickness, and my mother had to be called to my bedside. And when one night a stream of blood came from my mouth, she cried out that she was now going to have to give up her only child too.

But I recovered with God's help, and also received a church living in the north of our country, many miles from Schwabstedt, and served this community for over twenty years with an honest will and to the best of my abilities. I buried my dear mother there and mourned her dreadfully; after her death I had no one left whose love so visibly accompanied me.

I still heard about Renate from time to time; first, and soon after my departure, that she had run towards me across the water-lily leaves, which had supported her. But I know of no such thing; it must have been a deception of the evil spirit, for I had seen the water-lily leaves myself still in bud under the crystal clear water.

Then, a good five years later, I heard from a man who went about the country selling rush mats that an enormous black dog had come to her farm one evening, dirty, emaciated and with a broken rope round its neck. She had knelt down, put her arms round the old animal, and drawn its rough head to her breast.

Whether she is still on this earth, or whether God has already taken her mercifully to Himself, I have no further information.

* *

Here the manuscript ends.

But chance, which has permitted us to lift the shroud from a long-forgotten life, lifts it yet again; even though to a lesser extent than most of those reading this might wish.

The chest of drawers in the loft of our old ancestral home mentioned at the beginning of this narrative resounded with voices from the past as soon as one had the courage and patience to disturb the dust inside it. This I did not always have. A few years after finding the manuscript, however, I was sitting one autumn Sunday afternoon in front of its tightly closed drawers once more, pulling them open, often with difficulty, one after the other. Document after document, and almost everywhere that homely legible script of the last century. I had already untied the ribbon round many of the small bundles of papers, and after browsing through them returned each to its resting place. Then I came upon one that consisted of all sorts of papers concerning the inheritance of a long-serving priest in Ostenfeld; a brother of my great-grandfather, as I saw from enclosed letters to him, had taken up the matter on behalf of a preacher's widow living in Husum. Soon an unusually long letter, dated 1778, from a village in eastern Schleswig and signed 'Jensen, past.', captured my complete attention, for it was apparently the accompanying letter once sent with Pastor Josias's manuscript, with a request for its return, to my great-granduncle.

The first few pages, accompanied by a neatly detailed family tree, concerned themselves solely with the genealogical relationships of the Ostenfeld pastor who, it was soon apparent, was the cousin of our Josias, in whose house the latter wrote down his recollections of his early life. The letter continued:

> Our visit in our student days that you mention to my bachelor uncles at the parsonage in Ostenfeld I remember very well; and that you should feel such warm affection towards Uncle Josias is especially pleasing to me; as to the questions you have

raised concerning him, you will find them altogether answered in his own manuscript here enclosed.

They were in truth two quite different persons; Herr Josias, with his Johannine head, and the robust, quick-tempered local pastor. In the course of my own ministry I have often been reminded of the first Sunday I spent there; you did not come to us until that evening, whereas I had already been in the church at Uncle Josias's side in the morning. I can still see among the communicants before the altar the women in mourning who, according to the custom of the time, wore a black veil over their faces; and my uncle the pastor most impatiently tearing it off one of them with the words: 'Off, off with it!', audible throughout the church, while he held the Communion cup aloft with the other hand. Uncle Josias, though, calmly shook his head and leaned back, smiling, in his pew. All the same, as I noticed later during that last summer there when I was revising for the final examinations, the two cousins lived together on excellent terms. Each was a man who, as the saying goes, had learned his part and did not want to forget it. They often discussed learned subjects together, and argued about them, even in Latin.

But on one point they were in complete agreement; they still believed in pacts with the Devil and the black art, and considered such foolish delusion to be a necessary part of orthodox Christian belief. The pastor of Ostenfeld did so with the furious conviction of a well-armed warrior, while Uncle Josias, on the other hand, to whose naturally mild disposition these primitive beliefs were most distasteful, appeared to me to carry them like a burden. When we were alone, therefore, I often tried to talk him out of them on the basis of Holy Scripture and human reason; nevertheless, he would stoutly defend the godless power of the arch-enemy with all his acuteness, even if in a manner of painful submission.

As the summer drew to a close the utmost care was necessary for his health's sake; he was not allowed to attend church on Sundays, nor hardly ever to leave the house; but his gentle kindness and, if I might say, his melancholic cheerfulness, even then remained with him just the same.

It was shortly before my departure one morning in October; the first hoar-frost had settled and there was a fresh clarity in the air. I strolled about the garden, glancing occasionally at the newspaper which the messenger from the town had just passed to me through the fence. When I read that Petrus Goldschmidt, once widely celebrated but long since dismissed from church office for simony, had died a tavern-keeper in Hamburg, I hurried indoors thinking, not without a degree of malicious pleasure, to tell Uncle Josias about it.

As I approached him I felt as though the beautiful morning light had penetrated even this sombre room; for in spite of the burning stove, both window shutters stood wide open and the sounds from the neighbouring threshing-floor and the clear voices of children entered freely.

But I did not deliver my news as intended.

Triumphantly, with a radiant face, Herr Josias came striding towards me. 'My dear Andreas,' he cried, 'we'll never be in dispute again; I've just realised it this very moment: the Devil is simply a powerless spirit lying in the dark abyss!'

Dumb with astonishment, I noticed Thomasius's book on the crime of magic opened on his table. After our last disputation I had secretly left it there and now asked whether the salutary knowledge had arisen from it.

But Herr Josias shook his head. 'No,' he said, 'not from that good book; the light suddenly poured into my heart. I look at it this way, Andreas: death's shadows grow longer and longer; so all-merciful God will remove the other shadows from me.'

His eyes shone as though in supernatural transfiguration; he turned towards the light and spread out his arms. 'O God of grace,' he cried, 'out of my youth an angel came to me; do not reject me because of my dark guilt!'

I went to support him, for he had grown deathly white and I thought I saw him sway; but he smiled and said: 'I am not ill.'

Then he went to his chest, and from it handed me the

manuscript that you are receiving with this letter.

'Take it, my dear Andreas,' he said, 'and preserve it in my memory; I don't need it any more now.'

I departed shortly thereafter; and what now follows was told to me a long time afterwards by the son of the sexton there who was a teacher in the village of Ostenfeld for some years.

In the self-same month of my departure a rumour spread round the village: on Sundays, when everyone was in church and the streets were empty, a pale grey horse, the likes of which had not been seen in the community before, would stand tethered before the door of the parsonage. And soon afterwards it was further said that a woman would come riding from the south over the heath, tether her horse to the ring on the wall, then enter the parsonage; but that each time the pastor and the stream of church-goers made their way home from the church, she had already ridden away.

That this woman visited Herr Josias was not difficult to guess, for at such an hour there was no one else in the house. But there was something strange about it all; for although she was undoubtedly already in her late years, the few who saw her have disputed it and have asserted that she was still young, and others, that she was even beautiful; but when more closely questioned they turn out to have noticed nothing other than two dark eyes that glanced at them as the woman rode by.

There was only one person in the whole village who learned nothing of these things, and that was the pastor himself, for everyone was afraid of his quick temper and all had great affection for Uncle Josias.

But one Sunday, when spring had returned and the violets were already in bloom in the garden, the woman from across the heath was there again; and on this occasion too, when the pastor came home from the church, he saw neither her nor her horse; everything was quiet and solitary as usual as he entered his grounds, then his house. And when he went into his cousin's room, where he was now in the habit of going after church, it was quiet there too. The windows stood open so that the whole room was filled with the scent of spring from the garden outside, and the pastor saw Herr Josias sitting in his large armchair; but to his surprise, a small bird was perched unafraid on one of his hands, which rested folded in his lap. The bird flew off and out into the open air when the pastor approached with his heavy tread and bent over the chair.

Herr Josias continued to sit motionless and his face was filled with peace; only the peace was not of this world.

Soon a loud rumour had spread round the village, even the pastor was told about it by everyone he was ready to hear it from; it was now known that it was the witch of Schwabstedt who had come to the village each Sunday on her horse; indeed, some had certain knowledge that she had taken poor Herr Josias's life while pretending to heal him by her deceitful art.

But we, when you have now read it all, you and I, we know better who she was who took the last breath from his lips.

Notes

Locations of places and physical features mentioned in the Novellen and in the following notes are shown on the maps on pages 34–39.
Wording of biblical quotations is according to the Authorised Version.

The Village on the Moor

Page 43: *district judge's office*. The narrative is set in the district of Husum on the west coast of Schleswig-Holstein. The post of district judge at the time included the duties of a judge and chief constable, as well as the supervision of wards in chancery. Storm held this post, designated *Landvogt* in the Duchy of Schleswig, in Husum from 1864 until 1868 when it was officially abolished by the new Prussian administration.

Page 43: *Gas lighting was not established in our town then.* Street lighting by gas was not introduced in Husum until 1864, and even then only partially. The setting of the story therefore precedes this date.

Page 43: *will-o'-the-wisps*. Also known as 'jack-o'lanterns' – in local folk belief held to be the lights of the souls of unbaptised children; alternatively, the souls of those rejected by hell carrying their own hell coals on their wanderings.

Page 45: *resident of the community*. Original: *Eingesessener*, in rural communities a member of a family of long-standing in a village who owned his own property and land.

Page 45: *one of the villages to the east of the town*. Storm probably had the village of Rantrum, the real-life source of the story, between Husum and Schwabstedt, in mind (see Introduction, page 16).

Page 45: *which I knew to be heavily encumbered*. The responsibilities and duties of the district judge at the time depicted here included the handling of debt. The narrator would therefore have already been fully aware of the financial position of the deceased's estate.

Page 45: *sexton of the village.* The religious and popular authority in a village, often the schoolmaster and village elder.

Page 45: *the parish representative's desk.* The *Gevollmächtigter* was an influential landowner elected to the parish council to represent and act in the interests of the local farming community.

Page 46: *Amtsvogt.* An old judicial and administrative post similar to that of *Landvogt* (see first note to page 131).

Page 46: *holding a pocket handkerchief.* Many paintings of traditional dress in the Husum region at the time show a handkerchief being held in the wearer's hands. A black cap was also commonly worn as part of the traditional attire for a particular village or district.

Page 47: *twenty-four miles away in the town.* Six *Meilen* in the original. The *Meile* in use in the duchy of Schleswig at the time equalled some four statute miles; it varied considerably as between different parts of Germany. A possible reference to the much larger town of Schleswig, approximately the same distance away from Husum on the opposite coast.

Page 47: *Slovak.* A contemporary term for 'gypsy'.

Page 48: *the bonds of the old farming tradition.* The traditional requirement to perpetuate the farming line within a village by marrying into another local farming family, and not outside it.

Page 49: *Actum ut supra . . . and a sprinkling of sand on it.* A Latin legal expression used in official documents, and a reference to the old practice of drying wet ink with sand rather than powder.

Page 49: *the Neustadt.* Street leading north out of Husum. The sale of horses and cattle at the Neustadt market, then the centre of the town, played a key part in the economy of North Friesland in the nineteenth century. The Neustadt district was densely populated with inns, many of which provided stabling for horses and animals.

Page 50: *And with a slap the hands came together.* A customary way of sealing a bargain.

Page 50: *thaler.* Silver coin in use as late as 1876 when it was replaced by the Reichsmark following the foundation of the German Empire in 1871. One thaler varied in value between 30 and 40 schillings in the different duchies.

Page 50: *the harbour square.* The Schiffbrücke, a large busy square facing the harbour in Husum and a popular meeting place for the townsfolk.

Page 51: *he had left Hamburg on an emigration vessel.* Emigration from Schleswig-Holstein to America, primarily by steamship from Hamburg,

reached its peaks in the years 1872–73 and 1881–85, with a large proportion from the districts of Husum and Tondern. Compulsory three-year
military service, gold-fever and unemployment through overpopulation
were among the prime reasons for young farmers and craftsmen leaving the
land.

Page 52: *low hedgerows*. Original: *Wälle*, low grassy banks separating one
field from another, often covered with small bushes and shrubs resembling
English hedgerows. A distinctive feature of this region.

Page 52: *'Wild Moor'*. The moorland covering a wide area between
Schwabstedt and Ostenfeld south of Husum (see third note to page 156).

Page 52: *plover*. Presumably a golden or a grey plover, which is generally
found on the moorlands of North Friesland in the autumn.

Page 52: *I was reminded of something I had once read*. Storm was a serious
collector of ghost stories from around Europe and well versed in the literature and tradition of the uncanny, and his Novellen and fairy tales reflect
this interest. After being lost for over a hundred years, his personal collection of ghost stories was finally published in 1991 under the title *Theodor
Storm. Neues Gespensterbuch* (Frankfurt am Main).

Page 52: *demon*. Original: *Alp*, meaning 'nightmare', 'incubus', 'goblin',
'evil spirit'.

Page 52: *the village, the church spire and dark straw-thatched roofs of which
had long been visible to us*. Descriptions later in the story would indicate that
Storm here has the St. Jacobi-Kirche (St Jacob's church) in the village of
Schwabstedt south of Husum also in mind, which lies at the southern edge
of the Moor. For a detailed description of this village and church see
Renate, notes to pages 129 and first note to page 139.

Pages 53–54: *omen . . . roses . . . in the garland that the Slovak girl wore on her
black hair, there were my red roses*. In German folklore the associations of the
rose were not always agreeable. It is recorded having been worn as a punishment for immoral conduct.

Page 53: *ring-lancing*. Original: *Ringlaufen*, a children's game in which a
ring hanging from a suspended rope had to be pierced with a lance and
brought down; similar to the adult equestrian sport of *Ringreiten*, still
popular today in North Friesland.

Page 55: *the tidal flats*. The Wattenmeer: a vast area of islands, sand and
mudflats covering some 800 square miles off the North Frisian coast.

Page 56: *with ladders and poles*. Necessary in marshland for crossing broad
water-filled ditches, usually by pole-vaulting.

Page 57: *elder hedges*. Elder plays a dark role in European superstition, and is often considered an ill omen.

Page 57: *bounded fields and meadows*. Enclosed by low hedgerows (see first note to page 52).

Page 58: *the white sand in the hallway, the shiny brass knobs on the stove*. In North Frisian houses sand was strewn over the hallway floor in earlier times to protect it against dirt coming in from the barn which was generally an integral part of the house. The stove (*Beilegerofen*), a prominent feature, was often highly decorated with brass fittings and scenes from the scriptures. It was heated from the rear by the fire from the kitchen.

Page 58: *curtained wall-beds*. Alcove beds. An integral part of the main living quarters in a North Frisian house; set into the walls to provide greater warmth in winter. They were often elaborately decorated with floral patterns, maxims, biblical quotations or proverbs.

Page 62: *St John's Day*. St John the Baptist's day, 24 June.

Page 62: *when the night watchman blew nine o'clock*. It was common in many small towns or villages for most of the nineteenth century for the hour to be called by the blowing of a horn from a tower or the town hall.

Page 62: *sewing-stone . . . table-drawers . . .* A spherically shaped stone used as a darning mushroom or to smooth down the sewing itself. Tables in farmhouse living rooms often had two large rectangular drawers side by side beneath their tops. The couple here would therefore most likely be sitting next to each other.

Page 63: *geomancy*. Fortune-telling, palmistry, astrology or divination from the configuration of, among other things, randomly placed dots. Closely associated with witchcraft in the sixteenth and seventeenth centuries.

Page 63: *Then he stood up and offered me his hand*. It is still customary in North Germany to shake a person's hand when saying 'goodnight'.

Page 68: *the north-west wind was in full fury*. November is generally the time for severe storms in North Friesland, presaged by winds from the north-west.

Page 68: *hand-strap*. A rope, with hand grip, attached to the ceiling of a wall-bed to assist in sitting upright in bed.

Page 70: *the threshing floor of the house*. North Frisian farmsteads were commonly constructed as part living quarters and part stalls, threshing floor and barn, everything under one roof, the latter work areas being separated from the living quarters by a corridor or wide hallway. The threshing floor was often large, with the stalls situated down each side of it. It was therefore possible to enter the interior of the house directly from the threshing floor.

Paul the Puppeteer

Page 75: *wooden pin-cushion holder*. A fixture (*Nähschraube*) screwed on to the surface of a sewing table to hold a pin-cushion.

Page 75: *mechanicus*. An early nineteenth-century term for a specialist in the manufacture, operation and repair of mechanical objects and devices (see also first note to page 80).

Page 75: *forty years ago*. Around 1834 in the time-scheme of this narrative.

Page 76: *of Frisian descent . . . native language*. The local language is the most important feature of identity for North Frisians on the west coast of Schleswig-Holstein, the present setting of the narrative. The language consists of North, East and West Frisian branches; there is no standard source language.

Page 76: *an unmistakable south German ring*. According to Storm himself, in a letter to a friend dated 11 April 1874, 'from the region between Berchtesgaden and Munich'. See Translator's Note, page 31.

Page 77: *Paul the Puppeteer*. 'Pole Poppenspäler' in the original, Storm's title for the Novelle: the Low German form of 'Paul der Puppenspieler'.

Page 77: *In those days . . . the open fields beyond the town*. Around 1800. A reference to a house in the Süderstraße in Storm's home town of Husum on the west coast of Schleswig. The long cobbled street, with a mixture of town and small country houses on either side, lay at the southern edge of the town and ran from the market place with its church in the west to the then open fields in the east. The church in the market place might well have been the old St. Marienkirche (St Mary's church) with its extremely tall spire before its demolition in 1807/8 (see fourth note to page 133).

Page 78: *St Michael's fair*. A grand autumn fair held in Husum on 29 September, the feast-day of St Michael, following the harvest festivals.

Page 78: *the tailors' hostel*. The *Schneiderherberge* that once stood at 64 Süderstraße in Husum was a journeymen's hostel run by a craftsmen's guild both as a lodging and meeting place for guild members. Each guild hostel was run by a house-father (*Herbergsvater*). When an itinerant jour-neyman arrived in a town during his compulsory period of travel

(*Wanderschaft*) as laid down by his guild, he would proceed to his particular journeymen's hostel where he was temporarily lodged, sometimes at the expense of his guild. Journeymen remained in the town when their labour was in demand or were sent to another when not, often with money supplied by the guild (see second note to page 124). Through the first half of the nineteenth century, on average 1,500 journeymen journeyed through Husum per year.

Page 78: *in keeping with the reputation of that highly respectable craft.* The craft guilds were a powerful force in pre-industrial society throughout Europe (see Introduction, page 23), where an individual's place and social standing were generally fixed by his or her position in relation to a guild – as master craftsman, journeyman, apprentice, craftman's widow or simply wage-worker. Each guild was highly sensitive to its own status, and access to its hostels was strictly controlled, as recognised here by the narrator.

Page 79: *Lisei.* Affectionate term for Elisabeth.

Page 80: *The mechanicus.* See second note to page 75. Proprietors of marionette shows preferred to call themselves 'mechanicuses' in an attempt to sound more respectable to the public. During the late eighteenth and early nineteenth centuries these showmen travelled throughout Europe, often with quite large companies presenting a great variety of attractions, including puppet shows. By the second half of the nineteenth century smaller family troupes, like the Tendler family, had become the norm.

Page 80: *the royal capital of Munich.* Capital city of Bavaria, elevated by the Treaty of Pressburg in 1805 to the status of a kingdom. It was well known in the nineteenth century as 'the city of puppet plays'.

Page 80: *Schützenhof.* The centre and meeting place of the Husum Riflemen's Guild (Schützengilde), founded in 1586/7: a two-storey house at 42 Süderstraße in Husum, on the same side of the road as the tailors' hostel at number 64. Its assembly room (*Saal*), on the upper floor, was a large room serving as both a small theatre and a venue for the Guild's special occasions; its long rifle-range at the rear of the house extended across the fens, the Lämmerfenne, down to the river Mühlenau. The Guild still exists today in Husum as does the original house in the Süderstraße, its frontage much altered and modernised.

Page 80: *Count Palatine Siegfried and Saint Genovieve.* One of the best-known pieces in the entire European puppet repertoire, normally under the title *Genevieve of Brabant*. The plot is based on a well-known story from the Middle Ages. Count Siegfried, on his way to fight the infidel, leaves his wife Genovieve in the care of the knight Golo, who later falsely accuses her of adultery. She is banished to live in a forest with her son, and the two live off roots and herbs and hind's milk. Genovieve is forgiven by her husband when he discovers the deception, and Golo is executed.

Page 81: *bits 'n' pieces for the puppets' costumes*. It was common practice among travelling puppeteers at the time, whose incomes were low and unreliable, to make and repair the costumes for their marionettes themselves out of odds and ends. Much of the fabric, including velvets and silks, was recycled from worn-out or cast-off clothing, but the finished effect was enhanced by the use of trimmings and machine-made braids, accompanied by light-catching sequins and beads. The puppets were often clothed in costumes that could easily be changed during the play without involving restringing the figures.

Page 82: *two schillings*. One *Doppeltschilling* in the original: a silver coin of small value in circulation in Schleswig-Holstein, Hamburg and Lübeck since 1450.

Page 82: *footpath along by the river*. The Bürgersteig which ran beside the river Mühlenau in Husum.

Page 83: *for at that time such entertainment was eagerly attended*. The marionette theatre had been popular across Europe in one form or another since the seventeenth century. In the early nineteenth century travelling marionette theatres were the main serious form of entertainment for many. One element in their decline was the shift in emphasis from evening performances to matinées as the theatre itself developed and as audiences began to find other diversions in the evenings or to regard the puppet theatre as old-fashioned and even 'childish'.

Page 83: *our town's music director*. The *Stadtmusikus*. A Musicians' Guild position in most German towns since the fifteenth century, with the responsibility for the provision of music for festive or formal occasions. Like a master craftsman, the *Stadtmusikus* would employ a number of apprentices.

Page 83: *on one side a grim, and on the other a laughing mask*. Standing for Melpomene, the Greek muse of tragedy, and Thalia, comedy.

Page 85: *there was one dressed in a yellow Nanking suit called Kasperl*. By the early nineteenth century, in which period the main narrative of *Paul the Puppeteer* is set, Kasper, or Kasperl Larifari, was the most prominent puppet character in Germany and Austria, where *Kasperltheater* had become synonymous with puppet theatre. The character was developed in the eighteenth century through the Vienna Volkstheater from the amusing and extremely bawdy figure of the cunning peasant servant Hans Wurst, or

Hanswurst, into the more temperate, though still amusing Kasperl Larifari (the surname meaning 'stuff and nonsense'), who adapted his jokes to suit local audiences or make political attacks on local authorities. The figure was brought to Germany by travelling puppeteers.

Page 86: *'Doctor Faust's Journey to Hell'*. The most frequently performed puppet play in Germany during the period of the narrative. The celebrated travelling marionette proprietor Georg Geißelbrecht (see second note to page 94) performed it in Husum, for example, on 27 April and 4 May 1817. Storm kept many backnumbers of the Husum weekly newspaper and it is possible that an advertisement there for such a performance was one of the sources for his Novelle.

Page 86: *a two-schilling piece*. See first note to page 82.

Page 86: *the open garden of the Schützenhof*. The former rifle-range of the Riflemen's Guild (see third note to page 80). At one time enclosed.

Page 87: *over the tidal flats*. The Wattenmeer. See note to page 55.

Page 87: *Hans Wurstl*. A comic figure from the Vienna Volkstheater (see note to page 85).

Page 88: *hanging by seven strings*. The strings to manipulate the marionette were generally attached to *nine* places on the figure: to each leg, hand, shoulder and ear and the base of the spine. By adding further strings, more sensitive control could be achieved, some marionettes at the time having up to fifty. The strings, or wires, extended from concealed points on the marionette's body to the controls, a complex of wooden straight or crossed bars held in the puppeteer's hand(s). The practice of using only the fingers to control the strings (see cover picture) was primarily a Chinese one.

Page 89: *what an enchanting way of speaking* . . . See second note to page 76.

Page 90: *five feet above the floor*. In the original, literally 'five shoes high', the 'shoe' or 'foot' being an old unit of length in Schleswig-Holstein, equal to about 11 inches or just under 30 centimetres.

Page 90: *Doctor Faust . . . forces of Hell*. For his account of Tendler's performance of *Faust* Storm is said to have consulted the four-act arrangement by Karl Simrock (Bonn, 1846). Storm's text here is taken from the opening of the first act and is identical to Simrock's. Other passages from Simrock's version are used by Storm throughout the narrative.

Page 90: *"Your Magnificence"*. A respectful form of address for a rector of a university since the Middle Ages.

Pages 91–92: *"Just listen to that . . . Seifersdorf."* In Saxon dialect in the original.

Page 92: *"Am I supposed to ride to Parma on the back of the sparrow from Hell?"* Quoted from the second act of Simrock's version of *Faust* (see second note to page 90), in which Faust has already set out for Parma with Mephistopheles. In Simrock's play Kasperl is offered transport in pursuit of them, 'faster than a bullet from a gun'.

Page 92: *their home town.* Mainz.

Page 93 *"Fauste, Fauste, in aeternum damnatus es!".* Latin: 'Faust, Faust, you are damned to eternity!'

Page 94: *Gretl.* South German for Margarete or Gretchen.

Page 94: *"my dear father's!".* Reference to the most celebrated travelling marionette proprietor of the early nineteenth century, Johann Georg Geißelbrecht (1762-?1826). His troupe consisted of members of his family. His performances took him to Prussia, Mecklenburg, the Rhinelands, Denmark, Poland, Russia and Schleswig-Holstein; he visited Husum in May 1817, the year of Storm's birth (see first note to page 86).

Page 94: *"that godforsaken piece . . . My father never wanted to in his last years!".* Geißelbrecht's own version of *Faust* under the title *Dr Faust or the Great Necromancer* was published privately in 1832 in just 24 copies. A note added by him to the original manuscript stated: 'Everything that is underlined moved me never ever to perform *Faust* again.' The underlining referred in part to blasphemous use of saints' names and Kasperl's descriptions of his blasphemous and criminal relatives.

Page 94: *Resel.* Affectionate form of Therese. Written also as 'Reserl'.

Page 99: *Herr Tendler in front with the lantern.* Gas street lighting was not available in Husum until 1864.

Page 99: *"I'm not a mechanicus . . .".* See second note to page 75.

Page 99: *I'm actually a wood carver by trade from Berchtesgaden.* A wood carver and puppeteering family by the name of Tendler actually lived during Storm's time in Berchtesgaden, Bavaria. It was, and remains today, common for puppeteers to make and carve their own marionettes, and for their wives and daughters to dress them. Fresh marionettes have generally to be made for each new character in a play.

Page 99: *Reserl.* See fourth note to page 94.

Page 99: *"the famous puppeteer Geisselbrecht."* See second note to page 94.

Page 100: *Hans Wurstl Number Two.* See second note to page 87.

Page 100: *linden tree.* The tree of love and friendship, a common meeting place in folklore.

Page 100: *Had she been to school?.* Children of travelling show people were usually required to attend school. The records of one travelling puppeteer show he performed in 46 locations in one year, his children attending school for 1–4 days at each location. In an interview given in 1975 the daughters of Karl Winter (1863–1943), a fifth-generation travelling puppeteer in Schleswig-Holstein, described their schooling and early lives: 'As children we grew up in a travelling marionette theatre. We always travelled with it and attended the *Wanderschule* (from the age of 7). Occasionally that was not at all agreeable. We attended 160 schools. When we were at school, you can imagine how we were surrounded at break-times [. . .]. A parson once wanted to keep hold of one of our brothers and give him a proper education, but father said no. The Great War had reduced his income and he needed the boy's help.' (Quoted in Helga Werle-Burger, *Karl Winter's Grosses Mechanisches Marionetten- und Kunstfiguren-Theater*, Lübeck, 1997, pp. 19–20.)

Pages 100–101: *kissed my mother's hand . . . such strange antics in these parts!*. A common gesture of gratitude and admiration in southern Germany and Austria, but most unusual in the north.

Page 101: *The Children's Friend*. Christian Felix Weiße's *Der Kinderfreund*, published between 1775 and 1782, was the most famous children's educational periodical of the eighteenth century.

Page 102: *building my own marionette theatre*. Storm's daughter Gertrud recalls in her memoirs how, when young, she and her brothers had their own marionette theatre in their home, and how her father as a boy constructed his own theatre, making his own figures and performing popular plays of the time.

Page 102: *journeyman of my father's who had been with the family for as long as I could remember*. Here most likely since his apprenticeship. An apprentice, upon payment of a placement fee, would generally be placed in a master craftsman's household, agreeing to obey and respect him as a father. He would receive food, clothing, lodging and training in return. The apprenticeship (*Lehrzeit*) was as a rule for three or four years in the master's household. On its completion many began their compulsory period of travel (*Wanderschaft*) as journeymen towards their final qualification as master craftsmen. It was also possible for an apprentice, however, as here, to stay on with the master craftsman as his journeyman without wishing to be a master craftsman himself.

Page 103: *the high ridge of heathland outside our town*. The Geest, or uplands: extensive, frequently sandy, higher moraine land of Schleswig-Holstein stretching from Flensburg in the north to the river Elbe in the south. The town is Husum.

Page 103: *the cart.* Hilly districts with steep winding lanes and poor surfaces did not favour the use of the heavy four-wheeled wagon, which required a greater amount of room for turning. Such districts were best traversed by carts. Until the middle of the nineteenth century many of the unsurfaced roads in the duchies of Schleswig and Holstein were almost impassable in bad weather.

Pages 104–105: *It was about twelve years later . . . I found myself in a town in central Germany.* Around 1815 . . . The small town Storm has in mind is Heiligenstadt, set within beautiful forested hills some 14 miles south-east of Göttingen in the Eichsfeld. It was predominantly Catholic. It was ringed by walls, its three gates were closed each night, and a night-watchman blew the hours from a church tower. Street lighting was non-existent; in the main street water was drawn from the gully flowing past the houses. Storm's time in Heiligenstadt (as County Court magistrate, 1856-64) opened his eyes to the strength and influence of Catholicism in a small community and to the effects of extreme poverty among its inhabitants (see Introduction, page 19).

Pages 104–105: *the third year of grammar school . . . and had then been taken on by my father as an apprentice.* The Quarta, the third year of a *Gelehrten-schule* (grammar school), had pupils around 11–13 years of age. It was common at the time to allow sons of artisans to go through the lower classes of the grammar school, where they would sit on the same bench as the future professional men or merchants. It was equally common for a master craftsman to take his son on as an apprentice.

Page 105: *the master craftsman's certificate.* The *Meisterrecht* or *Meisterbrief*, an essential document for setting up in business as a master craftsman.

Page 105: *the widow, the good Frau Meisterin.* The customary title for the wife or widow of a master craftsman. Her title and its attached status were extremely important, affording her certain privileges within the community, such as wood for the winter (see second note to page 107).

Page 105: *the large prison opposite.* Storm's own house in Heiligenstadt, in the Wilhelmstraße, was situated opposite the prison (see second note to page 110), a bleak two-storey grey building housing up to eighty prisoners. Storm's wife Constanze was a frequent visitor. In a letter to his father dated 10 May 1862, Storm wrote: 'Constanze is across the road in the prison and mangling the washing with the prisoners . . .'

Page 105: *the tedious length of the journey at that time.* In the absence of the railway, the coach from Heiligenstadt to Göttingen, a journey of some 15 miles over difficult roads to connect with a train, still needed to be taken well into the 1860s.

Pages 106–107: *the narrow lane at the corner of the prison that led up to the church*. The present-day Vogelgasse in Heiligenstadt, a narrow lane leading to the fourteenth-century church of St. Aegidien, on the external choir wall of which hung the crucifix mentioned in the story.

Page 107: *the high hill that reared up at the end of the street*. The town of Heiligenstadt is surrounded by densely forested hills which can be seen rising up at the ends of most streets.

Page 107: *a rightful claim to five bundles of wood for domestic use*. The right to an agreed amount of wood for the winter from the adjacent forests was generally in return for work carried out for the local landowner during the year. A master craftsman's widow would seem to have had this entitlement by virtue of her guild status.

Page 107: *"and I almost believe He's sent me to you!"*. Paul addresses the girl in the polite form here in German but changes immediately to the familiar when he recognises who she is. Such telling shifts in personal communication are regrettably untranslatable into English.

Page 109: *mounted policeman*. A *Landreiter*, employed by the local authority to patrol the coach roads and to enforce its laws.

Page 110: *corporal*. It was not uncommon for former soldiers to seek employment as warders in prisons, particularly as here after the Napoleonic Wars.

Page 110: *spinning-machine*. The Heiligenstadt prison was well-known for its manufacture of bags, made by the prisoners for sale to the public. The prison used to be called the *Spinnhaus* after the spinning machines in use there.

Page 111: *the beggars' inn*. The *Bettelherberge*, a 'hostel' offering free accommodation under a poor relief system for tramps and beggars. Members of the 'undesirable professions', which included travelling show people, had to pay for their lodging in full. Such hostels were established in response to widespread pauperism following the Napoleonic wars and failed harvests. The worst years were 1816–17, the period of the narrative.

Page 111: *I asked Lisei if she had her passes with her*. Travel passes and permits to perform were essential documents for travelling puppeteers, particularly those frequently crossing frontiers. For the acquisition of a trade licence and permit to perform, personal references played a key role. Puppeteers endeavoured to get as many of these as possible from respected citizens in the towns in which they performed in order to vouch for both their respectability and the high moral standards of their shows. The wife or daughter of a puppeteer often negotiated permits with the authorities.

Page 112: *the best pillow there is in the world.* A reference to the old German saying: 'A clear conscience is a soft pillow' ('Ein gutes Gewissen ist ein sanftes Ruhekissen').

Page 114: *"But Paul, we're travelling folk. What will they say about it in your town?".* Here Storm highlights, without setting out to criticise, the social strictures imposed by the guild system at the time. Until well into the nineteenth century the travelling puppeteers across Europe led a poor life, stood on the same low social level as beggars, gypsies and bandits, and were generally despised. Show people were regarded with a degree of awe and mistrust, particularly if they led a nomadic existence. To be recognised and to take his place in the community it was essential for a master craftsman to have a wife and for her to come from the same social class as he. To marry 'the wrong' wife could lead to expulsion from the guild. Guild ordinances even demanded of every master craftsman that he be 'conceived of legitimate parents in a proper marriage bed' (Eda Sagarra, *A Social History of Germany 1648–1914,* London, 1977, pp. 71–2).

Page 115: *She still says "nit" as they say in Bavaria.* For High German *nicht*, 'not'.

Page 115: *footpath that runs behind the gardens of the town.* The *Bürgersteig* by the river Mühlenau.

Page 115: *the right wife for an established master craftsman.* See note to page 114 and Introduction, page 23.

Page 115: *'Master'.* The style of address for a master craftsman.

Page 116: *she travelled readily to the neighbouring town to Easter confession.* Possibly in Storm's mind was Friedrichstadt, south of Husum, a town renowned historically for its religious tolerance; Quakers, Catholics, Mennonites, Lutherans and Jews had freedom to worship there.

Page 116: *old silver coins . . . Kremnitz ducats.* These silver coins, *Harzdrittel* in the original, were in fact only a third part silver, from the silver mines in the Harz Mountains in north Germany. The Kremnitz ducats were Austrian gold coins from the gold and silver mining works near Kremnitz in the former Hungarian part of Slovakia. Such a collection indicates the extensive travelling of puppeteers of the time. Marriage being a requirement of guild regulations for mastership, an accompanying dowry was frequently essential to a master craftsman for setting up shop and buying tools.

Page 118: *Cripple-Lieschen.* Nickname involving word play emphasising the sharp differences between her and Lisei, with *Kröpel* meaning 'cripple' or 'lame' in Low German, and *Lieschen*, a play on the name Lisei meaning 'Mrs/Miss Average'.

Page 118: *the town hall where school-leavers gave their speeches around Michaelmas*. An old custom, the *Redefeierlichkeit*, dating back to the seventeenth century in Husum when rhetoric was part of the curriculum at the local grammar school (*Gelehrtenschule*); since the beginning of the nineteenth century a school function held in the autumn for pupils in the last class, who through prose- or verse-speaking gave proof of their attainment in learning (see third note to page 132).

Page 118: *The Beautiful Susanna*. Popular play based on the History of Susanna in the Apocrypha. The Babylonian Jewess Susanna is accused of adultery by two spurned old men; through Daniel's wise and skilful interrogation she is saved from being put to death.

Page 119: *the Cossack Winter*. The extremely harsh winter of 1813/14. Denmark's alliance with France during the Napoleonic Wars resulted in the invasion of Schleswig-Holstein by Russian, Swedish and Prussian troops in the autumn of 1813, leading to detachments of Cossacks being stationed in Husum during the following particularly cold winter which was thereafter called by this name locally. Following the wars, unemployment was rife throughout the region, leading to social unrest (see following note).

Page 119: *the poorhouse*. Following the economic depressions of the 1830s poorhouses were established in most regions of Germany. The Husum Poorhouse (*Armenhaus*) was established in the north of the town in 1856/57 for the penniless, destitute and those incapable of work. Its regulations, as in many other poorhouses, were strict, often penal, and governed the periods of work and rest. Those capable of work were given various manual tasks, or, following the Hamburg Poor Law of 1788 (*Armenordnung*), might have been sent to other institutions associated with the poorhouse, for example to local farms in summer, to earn their living.

Page 119: *The first row was almost empty, the second only partially occupied; but in the gallery the audience stood closely packed*. The avoidance of the costlier seats at the front is a clear indication here of the changing nature of the audience attending a marionette theatre coupled with the economic depression after the Napoleonic Wars.

Page 120: '*Beautiful Minka, I must away!*'. Beginning of a Russian folksong, 'The Cossack and his Girl' by Christoph August Tiedge (1752–1841).

Page 120: *Frau Meisterin*. See second note to page 105.

Pages 120–121: "*Lott is dead!*". The first words of a humorous North

German folksong.

Page 121: *"Paul the Puppeteer"*. See first note to page 77.

Page 123: *"For out of the ground wast thou taken!"*. After Genesis 3:19.

Page 123: *"And unto dust shalt thou return!"*. After Genesis 3:19.

Page 123: *"And together with my dead body thou shalt arise!"*. After Isaiah 26:19.

Page 124: *for the Blessed may rest from their labours*. After Revelation 14:13.

Page 124: *those eternally wandering journeymen*. Not every journeyman could hope to become a master craftsman. Some, who lacked the necessary capital, remained journeymen for life, wandering from town to town looking for work. Unemployment was particularly high during the so-called Hunger Years of 1846–47, and the number of journeymen increased throughout Schleswig-Holstein out of all proportion to the jobs available, and the ability of the guilds to support such numbers decreased. The old guild custom of giving aid when requested was no longer possible, and the journeymen affected, often begging with threats, became highly unpopular, being associated even among their fellows, as here by the narrator, with idleness and beggary.

Renate

Page 129: *the village of Schwabstedt*. A small picturesque village on high ground overlooking the river Treene, a tributary of the Eider, some seven miles south-east of the author's home town of Husum. Storm was a frequent visitor to the village both in his youth and later in life with his family.

Page 129: *according to some chroniclers*. Storm found this derivation of the village's name from the Latin *suavis*, meaning 'delightful', in the chronicles of Johannes Laß (Flensburg, 1750–52). The broad winding river through rich marshland forms almost a peninsula at the foot of the village, whose thatched cottages in narrow lanes, country church and inn on steep rising ground, and abundant yellow and white water-lilies by the river are as much an attraction for visitors today as they were in the author's time.

Page 129: *its old parish inn*. A small thatched cottage dating from the early eighteenth century that once stood on high rising ground overlooking the river; the Hotel zur Treene occupies the site today. Its views of the surrounding countryside are some of the finest in the district. As in

Storm's time, steep tree-lined granite steps lead down from it to the river where boat trips can still be made to the nearby town of Friedrichstadt.

Page 129: *Peter Behrens*. Three generations of Peter Behrens once managed the inn. The last in the line, Peter Behrens III, sold the inn in 1877, presumably before Storm began to write *Renate* in November of that year.

Page 129: *a harbour east of the village, used by the feared Vitalien brothers*. A location marked as 'Hollbek' or 'Holbek' on maps of the region. The Vitalien brothers were a band of notorious pirates which terrorised the region at the end of the fourteenth century (see third note to page 151).

Page 129: *the fortress-like residence of the bishops of Schleswig*. Schloß Schwabstedt, the official summer residence and refuge of the bishops of Schleswig from 1268 until 1624. The 'fortress-like' residence with its dominant octagonal golden onion tower, some 50 feet high, facing the river was pulled down in 1705. Huge depressions in the ground still remain today of the original dry moats and walls that not only once fortified the residence but also surrounded the entire village.

Page 130: *the bishop's rise*. The *Schloßwerft* – high earthworks by the river upon which the bishop's residence once stood.

Page 130: *ancient lofty oaks*. In mythology oak trees are evil and sinister – devils' and witches' oaks proliferate in German mythology.

Page 130: *farmstead . . . left to fall into ruin*. The 'Schwabstedter Hof', originally a large farming complex attached to the bishop's residence, was rebuilt in 1804 as a large stone farmhouse with adjoining barns. During Storm's boyhood it stood empty and in a state of ruin for many years, a condition he recalls here. A building stands today just off the main road into the village where Renate's 'farmstead' once stood: named 'Renatenhof' after the Novelle. A stone can be seen in its grounds bearing the inscription 'Schwabstedter Hof – Anno 1268 – "Renate" 1705'.

Page 130: *magpies*. In German folklore a bird of ill omen, which could change form into a witch, or a broomstick carrying a witch through the air. Magpies heard shrieking from a tree presaged the arrival of an unwelcome guest; if chattering, the advent of a friend.

Page 130: *'Mother Pottsacksch'*. Storm here uses the name of a Hollingstedt woman in the legends and folk tales of Schleswig-Holstein said to have been drowned as a witch in the river Treene. However, the real-life original he had in mind would seem to have been Christina Mommens (1800–88), a Schwabstedt woman, a photograph of whom, as a short hunched figure in a dark dress and white apron and with sharply pointed, stern face beneath a rough straw bonnet (the Schwabstedter *Peerkopp*), carrying a small wicker basket on her arm, can be seen today in the Schwabstedt Museum. She was nicknamed 'Stina Moßkranz' after her door-to-door selling of posies of flowers.

Page 130: *in her broad dialect*. The woman speaks in Low German in the original. After the Reformation the use of the Frisian language declined in favour of Low German (Plattdeutsch) and High German. The five languages spoken in North Friesland today also include Danish and Sønderjysk. Low German is frequently used by Storm to emphasise a person's rural origin.

Page 130: *'Were there witches here then?'* The chronicles of the region record the trial, torture and burning of two women convicted of witchcraft in Schwabstedt in 1619 (see notes to pages 131 (third) and 135 (first)).

Page 131: *the Amtmann and the Landvogt*. Senior officials in the administrative and judicial system of the duchy of Schleswig. Royal power was vested in an Amtmann, who might head several authorities; he was commonly assisted by a Landvogt, who had both judicial and administrative duties.

Page 131: *large burning eyes*. In North Frisian legends witches were said to be easily recognised by their burning red eyes.

Page 131: *'And was the horse she rode black?'* The Devil's colour. One of the two 'witches' burnt at the stake in Schwabstedt in 1619 was recorded as having ridden on a black horse to the Brocken, the highest point in the Harz Mountains; traditional rites were said to be enacted there annually on Walpurgis Night, or Witches' Sabbath (30 April); a scene enacted in Goethe's *Faust*.

Page 132: *the village of Schwesen*. The old name for Schwesing, a village five miles north-east of Husum.

Page 132: *his meagre income . . . he also had the duty of running the school*. In the early eighteenth century the country pastor's lot was often worse than a peasant's or craftsman's. His income usually consisted of tithes, paid with reluctance and collected with difficulty. Following the Reformation it was common for church duties to include running the village school, a task that was usually carried out by the sexton who was often also the church organist.

Page 132: *the Latin school in Husum*. The grammar school (*Gelehrtenschule*). Founded and built east of the old church in Husum in 1527 by Hermann Tast, the Protestant Reformer, for future clerics or civil servants; Latin was a principal subject. Nicolaus Rudlof was its rector from 1712 to 1727.

Page 132: *a 'Gergesene'*. A biblical reference to persons said to be possessed with devils from the town of Gerasa, east of the Jordan. See Matthew

8:28.

Page 133: *recently ended war with the King of Denmark.* The Great Northern War (1700–21) between Sweden and a coalition of its neighbours including Russia, Denmark and Saxony-Poland. Danish troops invaded the region in March 1700, besieging the local town of Tönning.

Page 133: *jack-o'-lantern.* See third note to page 43.

Page 133: *the town.* The town of Husum on the west coast of Schleswig-Holstein.

Page 133: *the old church behind the linden trees.* The huge late Gothic fifteenth-century St. Marienkirche (St Mary's church), whose steeple, before being destroyed by lightning, was the highest in Schleswig-Holstein, extending to a height of some 300 feet. The church with its three naves of equal height (Hallenkirche), almost as large as Schleswig cathedral, was demolished in 1807/8 because of structural defects. Surrounded by linden trees, it occupied a considerably larger part of the town's market square than the church of today.

Page 133: *Nicolaus Bruhn.* Organist in Husum from 1689 until his death in 1697. Born in the village of Schwabstedt, he was a talented pupil of the Danish organist and composer Dietrich Buxtehude (1637–1707), and his virtuosity as organist, composer and violinist was recognised countrywide. He was succeeded by his younger brother Georg Bruhn (1666–1742).

Page 133: *the so-called 'Mother-Linden'.* A tall linden tree that stood on the north side of the St. Marienkirche at the time of the Protestant Reformation in Husum and North Friesland (1520–30). A 'Daughter-Linden' also stood on the south side, under which the Husum-born Lutheran Reformer Hermann Tast (1490–1551) once preached in 1522. Before the Reformation it was common for services to be held outside a church under trees when entry to it was denied because of doctrinal strife.

Page 133: *the crucifix of the altarpiece.* A most richly carved and painted oak reredos that once stood in the old St. Marienkirche. Its centre panel depicted the crucifixion framed by four reliefs of the Passion, the wings on either side presenting the carved figures of the twelve apostles. Neglected and damaged during the Reformation, it was eventually acquired in 1834 by the St. Jacobi-Kirche (St Jacob's church) in Schwabstedt where it can still be seen today. The angels and other figures that Storm presumably saw in his youth adorning the top of the altarpiece are now lost.

Page 133: *the mighty equestrian statue of St George and the dragon, which actually belonged to the nearby home for the poor.* A remarkable six-foot-high, carved statue by Hans (Johannes) Brüggemann (c. 1480–1540) which once stood on a tall plinth against the wall on the north side of the choir in the St. Marienkirche. The armoured figure of St George, with right arm raised and sword in gauntleted hand, is shown sitting astride a rearing stallion above a dragon lying on its back. The statue was originally commissioned by Duke Friedrich to mark his accession to the Danish throne as Friedrich I in 1523. Storm assumed that it belonged to the nearby 'Gasthaus zum Ritter St. Jürgen' ('St George's Almshouse'), a home for the poor and infirm known locally as the 'Monastery' because of its historical link with an earlier Franciscan monastery in the town. The statue was given as a gift in 1830 to the National Museum of Denmark in Copenhagen.

Page 134: *Aegidius Herfort*. Mayor of Husum 1601–3.

Page 135: *black hound*. Black dogs were considered faithful companions of witches: metamorphoses of Satan, black betraying the presence of the Devil under the hound's skin. One of the two 'witches' burnt at the stake in Schwabstedt in 1619 was recorded as having been accompanied by a black dog (see seventh note to page 130).

Page 135: *A fight then ensued between a fourteen-year-old boy and an extremely strong and ferocious beast*. As source for this scene Storm used Ferdinand Röse's *Lebensbilder aus Süd und Nord* (*Biographical Sketches from the South and North*, Stuttgart, 1844) and Ernst Deeke, *Lübische Geschichten und Sagen* (*Tales and Legends of Lübeck*, Lübeck, 1857), both telling of a small boy, the son of a workman, inadvertently locked into the St. Marienkirche in Lübeck and attacked by its great guard dog. According to Röse's account, the child climbed up on to the statue of St George and defended himself with the sword before being saved. In Deeke's account the boy was terribly savaged.

Page 136: *a small glittering gold cap such as the girls in the villages hereabouts wear on Sundays*. A gold-embroidered velvet cap (*Haube*), worn at the back of the head over lace and secured by a coloured silk ribbon tied beneath the chin. An integral part of traditional dress, it was worn principally on Sundays and at major secular or religious festivals.

Page 136: *the old font beneath the tower*. A richly ornamented brass casting dating from 1643 by Lorenz Karstensen which once adorned the St. Marienkirche, Husum, before its demolition in 1807/8 (see fourth note to page 133). It is preserved and can be seen in the present-day church built in its place.

Page 136: *the sexton's, Albert Carstens'*. Pastor Albertus Carstens, born in Husum in October 1678 and appointed local sexton and preacher to the 'Monastery' in 1701 (see last note to page 133).

Page 136: *the Finkenhaus redoubt.* A fortification south-west of Husum which was destroyed in April 1700 during the Great Northern War. Its location is shown on today's maps as the 'Finkhaushallig polder'.

Page 137: *the Administrator, His Serene Highness Christian August.* Prince-Bishop of Lübeck (1673–1726), uncle, regent and administrator to the two-year-old Prince Carl Friedrich von Schleswig-Holstein-Gottorf after the death of the prince's father, Friedrich IV, in 1702 during the Great Northern War.

Page 137: *Councillor von Goertz.* Kammerpräsident Georg Hinrich Freiherr von Schlitz, born Görtz (1668–1719), from 1698 in service with the duke of Schleswig-Holstein-Gottorf. One of the most powerful politicians at court at the time. Storm made extensive use, often verbatim, of reports of his questionable business dealings with the church.

Page 137: *Böel in Angeln.* A village in the coastal district of Angeln some twelve miles south-east of Flensburg in the then duchy of Schleswig-Gottorf.

Page 137: *Schwabstätte.* The former name of the village of Schwabstedt.

Page 137: *the University of Kiel.* The Christian-Albrechts University of Kiel, founded in 1665.

Page 137: *Rockelor, with a sword.* The Rockelor was a travelling-cloak with a short collar; named after its first wearer, a Frenchman, the Duke of Roquelaure. The wearing of swords was not uncommon at German universities at this time and students often imitated as best they could the dress and manners of the courts.

Page 137: *theology . . . philosophy . . . professors.* In Latin in the original: *theologicis . . . philosophicis . . . professoribus.*

Page 137: *among the readers.* In Latin in the original: *magistris legentibus.* Here the younger teaching staff at the university, who were said to be more inclined towards enlightened and rational views of scripture.

Page 137: *Such opinions, however, were not to my and my dear father's way of thinking.* Post-Reformation theological teachings, in line with those of Luther and Calvin, had laid great, though differing, emphasis on the power of the Devil, particularly in regard to belief in magic and witchcraft. Such belief, however, was being progressively challenged with the rise of scepticism and rationalism, as indicated here among the younger members of the theological faculty.

Page 137: *two-year period of study.* In Latin in the original: *absolvirtem biennio*, a mandatory period of study at a university before an appointment to the church or state service could be made.

Page 138: *the famous University of Halle*. Founded in 1694 for the Lutheran Movement by the Elector of Brandenburg, Friedrich III, as a 'devout' counterpart to the University of Leipzig. Throughout the whole of the eighteenth century this university was the leader of academic thought and advanced theology in Protestant Germany. It renounced religious orthodoxy in favour of objectivity and rationalism, and its lectures were given in the vernacular instead of the customary Latin. Its fame owed much to the works and teachings of August Hermann Francke (1663–1727), the principal promoter of German Pietism, and the philosopher and teacher of law Christian Thomasius (1655–1728).

Page 138: *for the remaining eight miles conveyed myself in the manner of the Holy Apostles*. A reference to the Latin expression *per pedes Apostolorum*, meaning 'on foot'. Two *Meilen* in the original. The *Meile* in use in the duchy of Schleswig at the time equalled some four statute miles. The distance from Husum to Schwabstedt is eight statute miles as the crow flies.

Page 138: *first across the marsh*. The *Südermarsch* south of Husum.

Page 138: *former sea dyke*. A lowland dyke (*Lagedeich*) left inland after further dyking on its seaward side and frequently used at the time in which this story is set as a carriage and footway between Husum and Schwabstedt.

Page 138: *where it rose into sand and heathland*. The Geest: extensive higher, often undulating, broad belt of moraine land in Schleswig-Holstein to the east of Husum, stretching from Flensburg in the north to the river Elbe in the south.

Page 138: *the path wound up a hill*. The Mühlenberg. A high vantage point to the north-west of the village and site of windmills since before 1463, with a fine view from its summit over the village, the Treene river and surrounding region.

Page 138: *the tower of the bishop's old residence*. See sixth note to page 129.

Page 138: *a large two-storey building*. The 'Schwabstedter Hof'. See third note to page 130.

Page 139: *the churchyard on the high barrow on which the belfry stood*. The churchyard of the St. Jacobi-Kirche in Schwabstedt with its nearby wooden belfry built separately on a high prehistoric barrow, known locally as the 'Glockenberg' (belfry hill). The barrow in the churchyard stands some 21 feet high and provides a broad view over the village. The building of churches next to such prehistoric barrows, or burial grounds, was common practice in northern Europe, often on papal demand, to establish the New Faith over that of the heathen. A saying in the village today still links the barrow with the heathen practice of walking or riding round a grave three times: 'Whoever walks round our churchyard's belfry hill three times, can never forget Schwabstedt or leave it.'

Page 139: *a pleasant-looking house and garden on the other side of the road.* The thatched-roofed parsonage at Schwabstedt lay directly opposite the church as it does today.

Page 139: *studiosus.* The Latin word meaning devoted to learning, studious. An informal term for 'student'.

Page 140: *silver coin as a wedding gift.* '*Hochzeitsthaler*' in the original. The German monetary unit *Taler*, or *Thaler,* had been in use as currency in the Holy Roman Empire since 1566. It was customary in farming communities to give the married couple a gift of one or more of these large silver coins.

Page 140: *fens.* Tracts of marshland enclosed by drainage ditches.

Page 140: *The houses here are built in the old Saxon style . . . main doorway.* North Friesland is one of the richest regions in Germany for farmhouse styles, with no less than four basic forms, all straw- or reed-thatched, here the small *Hallenhaus* in the south-east of the region, with its particularly close mixture of family and animal accommodation. Storm's description of the Hallenhaus, which was stylistically classified in the nineteenth century as old or lower Saxon, is precise. A fine example of a lower Saxon Hallenhaus, the Ostenfelder farmhouse, exists in Husum today as a local museum.

Page 140: *two-step.* A quick, whirling dance in two-four time in which the partners held each other's shoulders. A popular dance at a village inn or barn.

Page 140: *The bride's gold-sequined crown.* The *Flitterkrone.* Chronicles for the region describe the bride's 'crown' as a tight-fitting cap (*Haube*) thickly decorated with gold sequins, bright multi-coloured ribbons and glass beads. It was worn high on the bride's head and was the key feature of her overall attire that included a black silk dress richly ornamented at the front with silver jewellery and white lace. Records date the use of the 'crown' as far back as 1563. As a village 'treasure' it was kept in the parsonage and lent out for the occasion for a small fee.

Page 140: *the farmer's living room.* Here the so-called *Döns (Wohnstube),* a living quarter generally built for this style of house at the side of the main threshing floor, containing the household stove (*Beilegeofen*), curtained wall beds and table and chairs. It was often richly decorated with Dutch tiles which also served as insulation in winter.

Page 141: *she was traditionally dressed . . . small cap . . . embroidered with gold sequins.* See first note to page 136.

Page 141: *Jungherr*. Form of address for a young nobleman or squire.

Page 141: *Jungfer*. Polite form of address to an unmarried woman at the time: 'Miss' in English.

Page 142: *Krontaler . . . Lübeck Mark piece*. Silver coins in circulation in the early eighteenth century. The Krontaler, a crown stamped into one of its faces, was minted by the dukes of Schleswig and Holstein, the Lübeck Mark piece in the self-governing city of Lübeck. One Taler was worth about three Lübeck Mark pieces.

Page 143: *Herr Studiosi*. A jocular form of address for a university student of the time, here no doubt indicated by the young man's dress (see sixth note to page 137).

Page 143: *Bauernvogt*. See footnote on page 51.

Page 143: *for at that time barley cost four thalers a tonne and wheat more than six*. The Northern Wars (1700–21) were raging in the region, with the nearby town of Tönning besieged and destroyed in 1700 (see first note to page 133). A *Tonne* was 200–240 lbs. On thalers see second note to page 50.

Page 144: *the pastor among birds*. In Christian tradition, and in many biblical texts, the raven is considered both a helpful bird and a messenger, contrasting with the pagan tradition of the ominous and sometimes diabolical bird.

Page 144: *so that she could learn a little more than what is on offer at the village school here*. Teachers at village schools were often poorly educated, in addition to being extremely poorly paid. The usual curriculum consisted largely of religious instruction, with some reading, writing, singing and simple arithmetic. At a time when the education of women was considered unnecessary, even frowned upon, since they had no role outside the domestic sphere, the girl's additional lessons give added emphasis here to the enlightened attitude of her father.

Page 145: *old mandate . . . Gottorf Calvinists . . . exorcise the Antichrist*. After the Reformation there were many savage doctrinal divisions within Protestantism, especially as between Lutheranism and Calvinism. Abolition of exorcism at infant baptism was among the reforms introduced to the region's Lutheran church by Johann Adolf (1575–1616), duke of Schleswig-Gottorf, but was discontinued after his death. Strict Lutheranism, however, which adhered to the long-held popular belief in the active presence of the Antichrist, in the medieval idea of the battle between God and the Devil, in the Devil's power over the world and in the prevalence of magic and witchcraft, always considered exorcism and other prayers against the Devil absolutely essential.

Page 147: *Glockenberg*. The 'belfry hill' next to the church, opposite the parsonage from which the 'bishop's tower' could easily be seen (see first note to page 139).

Page 148: *the village inn that lay above the Treene*. See third note to page 129.

Page 148: *Do you know what the black art is?* Both witchcraft and sorcery had their roots in the popular culture of the time, particularly in rural societies. Belief in possession by evil forces was a way of making sense of the universe, of providing an explanation for bad harvests, frequent famines, epidemics and recurrent outbreaks of the plague. It was also strongly reinforced by the church as a way of maintaining its authority and power over the people (see Introduction, page 26).

Page 148: *Medelbye*. A village some nine miles west of Flensburg in Schleswig-Holstein. Here Storm refers to the entry titled 'Die Schwarze Schule' ('The Black School') in the legends and folk tales of Schleswig-Holstein collected by Karl Müllenhoff (Kiel, 1845):

'There is much to be told about sorcery in North Friesland and Denmark. The Devil himself teaches it and prospective priests, in particular, are taught to be on their guard against it [. . .]. A pastor in Medelbye, in the administrative district of Tondern, by the name of Fabricius, was especially knowledgeable in this respect [. . .]. But the Devil lays traps for those with whom he especially wants to make a pact, and should pastor Fabricius choose to wear more than one garter he would be damned. But Fabricius was far cleverer than the Devil; he always took care in the morning when he saw two garters by his bed. The Devil had also often plagued with fleas the girl who knitted the pastor's stockings, so that she would miscount the number of stitches; the stockings therefore were generally too wide and would crumple round the pastor's ankles. The pastor, however, was not fooled by this. The Devil was never able to harm him.'

Page 148: *a pew for himself up in the church gallery*. A location generally reserved for leading members of the parish. The gallery in the Schwabstedt church is named the 'the farmers' floor' (*Bauernboden*), with some of the pews allocated to particular farmsteads.

Page 149: *Fingaholi*. Freely constructed name for a fetish. Some authorities suspect an influence from 'Ginquofigaholi', the name of the Devil in the fairy tales of F. Röse (1815–1859) which were well-known to Storm. There is also an echo of the legendary Irish figure Fingal. A red clay head with Asiatic features, similar to that described here, was found in the ruins of the Schwabstedter Hof (farmstead) in 1952, and thought to have belonged to a captain Peter Loff of the East-Asiatic Line who brought such things back for his family. It can be seen today in the Schwabstedt Museum.

Page 151: *Gottorp Bishop Schondeleff, whose residence was over there in the ruined tower- building where the King's administrator later had his seat.* Bishop Johannes Skondeleff, Bishop of Schleswig, who lived in the bishop's residence in Schwabstedt from 1372 to 1421 (see last note to page 129). *Gottorp*: a region centred on the city of Schleswig taking its name from the Gottorp palace nearby; often written today as 'Gottorf' or 'Schleswig-Holstein-Gottorf'. In 1624 the bishop's residence became the seat of a royal administrator, Amtmann, for the district.

Page 151: *they built the town down there and the great sluice-gate on the Eider in 1621 ...flood tides....* The town of Friedrichstadt was built on the Eider in 1621 following the construction of the Eider-Treene sluice-gates in 1569/70. Four sluice-gates were originally built, one of which was later abandoned. Storm refers here to one of the remaining three, the Kran (great) sluice-gate. The region had been particularly devastated by great storms in earlier centuries with much loss of life and livestock. One of the greatest storms in the region's history was to strike thirteen years later in 1634.

Page 151: *Likedeler they called themselves . . . the 'Vitalien brothers', led by Gödeke Michels and Störtebeker, the ones they beheaded on the Grasbrooke in Hamburg.* The Vitalien brothers and other pirates were active against the prosperous sea trade around Helgoland and the Elbe estuary, using the bishop's residence in Schwabstedt as a base and anchorage. Michels and Störtebeker were eventually caught and beheaded on the Grasbrooke (Grasbrock), an island in Hamburg harbour. Legend has it that before his execution Störtebeker proposed to his executioners that if, after beheading, he could run upright past his fellow prisoners, those he ran past would be freed. This was agreed, and the headless Störtebeker then ran past eleven of his fellow pirates before being felled. It is said the eleven were immediately freed. A life-size bronze statue of a naked Störtebeker in chains was erected in 1982 on the Grasbrooke in his memory. *Likedeler*, meaning 'in like shares', refers to the method of distribution of plunder among the pirates; see also notes to pages 129 (fifth) and 152 (first).

Page 151: *Ohm.* A shortening of the word *Oheim* meaning 'uncle'. Here Storm makes use of an old tradition in the family of his uncle Detlef Ohm, which he mentions in a letter dated November 1854 to his friend the writer Eduard Mörike (1804–75): '... during a battle, one of his forefathers hacked a way out for a Holstein duke who, because he had treated him as a friend and blood-relative, gave him this name, forest, fields and meadows as a gift.'

Page 152: "*Holbek*". In Low German *Hollbeek* means 'hollow stream'. Legend has it that pirates buried a gold chain in this sandy ravine that would have passed three times round the St. Jacobi-Kirche in Schwabstedt.

Page 152: *from the high hill . . . far and wide across Dithmarschen*. The Glockenberg is the highest point in the region, some 157 feet high, just over a mile from the village of Hude east of Schwabstedt. Dithmarschen is a vast coastal region south of the river Eider.

Page 152: *the moor to where his farm workers had been cutting peat during the week*. The 'Wild Moor' (see second note to page 52) was a main source of peat for the surrounding villages, in which each had an agreed share.

Page 153: *Senator Feddersen*. A senator was a municipal officer ranking next to the mayor; generally the head of a prominent and property-owning family in the community. Storm's great-grandfather Joachim Christian Feddersen (1740–1801) was both a senator and brewer in Husum.

Page 153: *... days' cutting ... stacks*. In the original *Tagesgrift* and *Ringeln*: the former an old unit of measure for peat equal to some 4,000 turfs, the expected daily output cut by one day-labourer, and the latter, circular stacks of nine turfs each built to dry them.

Page 153: *Ostenfeld*. Village some five miles east of Husum, between which and Schwabstedt lies the 'Wild Moor'.

Page 153: *Christian Mercacus*. David Christian Mercacus (1690–1739), pastor to the St. Petri-Kirche (St Peter's church) in Ostenfeld, 1718–39. The local chronicle records him as being 'a sincere man of fine reputation and pure thoughts who fervently stamped out improper use of the confession, communion and burial service'. He is further recorded as having expected each of the congregation 'to bring a bible to his services, open it, and follow his texts personally'. Given the extremely low level of literacy in rural communities at the time, however, such an expectation would seem to have been highly unrealistic.

Page 154: *crows*. In folklore the crow is considered to be the 'bird of death' (*Totenvogel*). Its cawing is generally interpreted as ominous, especially from the roof of a house in which there is a sick person.

Page 154: *the forest*. The Lehmsiek Forest north-east of Schwabstedt.

Page 154: *in Duke Adolf's time*. Duke Adolf of Schleswig-Holstein-Gottorf who ruled in 1544–86.

Page 155: *the dreadful business of convents in our land*. Following the Reformation many convents in Germany and Europe, which had previously been the enforced homes of many girls, were converted into hospices, or adapted for other uses, or acquired as real estate by neighbouring nobles.

Page 156: *'Lord, Thou makest darkness . . . Thou hast founded them.'*.
Combination of Psalm 104 verse 20 and Psalm 89 verse 11.

Page 156: *the firm uplands*. The Geest. See first note to page 103.

Page 156: *'The moor . . . We can't possibly cross it!'*. The 'Wild Moor' north-east of Schwabstedt could be crossed safely only in winter when the ground was frozen hard, and then only by restricted routes. The peat bogs and swamps were most dangerous places for the unwary traveller.

Page 156: *Petrus Steinbrecher*. Choirmaster at the St. Marienkirche in Husum 1687–1702 and at the Gelehrtenschule.

Page 157: *young choir boys and girls*. 'The old maxim, "Women shall be silent in church" (1 Cor. 14:34) still prevailed in seventeenth- and eighteenth-century Germany, both in the Protestant north and the Catholic south. In Hamburg around 1700 it was not thought proper for them even to sing in church although they were expected to be devout and instil piety in their children' (Eda Sagarra, *A Social History of Germany 1648–1914*, London, 1977). The Lutheran church here in North Friesland would seem to have been much more liberal in this regard.

Page 158: *salvo honore*. Latin: 'if you will pardon me for saying so.'

Page 158: *'Salve, Christiane, confrater dilectissime!'*. Latin: 'Greetings, Christian, beloved fellow in the service of God!'

Page 158: *Nitimur in vetitum*. Latin: 'We strive against the forbidden.' Quotation from Ovid, *Amores* III. 4, v. 17.

Page 158: *Petrus Goldschmidt*. Orthodox pastor born in Husum around 1660 and pastor in Sterup (a village thirteen miles south-east of Flensburg) from 1691. Author of *Höllische Morpheus* (*Devilish Morpheus*), published in Hamburg in 1698, a polemic against past and present atheists, naturalists, and especially the 'fanatic' Dutch theologian Balthasar Bekker, a pioneer of rational criticism against belief in the Devil, witchcraft and spirits, and his widely-published and translated work *De betoverde Weereld* (*The Bewitched World*, Amsterdam, 1691). Goldschmidt died near Hamburg in 1713. The cover of his book shows a grotesque figure, half animal, half man, with a tail and cloven hoof, symbolic of the Devil. Storm possessed the second edition of *Morpheus* and writes of Petrus Goldschmidt in his *Kulturhistorische Skizzen* ('Cultural-Historical Sketches') which appeared in 1871/72 under the title *Zerstreute Kapitel* (*Loose Chapters*). The chronicles Storm researched for it cite many 'encounters' between Goldschmidt and the Devil.

Page 158: *a second work, in this case rebutting the Halle professor Thomasius*. A reference to *Verworffener Hexen- und Zauber-Advokat* (*A Depraved Defender of Witches and Wizards*), published in Hamburg in 1705. Christian Thomasius (1655–1728), philosopher and teacher of law at Halle University, was a rationalist who systematically questioned the legal basis of witch trials and who in his influential treatise *De crimine magiae* (*The Crime of Magic,* 1701) spoke out against all superstitious ideas and belief in witchcraft, and attacked the 'scholastic fantasies' that had kept witch hunts alive (see first note to page 138).

Page 159: *Remigii's Daemonologia*. These teachings in demonology by the Venetian theologian Remigius appeared in German in 1703.

Page 159: *Christian Kortholt's tract on the witches' fiery circles*. Christian Kortholt (1633–94) was a professor of theology at Kiel University; his tract appeared in 1677 – on the subject of the magic circles of witches in which they were said to stand to summon the Devil and the spirits of evil; candles were often lit and placed round their circumferences.

Page 160: *'Get thee hence, unclean spirit! That is what you should say!'*. In 1665 a new hymn book and Ecclesiastical Statute was introduced in which the pastor had to ask the infant at baptism, not in Latin but in the vernacular: 'Do you renounce the Devil? – And all his works? – And all his ways?' and to say over the naked child: 'Get thee hence, unclean spirit, and make way for the Holy Ghost.'

Page 161: *witch . . . burnt to ashes in Husum twenty years before*. In 1687, according to the historical records of Johannes Laß (Flensburg, 1750–53), a twenty-one-year-old woman by the name of Margaretha Carstens confessed to sorcery and association with the Devil during harsh examination and torture. The criminal court in Husum, despite her death in the prison dungeon the day before, a not uncommon event, instructed that her body be taken to the place of execution and burnt as an example to others. The deep dungeon can still be seen today in Husum beneath the former prison-house on the edge of the town.

Page 162: *Flensburg*. Large and most northerly seaport in Schleswig-Holstein on an inlet to the sea, the Flensburg Fiord.

Page 166: *he dares wear only one garter*. To wear two would allow the Devil to take possession of his soul (see third note to page 148).

Page 166: *it's as if flies are dancing before her eyes*. Flies were taken to be common attributes of the Devil.

Page 167: *Halle . . . many celebrated theologians and other learned men*. Under the influence of notable teachers, the university at Halle soon expanded beyond the limits of its original Lutheran conception (see first note to page 138). The creation of faculties beyond those of theology and law enabled it not only to advance scholarship but also to train teachers.

Page 167: *black attire . . . exchanged for red*. Possible reference to a change of faculty. The study of law had begun to replace theology as the most popular and lucrative subject of study; the poorer students, however, continued to study theology since it was best endowed with scholarships and promised the best hope of employment.

Page 167: *river Saale*. River flowing close to the town of Halle.

Page 169: *Carstens, the sexton and preacher at the 'Monastery' nearby*. See last note to page 133.

Page 171: '. . . *he that loseth his life for my sake shall find it.*'. Matthew 10:39.

Page 171: *Superintendent*. An ecclesiastical post having responsibility for churches and schools in a diocese or district.

Page 171: *Güstrow*: a city in the state (*Land*) of Mecklenburg-West Pomerania, northern Germany.

Page 172: *Easter greeting*. In the original: *Auferstehungsgruß*, literally 'resurrection's greeting'. An echo of the festive greeting at Easter: 'Christ has risen!'.

Page 172: *O Lord, shew thy mercy upon us . . . And grant us thy salvation!*. In Latin in the original: 'Ostende nobis, Domine, misericordiam tuam' . . . 'Et salutare tuum da nobis!' .

Page 172: *Let us Sing Praises unto the Lord*. In Latin in the original: 'Benedicamus Domino'.

Page 173: *a pew in the gallery opposite . . . in spite of the balusters*. A feature of most North Frisian churches is the presence of a single wooden gallery along the north wall of the nave directly opposite and level with the high pulpit, enabling the preacher to see the faces of the entire congregation. A balustrade was a common feature, with often richly painted biblical scenes along the length of the gallery beneath it. The narrow winding stairs leading up to it were generally at the back of the church, as they are in the St. Jacobi-Kirche in Schwabstedt. North Frisian churches are some of the most beautiful in Schleswig-Holstein; simply decorated in greens, yellows and blues, they closely reflect the beauty of the surrounding sea and marshland.

Page 173: *And, behold . . . house of Israel*. St Matthew 15:22–24.

Page 174: *her white handkerchief clasped in her hand*. Part of a girl's traditional dress (see second note to page 46).

Page 176: *wedding glass*. Glass of wine drunk at a wedding celebration by the bride or bridegroom together with the giver of a wedding present.

Page 176: *'Exi immunde spiritus!'*. Latin: 'Depart, unclean spirit!'

Page 178: *Melanchthon*. Philipp Melanchthon (1497–1560), German theologian and Protestant reformer, leader of the Reformation together with Martin Luther.

Page 179: *Hude*. A village on the river Treene just over a mile south-east of Schwabstedt.

Page 179: *'Into the water with the witch!'*. Trial by water on suspicion of witchcraft was common throughout Europe at the time during which this story is set. The accused was tied hand and foot and thrown into deep water. If she sank she was innocent, if she floated she was guilty, the assumption being that the power of the Devil kept the accused afloat. It was not uncommon for the accusers to attach a rope to the woman to hinder her from sinking.

Page 180: *the Amtmann and the Landvogt*. See first note to page 131.

Page 182: *Schleswig*. Seaport capital in eastern Schleswig-Holstein and former residence of the dukes of Schleswig and later, until 1713, of the dukes of Schleswig-Holstein-Gottorp. A bishopric with cathedral (St. Peter) and five churches. Seat of the Danish governor of the duchies of Schleswig and Holstein (1721–1848) and capital of the Prussian province of Schleswig-Holstein from 1867 to 1918.

Page 182: *across the water-lily leaves*. Storm here makes use of a tale to be found in the legends and folk tales of Schleswig-Holstein by Karl Müllenhoff (see third note to page 148), in which a witch is said to walk on water-lily leaves.

Page 184: *the robust, quick-tempered local pastor*. See fourth note to page 153.

Page 184: *wore a black veil over their faces*. Ostenfeld women were renowned for the range, colours and styles of their traditional dress. A *Heik*, a veil of black material, was frequently worn by close relatives at funerals and during mourning.

Page 185: *Petrus Goldschmidt . . . had died a tavern-keeper in Hamburg*. See fourth note to page 158.

Page 185: *Thomasius's book on the crime of magic*. See fifth note to page 158.

Page 187: *The bird flew off . . . only the peace was not of this world*. The belief that birds are the winged souls of the dead, or that they carry/accompany the souls of the dead to the next world, is ubiquitous in folklore and mythology. In the original edition of this story (1878) Storm wrote: 'only his soul was no longer within him.'

In the preparation of these notes the translator has been greatly indebted to the following: Karl Ernst Laage's notes and commentary in the four-volume critical edition of the collected works of Theodor Storm used as source text (see Translator's Note); commentaries by Peter Goldammer in *Theodor Storm. Sämtliche Werke in vier Bänden* edited by him (Berlin, 8th ed. 1995); notes and commentaries by Rüdiger Frommholz in *Theodor Storm. Erzählungen* edited by him (Stuttgart, 1997); details of folklore and myth in David Artiss, *Theodor Storm. Studies in Ambivalence. Symbol and Myth in his Narrative Fiction* (Amsterdam, 1978); notes on *Pole Poppenspäler* in critical editions by Gerd Eversberg (Bange Verlag, Hollfeld, 1993, and Verlag Boyens, Heide, 1992), by Ingwert Paulsen (Husum, 1993), by Beate Lüttringhaus (Philipp Reclam, Stuttgart, 1996), and by Jean Lefebvre (Paderborn, 2000); the historical background, notes and sources for *Renate* in Magnus Voss's *Chronik der Kirchengemeinde Ostenfeld* (Husum, 1905), in Horst Appuhn's *Sankt Marien in Husum* (Husum, 1953), in *500 Jahre. Gasthaus zum Ritter St. Jürgen in Husum* edited by its Board of Management (Husum, 1965), in Hans Meyer's *Schwabstedt. 5000 Jahre Schwabstedter Geschichte* (Schwabstedt, 1986), and in Theodor Storm, *Renate. Zur 'Wald- und Wasserfreude'* edited by the Gemeine Schwabstedt (Husum, 1993); and the historical information and sources regarding the marionette theatre given in John McCormick and Bennie Pratasik, *Popular Puppet Theatre in Europe, 1800–1914* (Cambridge, 1998).

Also in Angel Classics

Nineteenth-century fiction

THEODOR FONTANE
Cécile
Translated by Stanley Radcliffe
0 946162 42 5 *(cased)*   0 946162 43 3 *(paperback)*

The first English translation of the second of Fontane's series of Berlin novels. At a fashionable spa an affair develops between an itinerant engineer and the delicate, mysterious wife of an army officer — to explode in Germany's bustling new capital. '*Cécile* is written with wit and a controlled fury and Radcliffe's elegant translation does it superb justice.' — M. Ratcliffe, *The Observer*

THEODOR STORM
The Dykemaster
Translated by Denis Jackson
0 946162 54 9 *(paperback)*

Der Schimmelreiter (literally 'The rider on the white horse'), set on the eerie west coast of Schleswig-Holstein, is the story of a visionary young dyke official at odds with his community. This narrative tour de force is one of the most celebrated works in German literature. 'Translations of the high standing of this one are more than ever in demand.' – Mary Garland, editor of *The Oxford Companion to German Literature*

THEODOR STORM
Hanz and Heinz Kirch; *with* Immensee *and* Journey to a Hallig
Translated by Denis Jackson and Anja Nauck
0 946162 60 3 *(paperback)*

Three contrasting narratives by a writer who may claim parity with Thomas Hardy, two of them here translated into English for the first time. As in *The Dykemaster*, maps and detailed end-notes enhance enjoyment of fiction strongly rooted in time and place. 'The quality of these translations is outstanding; they contrive to read like natural English and yet capture beautifully the sense and rhythm of Storm's German.' – *Forum for Modern Language Studies*

ADALBERT STIFTER
Brigitta
with *Abdias*; *Limestone*; and *The Forest Path*
Translated by Helen Watanabe-O'Kelly
0 946162 36 0 *(cased)*   0 946162 37 9 *(paperback)*

The most substantial selection of Stifter's narratives of the diseased subconscious to appear in English. 'Stifter's stories, richly symbolic and brushed with mystery, are presented in wonderful new translations.' – *Publishers Weekly*

Twentieth-century fiction

ANDREY BELY
The Silver Dove
Translated by John Elsworth
0 946162 64 6 (paperback)

This first modern Russian novel (1909), by the author of *Petersburg*, whom Nabokov ranked with Proust, Kafka and Joyce, depicts a culture on the brink, in the aftermath of the 1905 revolution. 'Bely depicts a world which is fascinating, full of strange imagery and tormented by passions.' – I. Montgomery, *The Guardian*

ALFRED DÖBLIN
Karl and Rosa
Translated by John E. Woods
0 88064 011 1 (paperback)

The self-contained novel forming the third part of the trilogy *November 1918: A German Revolution*, documenting the explosive events in Germany which ended the revolution of 1918, and the doomed but glorious struggle of Karl Liebknecht and Rosa Luxemburg. 'Döblin's ultimate novel, of magnificent narrative sweep and constructive power.' – *Washington Book World*

JAROSLAV HAŠEK
The Bachura Scandal *and other stories and sketches*
Translated by Alan Menhennet
0 946162 41 7 (paperback)

These 32 stories of Prague life written before *The Good Soldier Švejk*, most of them translated into English for the first time, revel in the twisted logic of politics and bureaucracy in the Czech capital which was also an Austrian provincial city. 'Animated translations . . . Hašek emerges as a prankster who carries his "what if" musings to absurdist heights.' – *The New York Times*

MIKHAIL ZOSHCHENKO
The Galosh *and other stories*
Translated by Jeremy Hicks
0 946162 65 4 (paperback)

These 65 short stories, nearly half of them translated into English for the first time, reveal one of the great Russian comic writers in their bitter-sweet smack and the fractured language of the argumentative, obsessive, semi-educated narrator-figure, trying hard to believe in the new Socialism of the early Soviet years. 'The translator's task is a high-wire act that Hicks performs with the utmost linguistic inventiveness.' – Zinovy Zinik, *TLS*

Poetry

GENNADY AYGI
Selected Poems 1954-94
Bilingual edition with translations by Peter France
0 946162 59 X (paperback)

Aygi's free verse stands at the confluence of avant-garde European modernism and the traditional culture of his near-Asiatic homeland, Chuvashia. This is the most substantial general selection of his work published in the English-speaking world. 'This book marks an important further step in the recognition of Aygi's extraordinary contribution to modern Russian poetry.' – J. Elsworth, *Slavonica*

HEINRICH HEINE
Deutschland: A Winter's Tale
Bilingual edition with translation by T. J. Reed
0 946162 58 1 (paperback)

This satirical travelogue on eve-of-1848 Germany is engagingly modern – on customs union, women, food . . . The wittiest work by Germany's wittiest poet. 'Reed succeeds beautifully in recreating the pointed, epigrammatic effect of the terse rhythm.' – A. Bunyan, *Jewish Chronicle*

FERNANDO PESSOA
The Surprise of Being
Bilingual edition with translations by James Greene and Clara de Azevedo Mafra
0 946162 24 7 (paperback)

Twenty-five of the haunting poems written by Portugal's greatest modern poet in his own name, the most confounding of his voices. 'The translators have succeeded admirably in the task of rendering this most brilliant and complex of poets into inventive, readable English.' – D. Pires and M. Tejerizo, *New Comparison*

MARINA TSVETAEVA
The Ratcatcher: A lyrical satire
Translated by Angela Livingstone
0 946162 61 1 (paperback)

The first complete translation of Tsvetaeva's masterpiece, a satirical narrative poem on conformism and material prosperity, using the story of 'The Pied Piper of Hamlyn'. 'In a finely tuned line of verse in translation, the style of the original not only shines through the dense layers of a foreign linguistic element but seems to stand on a level with it, as if two brothers were comparing heights together . . . This was my experience when I read this translation.' – S. Nikolayev, *Literaturnaya gazeta*, Moscow